The Unused Life
of Tito López

Luis Luna

Luis Luna Cortez was born in 1978 in a provincial city in Mexico. He grew up in that city. Since then, he has lived in Xalapa, Puebla, Veracruz, Mérida, Cancún, Brighton, Birmingham, Maidstone, and Whangārei. A journalist with degrees in literature and architecture, he lives today by a cenote in Quintana Roo. He wrote this story in idioma español mexicano; now he has translated it into South-English English.

The Unused Life
of Tito López

Luis Luna

Piwaiwaka
Press

Published by Piwaiwaka Press
www.piwaiwakapress.org

Cover Artwork: Sosa.kl@sosaenol
Cover Design: Maggie Tu and Madden Hay
ISBN (softcover) 978-1-7385926-4-7

1

'Wow, it's brilliant, Ángela! It's the best news! It's just so exceptionally – it's such exceptionally brilliant news!'

My sister laughs. She jumps up.

'And it's making you so exceptionally articulate, Tito.'

She grabs me. She looks at me hard. She starts to grin. Me grinning from ear to ear myself.

'They want me, Angelita! They like what I've got – me, that is, muggins – they like my work and they want me to start the day after tomorrow!'

She plants a kiss on my cheek. She keeps grinning.

'Course they like what you've got.'

'Ta, sis. You reckon they really do? You really reckon they like what I've got?'

'Course. Whoever they are.'

'Whoever – ? Oh, course, I'm carrying on like a right twat. You so don't know what I'm banging on about, do you? It's a job, Ángela. I've got a job!'

'Wow – a job? Wow   brilliant!'

So now I plant a kiss on her cheek.

'Your turn to be the one who's so exceptionally articulate, Angelita.'

She's holding me tight and looking at me harder.

'Bro, sweetheart,' she smiles, 'tell me the whole story from the start?'

Now you might be asking yourself why we're popping our tops about something as humdrum as my landing a job. Well, let's check me out, okay? Name in full: Matías López

Urbano. Age: twenty-two. Personal appearance: short, dark, skinny. Ordinary bod. Forgettable face. Nobody scouting for talent would look at me twice unless a talent they hoped to hook was for being overlooked. Personal attributes: lippy lad sometimes has way with words but brain basically second rate. Hang about – third rate! Qualifications: bachelor's degree in Spanish. Honours: none. Did okay in last couple years in literature of sixteenth and seventeenth century. Too late to fluke any kind of distinction.

Not a lot of jobs out there right now. And lots of others like me looking for work.

Fact of matter, past few weeks I've been just one unnoticeable little prat among hundreds – thousands! – of others, whole horde of new graduates, trawling the town for work. Summer has come on and kids queued for interviews are getting more and more down about their prospects. And the days have got hotter and hotter. This job – the job I've just sprung on Ángela – I tracked it down the other day. The bosses asked me to come in this afternoon for an interview. And they told me okay!

'First thing I did after they said they wanted me was snatch a bus going past and get myself straight back home and rush straight upstairs to tell you, sis.'

'Tito, I've always known you were born to be happy.'

'Born to be happy? Or born to be haphazard?'

'What? Born to enjoy lots of luck.'

'Lots of luck but no lucre.'

'Nobody says lucre any more, except in church or leftwing politics, so we won't count that one. I'll grant you haphazard.'

We've played this game of working out ways to speak weakly off-the-wall puns or half-homophones for years.

'Course they're not offering me a contract, not yet, it's only on trial.'

'You'll be great at the job, I know.'

She's speaking with so much satisfaction it makes me feel even more brill than when I first told her the news. I always believe Ángela. My big sis has always been my best friend. Biologically she's only three years older than me but in every other way she's at least a decade in front. Kinda pathetic, maybe, that my best friend is my sis. Ángela's so quick, clever, cool. How couldn't she be my heroine?

Also, maybe am myself not too together emotionally. Am kinda lonely really.

Well – really lonely.

Like, what have I got to offer anyone? Not a lot. You could say, like I've just said, that I've got a low key kinda gift as a guy who can be gabby. Written or spoken text, take your pick! Only apart from that I'm nobody. At uni I was always friendly but shy. So course my reward's everyone's friendly but shy with me. Don't suppose any of them would have a harsh word to say about me. Don't suppose any of them would have an ardent word to say about me. I don't seem to provoke any sort of ardour at all!

Yet goes without saying I'm longing for love.

Longing for love.

Ángela right now has dropped into her armchair again – keeping her eyes on me closely – and she's slipping a bookmark into the sociology text that she happened to have been reading when I first slammed into her room. She's reading for a master's degree and aiming for honours.

'I don't suppose I'll be great. Am gonna do my best though, Angelita.'

'They're fortunate to get you.'

'Right!' I laugh. 'Fortunate cause I'm so what they need in that niche – a hack.'

'Fortunate cause you're clever and creative and imaginative.'

I throw myself onto her bed. She's as pretty as always, her white skin, and a simple white dress. Ángela is really white, really pretty.

'They don't want creativity. They want product.'

'They'll see you've got something. Already seen it, probably – probably that's why they're offering you a job.'

'You better slow down, sis. You give me ideas about myself.'

'Good.'

'Seriously, creativity's not in the equation. We're not talking here about blank verse or deathless prose. We're talking about copywriting – trainee copywriting – in an advertising studio.'

Ángela stands up serenely.

'Time to tell the others the news.'

'Sure!'

Springing off her bed, I grab her hand.

The family house was built for our grandfather in the thirties of last century. Weird, isn't it, saying last century when the new century's only one year old? Anyway, the architectural style of the house is what you could call Spanish Viceroyal Revival. If you like the style.

If you don't like the style you call it Hollywood. A style sorta baroque, kinda kitsch.

Those who don't like the style aren't exactly scarce.

Stood on the street, looking up at our house from our outside, what you'd see would be swathes of white plaster and swirling whirlpools of stone, ceramics, wrought iron. Want to come inside? You gotta fight your way past a ferocious wrought iron palisade, painted black. Next, scratchy cypresses, spiky cactus, in pots. And next, step up into the portico. A portico topped with glazed red tiles propped by spiral columns carved by craftsmen from a soft pink stone common on the more showy sort of house in our city. Columns that kind of corkscrew upwards and make you feel seasick the way they twirl and snake.

Moorish maybe, you could say.

The tiles of the porch are glazed blue and white, with little lozenges of red. Toothed spikes sprout from agaves, also in pots.

We glimpse the portico through our open front door as we head towards the salon. We're giggling. We're still holding hands.

'Mmm?' says Mamá, looking up lazily from *El Universal*.

'Tito's got good news,' says Ángela.

Papá sets down his own newspaper, *Correo Católico de Villarreal*. He lowers his reading specs. He looks at us squarely. He likes looking at you squarely, does Papá.

'Good news?' says his carefully paced bass.

Ángela misses one beat only.

'Great news!' she says.

Mamá drops her magazine, crosses herself, grabs her shot glass. The glass is oily with tequila. Mamá downs the lot in one gulp. She and our father at this time on Saturday afternoons like to sit together in the salon and work their way through a bottle of tequila. Papá will sit silently tippling over the papers. Mamá will toss hers away, loll back smoking, or slouch forward to riffle through a fashion mag, and will talk. Well, more sort of ramble than talk. Rambling turns to raving soon as I've told her about my new job.

'Oh, wonderful news! Clever boy! What a clever boy you are, darling – oh, it'll be so lovely working at an advertising agency! How much are they paying?'

'Six thousand a month, Mamá.'

'Lovely! Just think of all the beautiful clothes you'll be able to buy!'

Papá cuts in here, a bit gruffly.

'The boy won't be wasting his money. Tito, keep your head down and work hard and work well. Don't waste time any more than you'd waste money.'

'Okay, Papá.'

My father nods soberly.

Sobriety is in scarce supply in our salon. Ma's family over two luxury-loving thirds of a century has ripely crammed it with leather and porcelain and cedar and majolica. Walls and ceiling are kind of crawling with fake baroque. Fat plaster grapes, pomegranates, oranges. Tortured brass chandelier rods plunge towards a marble tabletop. A typical sort of chandelier – drooping crystal teardrops, swooping arms moulded to look like heraldic serpents, opaque glass candles popping out of the mouths of the serpents. At night, electric filaments burn inside the glass candles. Well, not all the filaments burn – cause a lot of the bulbs have gone phut.

Nobody's got around to doing anything about the dead bulbs.

'You'll also need to watch your back, lad,' says Papá. 'Stay out of office politics.'

'Yep, will do Papá.'

'And stay away – those sorts of places are full of them – stay away from queers. Lots of queers in the advertising industry. They'll try to get their hands on a nice-looking boy like you, Tito. Let them know you're a real man.'

Nothing too novel, so I simply shrug.

'I'm not nice-looking, Papá. Me with my mug – they'll look right past me, I'll be okay.'

Papá always warns me to watch out for queers.

Whenever he comes back to ours from the hairdressing salon not far down the street he mutters about the guy who gives him his cut.

A guy his own age, with grey hair. A paunchy bloke who's sired six sons!

'That fellow,' mutters Papá.

'Mmmm?' says Mamá.

'Can't so much as say good morning without simpering like a woman,' goes on Papá. Yet my dad never speaks less than politely to the hairdresser. Papá knows it's not manly to be outright rude to a queer – not unless the queer tries to solicit you. Best to deal with those types simply by staying well away, says Papá. You're wise not to use the dressing rooms at our suburban sports centre, for instance. Full of queers, the dressing rooms at the sports centre.

Not that he ordinarily uses words a lot, my Papá. We hardly ever talk at any length about anything. Just minimally flick back and forth a few key phrases. He gives me orders, of course, in his dad capacity.

'Do this, lad.'

'Okay, Pa.'

'Now do that, son.'

'Sure.'

Our longest dialogues occur when he's interrogating me on what I've been up to, what I've been doing, how I've been spending my time, our money – or more often our fading credit.

'Tito – are there any nice girls at the agency?' ogles Mamá.

'One, Ma.'

'A single girl – a girl of good family?'

'Ma, I'll file a request for a copy of her pedigree first thing on my first day at the agency.'

Mamá writhes contentedly in heaped cushions on a

massive sofa upholstered in Italy. Cushions from Spain. Leather, oxblood.

'Oh, darling – we're so lucky you've landed such a lovely job. I'm such a lucky mother to have such a lovely, lovely son! Six thousand a month! Wonderful! How lucky, darling boy!'

Papá looks restless at the reiteration of that word.

'Luck comes as a reward to duty,' he says slowly, 'and duty involves duty to your family above all, son.'

María sticks her wrinkled head around the door and wags it for a while before telling us we need a top-up of our drinking water. A volunteer is needed, she says. Somone willing to nip down to More for Less. She shifts onto her chorus.

'I'm too busy slaving in the kitchen to look after it meself.'

Only she doesn't get a chance to finish cause we tell her my news. María with a throaty croak – like whooping cough – shuffles forward on her horny bare feet in a sort of jogtrot to smack kisses onto my cheeks. I smack big kisses back. She pulls down my head so she can make the sign of the cross on my forehead.

'We thank the Blessed Virgin for her ceaseless grace,' rasps María.

Bolting to the kitchen, grabbing the big plastic bottle, I tell everyone I'm off to get the water. The bottle – transparent, blue – is lightweight. Balancing it on my head I leap through the back doorway. I lope down the driveway.

I scarper out onto the street.

Our suburb mostly consists of stone villas and stucco bungalows, plus a few blocks of apartments rising no higher than four floors, set in walled gardens. Access to garages and entrance hallways is barred by mighty cedar or steel doors. Trees everywhere – jacaranda, cypress, eucalypt – climb up into a brilliant blue sky. On nearly every wall, flowering bougainvillea. Shops and stalls everywhere, too. A lot of little traders. A greengrocer here, flower seller there, lots of photocopy shops, unisex hairdresser almost every block. Streets right now being swept by little old men, brown skinned, deeply corrugated skin, sliced for years by blades of hard sun, whisking big brooms. Topiary clipped and snipped. Pyramids, this season, are a thing.

A tamale vendor crying her wares in singsong.

Ta-males! Ta-ma-a-les!

Topiary trim, tiny, sort of comic when you lift your eyes up above the rooftops, the treetops. Above the verdigris domes, the silver crosses, McDonalds Golden Arches, of Villarreal. Above the city. A dark green sierra, that's what you see. A dark green retreating sequence of sierra draped with forest on all flanks. Pine, mostly. I love looking up whenever I can – looking up at the lovely big shaggy sierrra.

Tama-aaaales!

A sign comes into view, painted in red letters on the white front of a shop.

Mini-Super More for Less.

Our family often find ourselves pronouncing those words. We need to name the place so constantly cause we're always running out of stuff. We tend to drop *the*. More for Less. Like it's a dog. Or a mule. I fancy a biscuit, María – get me a nice packet from More for Less. Back in a tick, ducking down to More for Less. A shadowy sixth person in our household. Next to it is the local sewing shop, which sells fabric and notions and toys and is called Divine Providence. Across the street is a poulterer called Chickenhawk.

The poulterer displays a cardboard sign today.

Heads and legs, four pesos.

My luck's holding good! Cause inside the corner grocery who do I find waiting at the counter? A groovy guy I know. Alejandro.

Well, I know him a bit.

He's really good-looking. And right now is waiting while an old lady picks her way through a beaded purse trying to find change at the counter. Alejandro lives nearby in his own apartment. Which the lucky sod can afford cause he earns good money working as a lawyer. He's about four years older than me, and taller, and smarter, and just generally is hardcore cool. Hanging from his hips are a pair of baggy white cargo pants. His hips are very slim. He wears his shiny black hair in a pageboy. He nods at me in a matey sort of way.

'Hi, howzit Matías?'

'Hi, Alejandro.'

'All cool with you?'

'Yeah, cool – it's all cool.'

My nerves are letting me down, right now, in a big way. Luckily it turns out I don't need to say much. Alejandro starts talking. About music. How this band is crap and that band is not so crap. Alejandro doesn't talk in a hurry. Ultra cool, Alejandro. After a bit I find myself stringing together the odd sentence that might seem marginally intelligent to that mule. Maybe cause I love music and I love dancing. My fave music is at the extremes – on the one hand I really get off on ultra pop, the shallowest most commercial pop, and at the same time I sort of swoon when I listen to classical guitar. Alejandro deems my tastes to be naff.

'Miguel Bosé is still cool,' he says, weighing his words very carefully.

'Yep, you're right Alejandro. Still cool, Miguel Bosé.'

'He's going off a bit, though.'

'Yep, just a bit.'

'Heard the latest from Savage Garden? They have their moments. Danceable music, and not stupid.'

'Yep, I've heard it. Production values the best!'

Alejandro frowns and thinks it over slowly.

'Production values passable.'

We go from music to football. The form in the latest game between ours and Guadalajara. Meanwhile the old lady at the counter can't make up her mind, she's in no hurry. Nor's the shopkeeper. Am feeling great, standing waiting. Am feeling the best! Alejandro seems to be treating me almost like a good mate. Course it goes without saying I don't tell him about my new job. He can't be expected to be too interested that this dude he knows barely by sight from the sports centre has got himself a job as trainee copywriter in a tiddly studio – that I'm about to try to make a living by brainstorming capitalist slogans.

'Their attack is strong but whenever we take the game forward it always turns out their defence is weak,' says Alejandro.

'Yeah, that's dead right Alejandro.'

We go from football to tennis. Alejandro likes tennis a lot. I like it okay. We've played before in mixed doubles. Now he asks me about maybe meeting for singles later today.

'Sure, Alejandro. That'd be cool. Sure!'

'How about eight?' says Alejandro. 'I reckon if I get organised I could make a game at eight.'

'Yep! Eight is cool.'

A big framed print of the Virgin smiles down at us like a sad ghost from the back wall of the grocery shop. Her sadness seems not mitigated by a festoon of tiny fairy lights twined not only around her dirty gilt frame but all over the flyspotted glass, the flyspotted smile, of the Lady.

A poster has been pasted onto the wall nearby.

This abode is Catholic. We do not allow Protestant propaganda. Long live Christ the King!

The poster, like the glass, is flyspotted.

'Eight. Okay. See you then.'

'See you, Alejandro.'

I dance with happiness back down the street. A tarred street, sticky in the heat. Concrete pavements, laid long ago on both sides of the carriageway, have been lifted and split by poking jacaranda roots. Birdsong overhead – twittering, warbling – while the background racket of traffic never ceases. Otherwise the street seems peaceful, sleepy. A thin stench of urban air pollution insinuates itself familiarly into my nostrils.

Swatting the air with our racquets, we meet promptly. We're both wearing whites cause the club rule is players must not wear colours. Alejandro looks strikingly studly. Short shorts. A handshake and then we head onto the court.

Play starts quickly.

Alejandro doesn't muck around at all and, with a swift pow of a fuzzy ball against the nylon net of his hi-tech racquet, opens service for the first game. Fuck! He plays hard! I need to work to meet his pace. Also it's tricky trying to keep an alert eye on the ball – which pows and pocks back and forth so fast on the artificial turf – cause my heart is sort of lurching about with the thought that maybe he likes me a bit, maybe this could become a regular date, playing singles with this cool guy. Alejandro pirouettes into a shot. His loose white shirt flies up. I catch a disorientating glimpse of a gleaming bare abdomen.

'Fifteen – love,' calls Alejandro.

He plays a really active and versatile game, turns out. Mixing his shots a lot, no doubt to keep me off balance. Working the racquet with his wrist, trying to get topspin. His backhand constantly in play. And almost more powerful than his forehand.

'Thirty – love.'

Alejandro aims for a winner with every whack. He slams away, twisting, turning, jumping, bouncing. My play by contrast is just a lot of quiet moonballing. Alejandro slams, slams. I lob, lob.

'Two sets to love, sorry Tito,' he smiles an hour later as we shake hands at the net. 'Nice playing!'

'Thanks, Alex. It's fun trying to run away from you.'

'Haha! Hit the showers?'

'Cool.'

The shower block for men consists of a courtyard with a sauna and plunge pool flanked on four sides by private stalls. The stalls are very roomy. Doors are high, opaque, and can be locked.

'Share a stall, mate?' says Alejandro.

'Sure – why not!'

Alejandro opens a door and steps into the nearest stall. I follow gamely. I'm shy. So shy I feel as though I'm about to be sick. Alejandro yanks off his trainers, whips off his shirt. He stands for a moment to grin at me broadly. Doing my best to look like a solid sort of bloke, squaring my jaw while wrestling with the laces of my trainers, I try to smile back. Alejandro, bending quickly, steps straight out of his shorts.

Fuck! I don't know where to look!

He's now wearing nothing but a white jockstrap.

I glance furtively at its cup. Fuck! I look away. Throat dry. My laces undone, I drag my trainers off my feet and straighten myself. I fumble my shirt up and over my head. Drop it onto a bench. Turn to look at Alejandro. What do I see? I see a gleaming young man standing completely naked in the centre of the stall.

I close my eyes. I draw down my own tennis shorts and with them my boxers.

I feel slightly weird – I've started to tremble. I open my eyes. The body inside this stall with me – a warm body, glowing – the cock, the balls – Alejandro looks a lot more of a man than me cause his chest and his legs are hairy. He looks almost white, at times, under the right light. My chest and legs are hairless and my skin is dark.

'You're fit, Alejandro,' I say, just about choking with the effort of speaking the words.

'I know, mate!' he laughs.

Not able to look any more, I stand shivering. I can feel his breath on my skin. I shiver harder. Standing so close to him makes me feel faint. It's like all my nerve endings are dilating. Alejandro reaches out with one hand and touches one of my nipples. It hardens.

I feel myself shudder deeply.

'Alejandro,' I whisper, 'it means a lot to me – I mean – I mean, I'm sorta – I mean – '

'You're a babe, Tito.'

He's saying that out of the goodness of his heart cause he's such a nice guy. I'm not a babe, I'm a baboon. My face is too pointed. My teeth are too big.

'You can keep touching, Alex.'

He grunts, very sexily.

My eyes are still closed. Keep them closed! Keep them closed cause you're so aroused that if you add sight to touch and scent you'll go into overload, your brains will blow out of the top of your head! Alejandro, taking his fingertips away, bends his head down to my nipple. He bites. A limber hand meanwhile working its way round my body and coming to rest on one cheek of my arse. A more or less muscled arse, thank fuck. Also, twitching nervously.

I let out a low moan.

Ángela and I always like to end any day, when we can get away from the rest of the family, with a short chat together. Tonight we meet in her room. Ángela sits cross-legged on the bed. I stay stood. I lean myself a bit shyly on the window sill. Am looking at sis. And at a wall of books behind her pretty head.

The room is orderly.

Ángela likes light. She likes simplicity. Her walls are porcelain blue. Spread and drapes are white.

'His name's Alejandro Valverde and I'm just totally gobsmacked.'

'He's the one who drives that new yellow Dodge? And he wears a Rolex? Okay. Why are you gobsmacked?'

'I'm gobsmacked cause by rights a hunk like him shouldn't hit on a berk like me – he should blank me!'

Ornaments in the room are notable by their scarcity. A small photo of our parents, framed in oak. A charcoal sketch of my sis, drawn by me last year, pinned on a wall. An amulet called deer's eye by proles and peasants. A seed, really from a certain species of tree. Deer's eye is known for its magic powers, course, and this particular specimen was a gift many years ago from María.

'He senses your vitality, Tito. He's like the people at the advertising studio – he sees you've got something.'

'Something? I wish! Sis, why has he picked me?'

'Maybe he deserves you.'

I laugh, and start to dance. Ángela jumps off the bed, grabs me, joins me in the dance. The two of us, chortling happily, begin voguing in the scent of summer blossoms and a low shaft of light from the setting sun. We vogue out onto the balcony.

'Angelita – it almost seems too much! I can't deserve to be so happy. Am sure priests would shake their heads and say it's a sin to be so happy. If they could see me so happy. Why isn't everybody in the world as happy?'

'Take it easy, though – before taking off to outer space. First make sure he's really lovable, and also loyal.'

'He's lovable and he's loyal.'

She laughs.

'How do you know?'

'I just – know! And he's – he's gorgeous. And he's so – he's so – hot!'

I stop, cause I can feel myself blushing.

'Hot – ?' she prompts, smilingly.

'It's not really something a guy can say to his sister – but the two of us, we've already – you know, just before, back at the club – we not only snogged but, well – with our hands.'

Ángela is busily blushing herself, now.

'Okay, you're right, we don't need to – ' she stammers.

'Anyway, he's so hot. And he's just lovely, he's really lovely – '

I stop once more, and look away. After a moment I burst out laughing.

'What's the joke?'

'You were right this afternoon. I'm so articulate, don't you reckon? Love, lovely, really lovely! My passion in inverse relation to my vocabulary.'

'Par for the course,' grins Ángela.

We stay stood for a while, our arms resting around our waists. Stood wordlessly breathing the bloom of bougainvillea climbing, wordlessly too, up the wrought iron grille of the balcony. A heaving welter of greenery. Flimsy petals, filmy, vermilion, like coloured crepe strewn freely for a party. Ángela, stood in the sinking low sunrays, breathes shallowly. Me too. One stray tendril of bougainvillea curls under my armpit.

'Ángela, all we need now to make life perfect is for you to find a good guy, too.'

'I don't want a good guy. I want a good grant.'

Cause that's her goal. Sis wants to get herself the best graduate degree possible – the best grades she can possibly score – good enough to win her a top grant for a doctorate. Ángela's always been a scholar, that's what she says. She loves being alone with her books.

'My wishes,' she tells me now quietly, 'are to be a sister, a citizen and a student. A good student.'

'And afterwards? Will you want a good guy afterwards?'

'Afterwards? Well as you know, bro, I pique myself upon the solidity of my reflections and after extensive observation have concluded that going for a good guy's too common a social and emotional failing. All that I've ever read convinces me that human nature is particularly prone to it, that very few of us don't cherish a pathological desire to glue ourselves to the skin and mucous membranes of some supposedly good guy on the score of some quality or other, real or imaginary, we believe he possesses. Good and a guy are different things despite their often being linked and indeed being sometimes used synonymously. So to sum up, bro, I think I can live without a good guy. Only that's me, darling. It's not you.'

You got to be quick to keep up with my sis.

'This is just unbelievable!' I burst out. 'I'm so happy! I can't believe how happy I am today! It's the best day in my whole life! Angelita, I'm the happiest guy in the world!'

2

Villarreal is a town that has been around for more than two thousand years. Temples and palaces and handball courts were first built here a couple centuries before Christ. Dynasties rose and dynasties fell. Peace followed war, and war followed peace, and sometimes the site was sacked and sometimes it wasn't.

Names came and went too.

Nobody now knows the original name of the city but what welcomed Spanish soldiers in the early sixteenth century were flowing aqueducts and flowering markets where vendors sold yellow dahlias and red chrysanthemums. A royal capital, plazas crowded with merchants, magicians, sandal makers, poets. Pyramids. And once more, course, the city got sacked. Afterwards it was built all over again in a new viceroyal style by the Conquistadors.

'We're lucky to live in such a beautiful city, aren't we Alex?'

'Could be worse, could be better.'

He slides his tongue between my lips and drives it back and forth, as though fucking my mouth.

The two of us are together on the top of Cerro del Calvario, looking down at the city. Making the most of a secret nook tucked between buttresses bolstering a wall on a church built soon after the Conquest. We've got a whole afternoon ahead of us, cause it's Sunday. Only yesterday we played our game of tennis, and tomorrow I start work at the agency, and right now I'm feeling this mood of peace, feeling like I'm at a point of balance, a sort of beautiful equipoise. The walls are granite. The church stands on the site of a temple built in the tenth century when the city was ruled by Toltecs.

Elated, swivelling on the balls of my feet, I look out north, west and south across the whole of Villarreal.

Domes, crosses, shimmering in the heat.

Alejandro starts tickling me, first my neck, my abdomen, so I laugh and struggle to pull away. Only he holds me tightly. He reaches down and starts to caress my arse cheeks.

'Mmmm,' I say.

He slides his hand inside the seat of my cargo pants, under my boxers, and strokes my bare skin.

'Wow!' I say.

'Like it, don't you babe?'

'Love it, Alex.'

The oldest part of the city's right below. A tight geometry of tiled rooftops crowded around the Plaza Mayor. Villarreal was a stronghold of the church for centuries under the Hapsburgs and then the Bourbons. A church so well endowed it weathered every political storm in the first half century of the republic. And then the see's prelates stepped forward as one body to welcome the second coming of the Hapsburgs. The Empress Carlota and her courtiers stayed in the city for one month at the palace of the Marquess de la Tijera, biggest of the very big landowners of Villarreal.

A lady diarist of the imperial court claims that when in our town the Empress suffered from her first publicly witnessed fit of insanity. A chat with the spout of a silver coffee pot.

Apparently the spout was quite witty because the Empress laughed animatedly.

'Okay,' says Alejandro. 'Now I want you to give me your arse like a good little brother.'

'Hey, can we kiss a bit more, Alex? I love your kisses.'

Half a million people now live in the city. Most of us live not in the historic core but in the new suburbs. You can look out at the suburbs from up here on Cerro del Calvario. Suburbs stretching five or six kilometres or so into the remote hazy hot distance of the altiplano.

'You're giving your big brother your arse.'

'Am I, Alex?'

'Yeah, mate. You're asking for it – this arse is so totally nice and yummy, like a peach.'

'Okay, it's yours big brother.'

'You better believe it, little sis,' he laughs.

Arses are crucial in the life of any guy in Villarreal. A guy's obsessed with his arse. Only a few guys are willing to give their arse away. And even then only to the right guy, a guy who's a real man, a guy who's one hundred percent manly.

That's the phrase they use, the silly tits.

Straight boys will give gay guys a looking over late at night on the way home from spending time with their girlfriends. Straight boys whose girlfriends won't even allow a kiss until the fifth or six date. Those are the rules for good girls in Villarreal. Straight boys, saying goodnight to those chaste girlfriends, go away with cocks rock hard. Horny and angry. Horny over girls. Angry at girls. So horny that if a boy offers them a hand job then often as not they'll undo their flies willingly. And so angry that maybe instead they'll punch the boy's lights out. And maybe if the straight boy's had a bit too much to drink – or he's downed enough to fake that he's had too much to drink – then he might give a gay guy's arse a good fucking.

Not that he'll want to know the guy the following day. He'll be straight, tomorrow.

We bent blokes call those guys pullers.

We've got a complete lexicon here in Villarreal. A puller is a guy who goes with girls but, when randy, will fuck a guy. Fuck, not be fucked. *Only two types of guys in this world*, goes one saying, *guys who will and guys who pull*. Also you've got your mayate. A married guy, or a guy with a girlfriend, who regularly has sex with guys, not like a puller. A mayate often has his regular wife or girlfriend on one hand, and on the other hand his regular boyfriend. His boyfriend is always bottom, course – the mayate has got to be top. And how about buga? A buga is a guy one hundred percent straight who never in his life would fuck a guy, even when very horny.

Anyway, every guy who wants to look manly can prove it to the world – and to himself – by fucking the arses of other guys.

Go figure!

A guy's arse is the core of his manhood, more even than his cock. Your arse is your secret weakness. Pump another guy's arse and you make yourself more of a man. Give away your arse – or let it get taken from you under duress – you're fucked! So most guys give a lot of emotional and imaginative energy to guarding their arse from other guys. And will fight to stop being thought someone who might get filled by cock.

Well, all that's a crap way of thinking from the past. We don't think that way any more, we're educated young guys.

'I've never been fucked before, bro,' I whisper. 'So you'll need to take it really easy.'

He plants another kiss on my lips.

Alejandro isn't one of those dickheads who think that by taking a guy's arse they can steal his manhood. A lot of young guys still think that way! I know I can trust him completely. Am going to let myself be fucked – know am going to love it, cause it's Alejandro! He's yanking up my polo shirt right now. He's bending his teeth to my nipple again, the way he did in the shower yesterday. And he bites. As before I start to moan with pleasure.

Alejandro looks up from my nipple.

I look down.

Startled, I catch a swift glimpse of something sharp – sly – in the eyes of the guy.

'I'm falling for you, babe,' he says.

My heart bumps so fucking hard it makes me want to jump.

'Are you, Alex?'

'Yeah.'

'I've fallen for you too, Alex. I mean – totally fallen!'

'Cool, cause I'm yours, little girl.'

'And I'm yours, Alex.'

3

Dawn chorus in our suburb. Cockerels crowing. Cock-a-doodle doo. Doves cooing. Coo coo coooroo. Wheeling flocks of littler birds trilling and whitling and piping. My first day at the agency! Am sick with nervousness. Am excited, filled with hope, and – better get moving!

Bounding off my bed, run to my sunny window.

The blinds aren't down. Hate sleeping with blinds down. Look through the glass to see a fluffy little ball of feathers balanced on a branch of a jacaranda. A pair of turtledoves, still asleep. Two tiny tails poking out of the feathery ball. The sight of them makes me go all soppy.

Church bells start chiming.

Dong, doooong, they chime at dawn for the first of three morning masses every day of the week.

I better get dressed now. Only for a couple more minutes I stay at the window. A young woman, dark brown face, blank look, unlocks a gate in the black steel palisade of the house opposite. A maid. Slaps with yellow rubber flipflops across the pavement. Drags bags of rubbish from inside the property.

'Okay mate – look sharp,' I tell myself.

A few seconds get me out of my room and onto the top of the staircase. Papá can be heard from the bathroom across the landing where he's shaving with his electric razor.

'Blessed art thou among women – '

Always while shaving he prays. You can set your clock by the way he starts his day with muttering appeals to the Virgin, blurred by the buzzing of the razor. Mamá, other side of her bedroom door, snoring obliviously. She sleeps apart from Papá.

Don't think they've had sex for years.

A few more seconds get me down the stairs, two treads at a time, and along a passage into the ground floor shower. Afterwards, three treads at a time back up to my room where my clothes for the day have been laid out on a chair. Got them sorted last night. Wanted not to have to think it through first thing in the morning of my first day. So – here we go! Start slipping on a pair of green linen pants, a white cotton shirt, a tie of yellow silk –

'May it please God to watch over your journey,' says María twenty minutes later while stretching up with a calloused mitt to make the sign of the cross. The old love always makes the sign of the cross over Ángela or me whenever we're leaving the house. I bend forward, feeling more and more nervous, more and more excited, and give her a smooch on the cheek.

'Have a great day, María!'

'God willing, darling.'

María has been our servant for a lot longer than I can remember and though I could do nicely without her holy mumbo jumbo, I couldn't do without her love. Ducking out of the house, I catch a quick whiff of the bougainvillea. Wow! Next my hips are brushed by a bush of widow's veil – you know, a verbena, not in flower now, pity. My mood today suits flowers. My mood every day suits flowers! The widow at this time of year isn't veiled, she's wearing nothing but her scrawny leaves, saw-toothed. Wheeling round a corner, I catch the scratchy sound of a twig brush. Next-door's gardener sweeping outside our front gate. We can't afford a gardener so the bloke does ours out of the kindness of his heart. He's short and dark, and squat.

'Hi, Juan,' I say.

He doffs his red baseball cap.

'Morning, Señorito Tito.'

Bounding along the street, weaving in and out of the feathery shade of jacaranda – and now the boughs of eucalypts – smiling at the sensation of my head being combed by lightly clattering leaves, little olive-green dusty sickles. Quickly passing house after house, come to More for Less. A woman stands in the doorway holding a bowl filled with suds. A plastic bowl, dyed lime green. The woman scoops the suds out by to toss it across the pavement with wide swinging gestures – like a peasant sowing seed.

A couple more blocks to my bus stop.

Parrp! Blatt!

Cars, bikes, trucks, vans, buses, minibuses. Sounding their horns. Whenever traffic slows or snarls – and traffic often snarls or slows in Villarreal – count on guys behind steering wheels to start tooting. A well-known way to speed up snarled traffic. A sure way to soothe the temper of your fellow motorist.

Parrrp! Parrrrp! Blattt! Bla-aa-aaaatttttt!

A crowd waits at the stop. I feel exhilarated. We're workers on our way to work! I love the faces of my fellow workfolk. Their faces, their stances, the set of their shoulders. Well, to be honest, the droop. Anyway, a bus fumes to a stop and we push forward. It's already packed. We squeeze up the steps.

We cram into a crammed aisle.

A transfer stuck by the driver on his window shows a head of Christ. Christ nearly large as life and wearing his crown of thorns. It's bloody. He's in agony. Also the driver's hung from his rearview mirror a small Virgin. She simpers inside a plastic frame, fake silver, flanked by tiny vases. Two posies of plastic flowers wired into the vases. A toddler's sandal hangs from the handlebar behind the driver, for good luck.

'I says to her,' jabbers a girl by my right elbow, 'Carmelita, what you gotta do with that guy is this, you gotta tell him where to get off. '

The bus fumes towards the centre of the city. An old man, clutching an armful of dog-eared books of astrology, jabs and worms his way down the aisle.

'Señores passengers, learn all about the signs. The lion and the scales. The virgin and the crab.'

A tired voice, singsong. Nobody buys.

'Carmelita, I says to her – that's what I says – I says, Carmelita, you're gonna get nothing but grief from that bloody guy – '

'Five pesos it's worth to you,' chants the old man, 'and five pesos it costs you.'

He climbs off at the next stop.

Carmelita's confidante sticks to her seat and her story.

On board we're a motley lot of odds and sods. Workmen squatting on benches of battered vinyl, nursing plastic bags. You can see their midday meals inside the bags: a torta, a bottle of fruit water. Or maybe something cooked by the wife, popped inside a little plastic pot and eaten later with a plastic spoon. Charwomen, washerwomen, maids, cooks, squatted on the vinyl too. Gripping vinyl handbags. Jolts of the bus make the big hair that blooms on their heads, glowing with spray, swing and sway.

A lot of potholes in Villarreal.

One girl, scowling into a tiny mirror, fixes a fake eyelid. A girl opposite makes the most of each bus stop or red light to wield her mascara wand. After putting away the wand she rubs the back of a spoon over her lashes. Girls on all sides are combing and patting hair, gingerly fingering their fringe curls. Prole girls in this town almost always sport a fringe curl. At night when going to bed they screw their front hair onto a big plastic roller, and then in the morning they snatch a can of hairspray and spray the shit out of the fringe. Afterwards they wait for it to dry, then slide the roll out sideways – painstakingly, so as not to wreck the curl. A dodgy enterprise, which means all day you keep touching your fringe with the tips of your fingers to check it's not gone lank.

Hey, something wrong under my shirt. A sort of small worming movement. A caterpillar fallen from a feathery jacaranda? Or an olive-green lightly clattering eucalypt?

I make a quick grab.

A hand.

A small hand. Dark. Gnawed nails. Pickpocket, course, some kid feeling for my wallet. A kid who turns out to be a scared little boy about nine years old. Wearing a baseball cap printed with a phrase in English. *Punk is Dead*. An orange and indigo cap, streaked with black grease.

'Your name?' I say.

'José Gallego,' says the kid.

'Here, José Gallego,' I mumble, palming him a peso.

'Thank you,' answers the boy, lowering his eyelashes, and then looking up at me a bit more boldly. 'Your name?'

I grin at the kid and hold out my right hand for him to shake.

'Matías López at your service, Señor.'

A couple minutes later I get off at a bus interchange. Crowds of commuters waiting, walking, wherever you look.

Vendors spreading blankets on concrete pavement,

laying out goods. One sells compact discs. Another carpentry tools. Another straw hats. One young guy in a dirty tee lays out a job lot of latex dinosaurs, chromed ballpoint pens, high heeled shoes for women – violet and scarlet and jade. Ceaseless traffic whirling back and forth, pouring poisonous fumes from exhausts.

'Got the time, squire?' asks the young guy.

'Sorry, don't wear a watch.'

'Okay, go with God.'

Any man in this town who can afford a wristwatch tends to buy one and wear it proudly. Preferably one that's chunky and looks costly. Me, I pride myself on not buying into product. As does Ángela. Well, course am only copying Angelita. Hah! Anyway apart from that I hate straps, belts, necklaces, piercings – can't stand any kind of restraint or weight on the free play of my body.

I want to run free – that's what I like to tell myself.

Quickly, now that my target is close, I try to prove my maxim by scarpering along the pavements of the central city. Feeling great. Scared, but – feeling great! A block, one more block. I come to a nondescript concrete structure. I look up to the first floor. The agency.

Fuck –

Oh well, go for it!

I bound into the lobby, nod at the guard, and pound up the stairs.

Diana is a tall, skinny, slightly ravaged looking woman about forty years old. Her hair is already grey. She's focused, intense and seems very faintly dirty. She owns the agency.

'Welcome to what one hopes will be the commencement of a long and happy career in advertising, Matías.'

Diana speaks very precisely.

'Thanks a lot, Diana. Okay if you call me Tito?'

'By all means. Now, as you no doubt recall perfectly your main task will be to help our two experienced copywriters to brainstorm, draft and edit text. We've alloted you that desk and computer in the corner. Also we'll employ your services as office boy generally.'

'Sure.'

'Don't look so worried, mate,' laughs the assistant director of the agency, coming up behind Diana. 'We're not slavedrivers.'

'Sorry! Do I look worried?'

'A bit, mate,' he says, slapping a meaty paw on my shoulder.

'I'm not worried, Miguel. I'm over the moon!'

'Sweet,' he nods.

Miguel and Diana are husband and wife. She married him, my mother has already found out, against the wishes of her own family. Diana comes from one of the better families of the city. A family like Mamá's. And not like Papá's. Diana's eyes are pale blue. Skin, beneath the slightly soiled film that seems to make it drab, looks almost wholly white. A svelte bod. Correct outfit. Miguel, though, he's brown, short, round, about thirty years old and a son of the working class. Got a degree in philosophy but speaks slang.

'Where do I start?' I say as eagerly as could be desired by any employer.

'Nose away from the grindstone, mate, at least for a bit longer,' says Miguel. 'Come and meet the team properly.'

Four boys and one girl work for the agency. Two of the boys are graphic designers. The other two and the girl are copywriters. Diana handles sales and accounts. Miguel runs the rest of the agency, keeps us happy. The four boys and the girl are smiling and friendly. We start brainstorming a new ad for a tequila company.

All our clients are in the food and drink industry, turns out, and the biggest punter by far is the tequila company.

'Think this concept will go down with Mother Superior?' one of the graphics designers asks Miguel.

'Tidy it up a bit, mate before we fax her a draft. We got to watch our arses with Mother Superior. She don't like a draft to look like a draft – she always likes it to look printer ready.'

'As if she knows anything about it,' growls the graphics designer.

'As if,' agrees Miguel.

'Mother Superior?' I ask the girl copywriter.

'A cow,' says the girl. 'No, hang on, she's not a cow – she's a bitch.'

The others laugh.

'Mother Superior is head of the tequila company,' spells out Diana, snapping her phone shut. 'A woman whose understanding is scanty, who dominates our lives with her caprices, and who has just told me that we must alter the balance between copy and image on the brochures we completed last week.'

Everyone rolls their eyes.

'What balance does she want, sweetheart?' asks Miguel.

'Twenty percent less copy, twenty percent more image.'

'Okay,' says one of the graphic designers. 'More pix, less sense.'

'Quite,' says Diana.

Not that the copy we write makes all that much sense, course. Not, in fact, that it's any more than specious crap. I get a kick from writing it though, from squeezing almost all meaning except for the primal, the subliminal, out of words. We all have a lot of laughs, us copywriters, writing our copy.

On my way home at end of a good day a beggar holds out his hand. We're outside More for Less. A beggar who's dark, listless, skinny. And seems not to have any legs.

'Take pity on this poor soul abandoned by the hand of God.'

I palm him one peso.

One peso is worth sod all, course, only it's one peso over my daily allowance for charity. I budget five pesos a day to beggars. Money is scarce not only in my pockets but in every pocket, purse and wallet in my family. We try to keep up a show of solvency. Really, though, we're just scraping by.

'Typical of her ladyship!' snaps María not a lot later on the landing. 'Wanting a soul to wait on her hand and foot when who knows what work's still waiting to be done downstairs.'

'Sorry, María,' I mumble.

'Not your fault, baby.'

She's carrying a tray of chamomile tea to Mamá. Who's lying on her bed for a rest before getting ready to greet a group of friends for a game of canasta. A card party circulates weekly among the set she calls the *nuns*. Ma belongs to three sets. The nuns she knows from church. A second set, the *girls*, old friends from college, also meet once a week. Also for canasta. A third set – the *snobs* – are too sophisticated for cards and meet mostly to drink. All three sets live on the phone, gossiping endlessly about daughters, maids, husbands, grandchildren, taxes, exes, varicose veins, hysterectomies, breast cancers.

'Women shouldn't loll on beds thinning the blood with tea,' says María. 'Women are made for work.'

'Okay for men to loll though, is it?' I say, trying to tease her a bit.

She's especially crabby this evening because the canasta party will turn the whole household upside down. María's nickname for the nuns is the *witches*. She's grimly anticipating the way we'll all have to snatch a quick supper, and she'll have to rattle quickly through the dishes, and afterwards the nuns or witches will swoop through the front door, smiling, lipstick, white power, silk, and stay till midnight eating pâté sandwiches and drinking sherry.

'Neither woman nor man lolls in Tres Madres.'

'Well – you know, María.'

I dart a kiss onto her bony cheek. She grunts. María came to the city years ago, when she was a girl, from a pueblo sunk in the dark forested depths of the sierra. Nobody in our family has ever been to Tres Madres. Why would anyone want to visit that lost little spot in the pine forests? Yet almost every day of our lives we hear about it. Tres Madres, for María, is the benchmark of domesticity, decency, moral authority.

'The Señora could do a lot worse by just getting stuck into her darn housework.'

'Here, let me take the tea to her.'

I reach out for the lacquered tray. María grips it tighter and gives me a broad grin. The two of us understand one another inside out.

'Don't worry, darling,' she laughs. 'I'll give her ladyship her weak bloody tea, and watch me not say a word.'

María clumps forward. I follow. Our house was built to be tended by many brawny and poorly paid hands for the comfort of our family. I don't feel great about the way we work her so hard. Only she kind of connives at her own exploitation. Gets off a bit on being a martyr to her mistress. A mistress who right now turns out to be pouting on top of her massive old bed – bedspread as slippery with satin as my mum's bum is slithery with silk.

María sets the tray down on a cabinet. She pours a thin yellow trickle into a cup of fine porcelain. She hands it to Mamá.

Mamá sips.

'Ugh, María! I said weak!'

'Make it yourself next time if you want weak.'

I nudge the old woman to let her know that this a funny way of not saying a word. María lets out another little grunt. Mamá lets out a long laboured moan.

'María, please try to be less of a native – my nerves! Draw the drapes on your way out. I find the sunlight gives me a splitting headache in this nasty glary room.'

'If it's so nasty why was it good enough for your blessed father and your poor blessed saint of a mother?'

'What are you talking about?'

Our house was built by my mother's father, who was the son of a good family gently sinking in the world. Two elderly aunts of my mother when I was a little boy lived on an old hacienda in the country. Ernestina and Techa. Maiden ladies, as people say. Very white ladies, they were. White skin, white hair. Their fingers I especially remember – not the common fingers, they were long and thin and pallid.

'Your aunts would never speak to me so rudely,' snaps María.

Techa and Ernestina were extremely courteous, extremely sweet, always giving me cakes, touching me gently. And speaking in a sort of falsetto. And those pallid old fingers weighed down with masses of gold rings. Techa wore a slender string of pearls, too. Antique pearls, handed down for generations among the women of the family. Techa had a habit of fingering that lustrous, creamy little string while sighing mournfully.

Now they're long dead and the hacienda's gone out of the family.

'My aunts lived in the past, for heaven's sake!'

'And you're supposed to be living in the present, are you? We'd reckon you was living in fairyland, us dimwits from Tres Madres.'

María stumps out.

Mamá slumps back onto her pillows. Sighing, crossing herself, she starts asking me about my day. I give her an upbeat account. A cedar crucifix screwed above the bedhead, draped with her personal rosary. Carved from ebony, bought in Rome when we were there on holiday.

'She's a lady, this Diana?' asks Mamá.

'Totally a lady, Ma.'

Also above the bed you can scope a crowd of saints. San Martín. San Lucas Tadeo. The Virgin of Succour. The Black Virgin. Also family portraits framed in silver and ivory. Centrepiece is a black lacquer fan, painted with pink roses, framed, brought back from a shopping trip to Madrid. A glazed frame of mahogany.

Mamá turns her eyes towards me, sighing theatrically.

'Tito, darling boy – we all depend on you, you know. You carry the hopes of the family on your shoulders.'

Not the first time this has been said to me by Ma. Or Pa. Always they're laying good hefty burdens of guilt and obligation and duty onto my back. Also onto the back of poor Ángela. The two of us are supposed to save the family. Get great jobs, earn top money. Climb ladders. Marry. Not just marry anyone, course. Marry well. Marry right. Marry into an old family with old money – or at least a new family with lots and lots of new money. We're meant to do this cause it's natural law that dutiful sons and daughters behave that way. Also cause we're so skint we need to be dragged quick as we can out of an impending pool of deep shit.

'Want me to help with the drinks tonight, Mamá?'

'So sweet of you. Don't worry, leave that to María. She needs to earn her keep.'

'She earns her keep in spades and more, Ma.'

'Heaven knows she taxes us enough in backchat and cheek! Oh it's so shameful having to make do with just one maid. Why can't we live the way I'm accustomed to live? It's my birthright. My family is just as good as the de la Tijera!'

She points at a copy of the city's conservative newspaper lying on one of the satin pillows. A black border enclosing a whole page. Black script inside the border tells us about the death of some aristocratic old lady.

The grieving Family de la Tijera de Lago acknowledge with gratitude all condolences received on the recent occasion of the decease of the late Sra. Aurelia Lacanzo de la Tijera. Comforted by Papal Benediction. We pray for her. Palacio de la Tijera de Lago.

The words Palacio de la Tijera make me think about the Empress Carlota enjoying her psychotic natter with the spout of the coffee pot.

'We're better than the tiresomely boring old de la Tijera de Lago, Ma. We may not be Comforted-by-Papal-Benediction, but *we got rhythm, we got soul.*'

'Darling, nobody's better than the best. And the best of the best families are the de la Tijera. And stop talking lazily ignorant English like a Yank. Now, mind what I say, my sweet boy! You really are the shining hope of your mother and your father!'

'Papá may make a comeback. He's a middle-aged man in his prime, Ma.'

She looks at me sharply.

'He's going nowhere. He's as broken as my poor bleeding heart.'

My father in his heyday was a civil engineer working with one of the biggest construction companies in Villarreal. Not his day any longer, mind you. Papá has become quite a pitiful person. He does the odd job as a consultant and he drinks too much. Well, he drank too much in his heyday, too. He's a man who suffers from stress badly, Papá.

You can read the traces of years and alcohol in his body. Got no energy. Tires easily. Shows not much interest in business or politics. Ten years ago he was a bold character, dominating the family and it seemed the world.

We sit down for an early supper, Mamá, Papá and me. Ángela is studying late at university.

Squawk! Skre-eek!

The dining table has got eight mahogany chairs and all my life I've heard those chairs squawking. Pull out a chair from the table so you can sit, or push a chair back from the table so you can stand, there's this unholy racket. The wood in the curved legs of the chairs is highly tensile. Drawing a chair across the marble paving of the dining room is like playing a fartbox.

Skre-eeeek!

Our evening meal we always eat at the big mahogany table, cause no matter how down on our luck we may be my mother is determined to keep up standards. All members of the family always must seat themselves in precisely the same place around the mahogany. Mamá at the top of the table. Papá at the bottom of the table. Daughter of the house to the father's right. Son of the house to the mother's right. A small silver bell sits on top of the table between me and Mamá. She tinkles it from time to time to summon María.

María, who after she's finished serving the family, will snatch a bite by herself in the kitchen.

'Tito, stay out of the sun,' says Papá as soon as we've sat down and started on a salad.

'Papá?'

'Your face is looking too tanned.'

'Okay, Papá.'

Papá is very aware of skin colour. He's always felt less than acceptable in the right circles of the city because his own colour is dark. Not that he ever talks about the fact. Tell him that he's swarthy and you've made an enemy. He's an educated man – how can he be dark? He's not a native! He shuns the sun. He can't bear to see his daughter or son making friends with dark skinned girls or boys.

'You're getting around with an Indian!' he'll cry.

Papá admires families whose blood is pure white. Families like the de la Tijera Comforted-by-Papal-Benediction. Papá loves Europe. He's always insisted on promoting customs in our family that come from Spain. Certain dishes are served at table – paella, chorizo, goat guts with green peas – because they come from Spain. Yet he's got no social skill. He doesn't know how to make conversation. He prefers a drink to a talk.

Whisky, cause it's European. He won't touch beer – too Indian.

'What are your plans, lad?' he says to me now, looking very sober while taking a swallow of Chivas Regal.

'Plans, Papá?'

'How do you see your future, son?'

Tequila he likes, too. Herradura, his preferred tequila, comes in a crystal clear bottle, colourless, pasted with a white label. A horseshoe is printed on the label, and a peasant wearing a straw sombrero. When a kid, I loved looking at the label. The peasant is about to start peeling a big green agave.

'Licenciado Jiménez on the phone, Señor,' cuts in María.

'Tell him I'm busy,' says Papá.

Licenciado Jiménez is a crony. Papá has no close friends, only a small circle of cronies – men of his own age and profession. You require a university degree to be a crony.

Papá's question about my future has left me a bit stumped. How do I see my future? Well, course I see myself having a successful career – not in commerce, though, and that's not something I can talk about too fluently with Papá. I see myself making my mark quickly at the advertising agency. Diana will soon work out that there's more to me than just writing copy. Won't she? She'll work out that I've got a way with words. And she'll talk about me among her business acquaintances. And after a while I'll get a job in a publishing house. I'll become an editor in a publishing house, one day. Maybe one day I'll even become a writer. A novelist, writing perceptive stories about the daily life of Villarreal.

Downer is that I'm not really too sure there is more to me than just a copywriter!

Papá would hate to know I've got anything in mind so nebulous as being a novelist.

Well, no need to sweat. Maybe nothing will happen other than that I do a decent day's work at the agency, earn my pay, week in, week out, and slowly over the years climb the advertising hierarchy. That's okay. That's awesome! A cool place, the agency, with cool bosses and cool workmates.

'I see a secure career ahead of me in advertising, Papá.'

'No such thing as security, son. Life's a battle. You've got to be bold, and fight.'

Papá feels he always had to battle. My mother's family may be classy but my father's were very ordinary. A clan of small shopkeepers in a country town far away from Villarreal. We never visit that family. Our country cousins are much too low. Papá dreads the thought that after all his toil as a young man we may end up just as low. Or even lower. After all, we own nothing, not even a small shop – only debts.

'Alex, it's my turn to fuck you. We're both guys – why don't we take turns?'

He laughs teasingly.

'Cause you're not a guy, you're my cute little sister.'

The two of us are inside his apartment, tangled up together, naked. Alejandro is smoking dope. I'm not smoking. Don't do drugs, not even weed. I want to stay healthy. Alejandro gets his way, course. We kiss, and we stroke, and soon he's pumping my arse. He pumps forcefully. Moaning, he fills the condom. Afterwards, he smokes more dope.

'I'm looking out for number one,' he says. 'Nobody will look out for anyone else when you're in the fast lane, you need to look out for yourself.'

'True – till your car runs out of gas.'

'Eh?'

'I mean making and maintaining a car is a social act based on complex social contracts. Not to mention making and maintaining a motorway.'

Squeezing me hard, and kissing my shoulder, he lets out a laugh.

'What the fuck do you think you're talking about?'

'You're a lawyer, Alex. You know about contracts don't you?'

'Sod social contracts. What matters is the letter of the law.'

'Also when talking about fast lanes we need to factor in what happens when our eyes pack up and presbyopia sets in and we can't look out for ourselves any more.'

'Presbyopia? What's that, little sis?'

We've been together long enough now, a couple weeks, for me to have lost my first feelings of awe. He's a cool guy, Alejandro. Only I can see I'm gonna have to keep my end up otherwise he'll maybe start believing all this crap about my being the girl. At the moment he doesn't believe it, course. Am pretty sure he doesn't believe it. He's too intelligent to believe it. It's just a sort of game. So it's up to me to bat the ball back at him across the net.

'Long sightedness. You won't need to worry about it for a while – not even in your fast lane.'

4

Sanborns near the Plaza Mayor. We've driven up this evening in our worn old Chevrolet cause we're invited to celebrate the name day of a close friend of the family. Our car was bought new, twelve years ago. Now it looks every year of its twelve, plus a few more.

'Notice that knocking noise, Tito?' murmurs Ángela.

'Yep – it's on the left under the bonnet.'

'A bad omen, you think?'

'I only know about benign omens, Angelita.'

'You've got to get over this pathological optimism,' she says with a laugh. 'Omens can be cruel.'

'Nope – all omens are cool!'

The restaurant has been built inside the shell of a palace from the sixteenth century. A neighbouring palace, also dating from the viceroyalty, was flattened by bulldozers and the site paved with slabs of concrete to make a convenient parking lot for customers.

'Stop trying to be clever and find a space close to the front door, darling,' says Mamá.

I salute her in the rearview mirror.

'Señora, your wishes are my command!'

The steering wheel is my responsibility cause Papá prefers to stay home and watch football on tele rather than come with us to Sanborns. He always prefers to stay home to watch tele. Now, enjoying myself, I spin the wheel in a satisfyingly tight circle and slip into a space not so far from the front door to give cause of complaint to Mamá. The parking lot displays plenty of those big bullet cars they call sports utility vehicles.

You know, Yank tanks.

Dark, needlessly massive, powerfully pointless, windows with tinted and polarised shatterproof glass behind which nobodies can protect their precious privacy. Snub hoods, sorta snouts. Car manufacturers glamorise these ugly awkward things with names implying that owners lead ample, outdoorsy lives spent speeding between town and country. Lincoln Navigator. Chrysler Voyager. Ford Windstar. Cars made for movement, adventure, for zooming away.

Cars packed tight, right now, inside the scant spaces marked on concrete with white paint on the site of the flattened palace.

We get out of our poor old banger. Ángela is travelling light in white cotton. Mamá is poured into a sort of tube of red silk. Me, am cool in cargo pants. We walk into the restaurant, where it's up to me to be the man of the family.

'Fuentes,' I say to a guy in a suit.

He shows us to a table where two women are already seated. One of the women a correct matron of fifty. Her companion a girl my own age, dressed as correctly.

'Darlings!' says Mamá, airkissing near their cheeks.

Smooches, smiles, all round.

Señora Fuentes and her daughter Magdalena are our neighbours. They live in an old family house down a bit from ours and for the last few years have let the lower floor to a woman they don't know cause their finances are as definitively in decline as ours. We've always been intimate. Señora Fuentes is tall, meagre, fancies herself wise in the ways of the world, and smokes costly little cigarettes. We're here for her name day – and she's moaning about money.

'Sweetness, why must one spend one's whole life

counting every tiny centavo?' she asks Mamá.

'*Darling, don't!*' replies Mamá in crisp English. 'Let's simply eat, drink and be merry!'

'Don't mind a drink, certainly,' says Sra Fuentes.

'Never do mind a drink, darling – do you!'

'*Anyway, who cares?*' comes an answer in English.

Sra Fuentes and my mother despise the Yanks yet always compete to pepper their speech with as many phrases as they can possibly shake out of the lexicon of chic English. *Sorry. Okay. Cool. Next week. The weekend.* Sra Fuentes and my mother while talking this sort of baby talk are turned out from top to toe, like all other matrons in the restaurant, in the standard style for a lady. Fingernails grown into long talons and painted red. Mouths greased with lipstick. Big hairy false eyelashes pasted on top of their meagre real ones. Hair permed, bleached, dyed honey or cherrywood or mahogany. How the fuck can straight guys bear to kiss such weird artificial creatures? Must be like kissing an inflatable doll. All nylon. How can a guy help from bursting out laughing when he moves in for a clinch and feels the batting bristles of the fake eyelashes?

Not a problem for Sra Fuentes. Divorced, she likes to sharpen her wit on her ex.

'He phoned me yesterday, asking for a loan,' she says now to Mamá.

'Darling!' says Mamá.

'Only the littlest loan, he said. Well needless to say I asked him why he should need even the littlest loan from his skint ex-wife when he's already got his grasping greedy ex-grip on her ex-matrimonial ex-chattels and her ex-matrimonial ex-car and her ex-matrimonial ex-maid.'

'What did he say, *the loser*?'

English word, again.

'Well he wanted the loan, sweetness, to buy me a name

day present! She's had an abortion, by the way.'

'Who?' boggles Mamá.

'My ex-maid. My ex paid to have their baby aborted and the poor girl let him have his way. By the bye, I notice that dear Tito, with our two girls over there, is laughing and talking ninety to the dozen, as per normal.'

'Matías is an enthusiast,' sighs Mamá. 'He's enthusiastic about everything he does or thinks or feels – it's – it's fun to be around him – he's very refreshing.'

'To me he's tiring,' says Sra Fuentes.

My mother, silenced, chooses to squint into the sugary depths of a sorbet. A crowd of men and women meanwhile glow like flowers outside in the patio. Cottons, linens, silks in pastel colours worn by attractive people whose skin is white or cream or olive. Sra Fuentes and her daughter are whiter than most, nearly as white as Ángela and Mamá. Women in the patio are smiling, laughing, blowing kisses. Boys are clapping one another on the shoulder. Plinks and plunks of guitar strings. A fountain, a real granite waterspout from the viceroyalty, plashes in the patio. Waitresses swish back and forth in their stylized peasant costume – a white blouse with puff sleeves and a pleated cotton skirt, flouncing down to the ankles, candy striped. A vast collar, shaped like a V, dyed fuchsia pink. A folded kerchief, also fuchsia pink, pinned to the back of the head. A plastic name tag dangling from the neck onto the pink collar.

Hello, my name is Silvia.

Silvia works her way around our table. She sweats beneath a thick layer of makeup smeared onto her face laboriously yet inexpertly. Her skin is dark. The features seem Mayan. Bracelets of little linked hearts, moulded from fake gold, let out tiny tinkles as she grips a black pencil and writes on her white notepad.

'Steak, Señoras? We recommend the steaks.'

'*Okay*,' says Mamá. 'Steak for me, medium rare.'

'Steak for me too – rare!' snaps Sra Fuentes.

Silvia knows her work. She easily talks us into ordering more courses than we can afford to pay for comfortably. Soups, salads, tortillas, poultry, beef, pork. Cocktails, wine.

Her cut will be ten or twelve percent on top of the price printed on the menu, assuming we judge her service up to the mark. Well, if you ask me she looks pretty sure to keep up to the mark.

She tucks away her pad, pads off on soft rubber soles.

'I hope she got it all down correctly, she looks a little slow,' whispers Mamá.

'Silvia looks positively simian!' sneers Sra Fuentes.

Magdalena cringes a bit and asks me about my week at work.

'Wicked – really wicked, Magda! The agency gets more and more interesting every day. And the more clued up I get about copywriting the more I like the work!'

'How about your workmates?'

'The blokes in the agency are all cool.'

'How about the girls? Didn't you say one of the copywriters is a girl – and that she's directly responsible for training you?'

'Rosita, yep. She's cool, really sharp – classy.'

'You're lucky to have landed on your feet. Mind you, couldn't have happened to anyone who deserved it better.'

'I dunno about deserving it Magda, but you're right about lucky.'

'Spose she's quite pretty?'

'Pretty? Who?'

'Rosita.'

'Oh – sure! She's got these great big gorgeous eyes. Always looks kinda carefree and happy, too.'

Which is the opposite, right now, of how you'd want to describe the facial expression of our Magda. Almost like she's wearing a mask. Not that a masked look is new. Not on Magda. Often you can't read Magda. Nobody who knows her would think it out of line to claim that her eyes and mouth are enigmatic on a daily basis and at times of crisis turn totally opaque.

She's intelligent, observant, concise.

'Nice.'

'Not that it's one hundred percent groovy at the agency. We tend to have issues with the person we call Mother Superior.'

'Oh – and who's Mother Superior?'

'A gorgon with a bank account. She's our top client and she's also our trickiest client. Right now she's dissing our concepts.'

'Magda darling,' cuts in Mamá, keen on stirring. 'When will *you* be out in the workforce?'

Magda laughs lightly.

'Never, I hope.'

Magda graduated in anthropology at the end of last academic year but so far has shown no sign of starting to look for a vacancy, let alone landing a job.

'One can't live on air, dear,' says Mamá.

'I hope to live on love.'

'What?' says my mother with a blank look.

'Love, meaning – what, precisely? says Sra Fuentes.

'Love,' says Magda. 'Only love.'

'Tito, want to come for a wander out to the patio?' asks Ángela. 'I'm keen to dip my fingers in the fountain.'

'Sure, Angelita.'

We head out of the airconditioned restaurant into the

heat of the patio. We dip the tips of our fingers into the tepid water. Turns out, though, that we've come not to wet our hands but for me to soak up some sisterly words of wisdom. Words that wait till sis has looked at me slowly.

'Magda's careful not to show any weakness, don't you think?'

'As careful as anyone needs to be who's been stung so often by such a waspish mother.'

'Tito, I don't want to be nosy, but – '

'Yep?'

'Well, you know how much I care about your happiness. Also about Magda. She's nearly a sister, too. Anyway, you don't seem to have noticed – ? Well, what I mean – do you think when she's with you she's okay?'

'Magda?'

'Mm, Magda.'

'When she's with me? Yep! Magda's always okay, far as I know. We needn't lose sleep over Magda – need we?'

'No, we needn't lose sleep over Magda – but Tito – well, have you ever asked yourself whether she's losing sleep?'

'Come again?'

'Losing sleep over you?'

It hits me with the weight of its own obviousness. Clam up for a second or two. Magda and – and me! Of course. My mind scoots quick as a wink across the memory of lots of recent scenes, and lots more scenes less recent, and speeches spoken, and speeches not spoken, and course it's clear and simple as four aces in a hand of poker. Our old playmate from down the street is stuck on me, poor kid. Shame flashes through my brain, briefly. Have I led her on? I think maybe I have. Not consciously – at least I can let myself off that hook – but for years we've kinda flirted with each other for no particular purpose.

No particular purpose from my point of view, at least.

Except that flirting with her has suited me nicely as a smokescreen. Easy to get off with guys when everyone in the neighbourhood thinks you're soft on the girl down the street.

Fuck!

Shame followed now by blame.

'Sis, I gotta backpedal with Magda, don't I?'

'You've got to do more than that, bro. You've got to make it completely clear. You've got to let her know why it can never happen between you two.'

'You mean – tell her about me and guys? Why?'

'She won't believe you otherwise,' sighs Ángela. 'Well, maybe she'll believe you but she'll still hold out hope. She needs to know that for you it's boys.'

I find myself at a loss, almost shy.

'How can I tell her?' I say in a small voice. 'I've never said it to anyone except you.'

'And you only told me cause I'd guessed already,' she smiles gently. 'Just make it clear in an indirect way, Tito.'

'Will she get it?'

'Magda's not slow, she'll get it. And you're clever – you can work out a code.'

'I'm not clever, I'm in a cleft stick.'

'You're not hapless, you're hip.'

'I wish! Okay, consider it done Angelita.'

My smart sis kisses me quickly and we slope back into the restaurant, where we find the three others laughing about the woman who rents the rooms downstairs in the Casa Fuentes. Sra Fuentes calls the woman the Screamer.

Mistress of some married man, apparently.

Who drops in on her every second night, at exactly the same time, and ten or twenty minutes after he parks his Ford in front of the house you hear the sound of the woman screaming in faked ecstasy. Well, we assume it must be faked because it seems to be scream-on-cue, dial-a-scream. A scream to make the businessman feel a real hero before he farts off in his Ford. A scream to make him want to keep coming back, and keep forking out the money.

'She's clever at buying the most expensive clothes,' says Sra Fuentes. 'And when she puts them on she's even cleverer at making them instantly look like tat.'

'Dunno how anyone can sell their body for status or security,' I say.

'I feel sorry for the poor woman,' says Ángela.

'Not that anyone in their right mind would ever want to waste a penny on a guy as homely as me, even if I did offer to sell myself for a fast boff.'

'I feel sorry for her too,' says Magda.

'No need to feel sorry for a tart,' jeers Sra Fuentes. 'She's got her head screwed on and her hand held out.'

A screamer ends my day. Alejandro tonight agrees to be the girl for the first time since we started to shag. We're in his apartment. He's given me a key. Not in any ceremonious sort of way.

'Here, this'll come in handy,' he says.

'Oh, sure – ta,' says I.

So it's no big deal. Nice, though. Nice he's trusted me with the key. And now I do my best to push into him slowly and smoothly. He grunts. He grimaces. He groans. He won't let me get into the right rhythm. He clenches his arsecheeks when I want to thrust. He swears and curses. He bites the pillow.

Finally when I push in really deep he lets out this bloodcurdling scream.

'Shi-i-i-i-i-it!'

'Sorry to hurt you, Alex,' I say afterwards. 'We gotta take it easy – it'll all come right after a few more tries.'

'Never again, mate!' he says, scowling at me before hitting the shower.

'Never's a big word,' I grin.

'It's a sodding short word,' he says, grinning back and chucking a towel at me from the bathroom.

5

Heat slams down from a naked sky. Heat slaps back up from the white concrete of our driveway. A hummingbird hovers at the purple lip of a flower-of-paradise. Black windows open onto the street from neighbouring houses.

Black, blank.

Open yet sealed, secretive.

The agency has been closed for rewiring for the first few hours today, so now am heading in to work at pretty near midday. Hot! Sweat already rolling from my armpits and soaking into the cotton of my polo shirt while I swivel from the driveway onto the patio. My polo shirt is too heavy for the heat. My jeans are too heavy for the heat. Levis should be outlawed in this city.

My head aches. I smell petrol from the traffic in the street, cooking in the heat. Frowning down at my leather loafers, I stride towards the palisade of steel spears – brittle, hard – that struts between our front garden and the street to ward away outsiders. Square plots of grass, glistening in front of each house, have been mown into spiky green buzzcuts.

'Good morning, Señor,' pipes a small voice.

I look up. A small heap of rags on the street side of the palisade. Dirty rags, black and musty. The pile trembles a little, which means that inside it there must be rats.

Rats, or – an old woman.

A crone dressed in dirty rags, that's what's heaped on the street side of the palisade. A crone clinging with one gnarled brown hand to a black plastic bag inside which have been stashed empty bottles, sticky glass bottles pasted with labels like Pepsi, Corona. The old woman is fumbling with the lock of our gate. She looks baffled.

I feel sad, obscurely.

'May I be of some help to you?' I ask.

Her face is as brown and dry as a cocoa bean, as furrowed as a walnut. No teeth inside her jaw. Scratch that! One tooth – a back molar, which is yellow.

'Señor,' she mumbles, 'householders are kind enough to allow me into their driveways to collect any empty bottles they may have to give away, but Señor – how can I get past this gate?'

Well, it makes me feel still sadder. Sad cause of her rags and cause of my loafers and my Levis. I even feel sad about my headache, which seems suddenly a sort of luxury. Yet it's not only shame that I'm feeling, now, it's also something different. Relief! Thank fuck it's not me – thank fuck I'm not this dirty crone! Which warps into a renewed sense of sadness, course. How dare I feel relief that it's not me? Who am I to – ?

'The gate isn't locked,' I say with what I hope is quiet respectfulness.

She squints at me quickly, suspicious.

'What do you mean, Señor?'

'We leave the gate unlocked during the day. We find it too much trouble. You know – poking around in the heat with keys? We only lock it at night. Right now you're free to come and go as you please.'

'Thank you Señor. God go with you.'

'And with you.'

Diana is not looking too happy about the state of the world when I step across the threshold of the agency. Seated alone on a chrome stool inside her office, she's leafing her way through sheafs of paper, scrolling her way up and down the screen of her computer. She calls me in and closes the door dolefully.

'Not good news, dear Tito,' says Diana.

I gape like a little kid, I think.

Not bad news either – she hastens on – no need to be alarmed – just not entirely good. Turns out one of our contracts from the tequila company hasn't been renewed. Worse, the contract has been awarded to a rival advertising agency. An agency whose chief, she thinks, may well have been slipping a bribe to Mother Superior.

'Honestly you know, Tito, one doesn't like to cast aspersions but can you think of any other reason why the contract should have been transferred to our rival?'

'Um, well – '

'Of course you can't! Our work is at least as good as theirs – better, in my opinion.'

'Sure!'

'Unfortunately we have to cut your hours, Tito. We're sorry. You've been a real find for our studio. Your vocabulary alone has proven invaluable. We'll do our best to make up the shortfall in your hours as soon as we can secure a comparable contract from some other company.'

'Okay, thanks Diana.'

She touches my cheek lightly with the tip of one gnawed and nicotine-stained finger.

'Poor boy, don't you worry. We've an excellent name and everyone in this town knows it's merited. I've already drawn up a shortlist of companies which we can target in a campaign to get contracts transferred to our agency.'

'Cool!'

Frowning in a distracted way, she turns back towards her desk.

Me, well what's there to do but make my way across to

my own desk? Rosita and the others look at me sympathetically. We try to brainstorm a slogan for slimming tablets. Not a lot of luck. Afterwards we need some bulk photocopying to be done so I'm sent out in my capacity as junior.

Holding an armful of papers, I boogie my way down the street.

The heat has abated a bit because the sky has filled with a smoggy haze. Often happens in the middle of the day. And the pace of passersby has slowed. A lot of people in the city still take siesta at midday. My mood, for some reason, has become kind of perky.

Temp setback, all it amounts to, at the agency.

Diana very likely can poach us some new contracts. Diana, dammit, will poach us some new contracts, cause she's a woman with a will and a way! Right now it feels sorta nice to be cruising to the photocopyist, and handing across the papers, and standing under a shade tree outside while waiting for the work. I look at a chalked board poked onto on the pavement in front of a family caf.

Plate of the day: French fries with cheese, costing eight pesos.

A couple of workmen are counting out pesos one by one to see what they can afford to buy and leave enough for a beer. Nearby an old man wearing a pair of specs is seated on a white plastic chair reading the sonnets of Petrarch. On the pavement a couple of little lads aged about twelve, very dark, have set up a snack stand and stocked it with bags of peanuts, packs of gum, boxes of the fruit juice called Boing. Nobody wants to buy. So the boys are feinting punches at one another and laughing loudly.

'Come on Pedro – hit me where it hurts!'

'I'll make you hurt, hurt fucking everywhere, you queer!' laughs Pedro.

A lot of students aged seventeen or twenty are out and about. All look like clones, really. I scope the guys. Jeans or cargo pants. A backpack. A backpack is a fashion accessory. A guy shows his style with his backpack. Backpacks of leather or imitation leather, of canvas or imitation canvas, heavily stitched. Or nylon in bright colours. Twink boys wear big baggy backpacks and big baggy jeans and loop steel or brass chains from belt to pocket. A tight little clinging tee squeezing their skinny chests. A beanie dropped on top, maybe, tugged low over the eyes. Many guys wear rings or studs on the earlobe. Around the neck a small string of beads. Or a leather thong. Also thongs or beads around the wrist.

'Hey, you loser, Pedro – stop hitting out wild – poke me like a man, not a queer!'

'Stop dancing round like a queer and I'll poke you all right!'

The feinting boys are ignored by the students, cause their feints are pathetic and students are way cool. A big deal among the guy students is how they coiff the hair on top of their head. Hair is totally important among guys. Nearly all of us have jet black hair, course, so we shell out shekels trying to get a cut to make us stand out from the ruck. Gel is big. We slap on the gel. Gel tugged into points so we cover our whole head with spikes. Gel swirled sideways. Gel combed straight back. Boys of a prole type are keen to use gel for a particular style. Dipping their fingertips into it they twist a sort of tiara of sticky hair above the forehead and slick the rest of their hair dead flat.

One guy student, clocking me scoping the talent, steps up pointblank. He lifts his lips, sparkles his eyes, cutely smiling. Wow!

'Hey,' he says.

'Hey.'

'You got a place?'

Fuck! Why the fuck has such a hot guy hit on me, for fuck sake! Fuck!

'Um, sorry – nope.'

'Okay. Me neither. Bummer.'

'Yep, bummer.'

'See ya.'

'Oh, um, yep sure – see ya.'

Winded, stumped, gobsmacked, I stand stupidly outside the photocopyist and watch while the guy walks away. Well to speak accurately not so much watching as perving at his backside. A babe. Hot! Not that this come-on has strained my loyalty to Alejandro. Okay, not more than a nanosecond. Maybe a couple nanoseconds. Ask yourself, why would I want to grope some guy picked up on the street when I've got Alejandro? Fuck, look at that arse squirming inside those tight jeans! Alejandro, of course – well, he's simply the best, is Alejandro.

6

Saturday night, one week later. Alejandro has been lumbered with a big case load at the legal office and has told his boss he'll work late to cut through the backlog. Ordinarily the two of us go clubbing. Ángela's upstairs reading academic texts. Mamá's nagged Papá into assenting to an evening out with Sra Fuentes. All three of them right now are sat in the salon sipping tequila before setting off. Magda's tagged along with her mother, too, saying she'll join a girlfriend in a bit to catch a movie.

Cool. Optimal time to come clean with Magda.

'Want to take a look at my cypresses?' I say.

'Why? You want me to pretend that I can tell a cypress from a cactus?'

'Can't you?'

'Not even for money.'

She comes with me readily enough, mind, to the patio.. Bald walls, naked concrete. Last year, making up my mind to turn it into a bit of a beauty spot, I dragged two big glazed terracotta tubs from the front portico and sat them in the centre of the patio. The tubs are deeply lovely. Puebla tubs, massive, white and azure, planted with a couple of tall cypresses.

Now, when we find ourselves in front of the terracotta tubs, the atmosphere feels sort of peaceful.

Gently as I can, I take her hand.

She looks at me, cool like always, calm, only her hand starts twitching like a little animal. All of a sudden I'm nervous as fuck. Violet shadows from the cypresses are wafting back and forth, stirred by a breeze, noiselessly brushing across the glazed tiles of a low wall. Water spouts from the mouth of a small bronze cupid.

'Magda, um – I've always liked you. You know, it means a lot that we've known one another since we were brats. I've always – loved you – '

She leans forward swiftly, startlingly.

'I love you, Tito.'

Oh my god!

'Magda, you're so – I'll always feel that you're my – my sister. Magda that's what you are, you're my – my second sister.'

She steps back smartly, looks away.

'Oh, thanks,' she says. 'Naturally, I badly need a fake brother. What are you trying to say, Tito?'

'What am I trying to say? Well – well, what I'm trying – the thing is, Magda – like, I mean – the closest possible relationship for me with a woman my own age isn't as a – as a, you know – it's as a sister.'

'A sister, yes. You're repeating yourself Tito.'

She looks at me angrily. She hasn't got it. She hasn't worked it out.

'Magda, I'm sorry – but – '

'Why are you sorry, Tito? No need for anyone to be sorry.'

'Well, I feel sorry – '

We stand silent for a few minutes, looking at the cypresses and the stupid bronze cupid. And am kicking myself cause am a coward. Am a pathetic prick of a coward cause I know, now, that I haven't got the nerve to say what I'm trying to say. I just sort of stand there, drooping gormlessly.

'What on earth are we talking about anyway, and why don't we go back and join the others for a tequila?'

'Magda – '

'Tito?'

'Okay.'

'You two look guilty,' says Sra Fuentes when we shuffle back into the salon. 'What have you been getting up to?'

'Tito's adopted me as his sister,' says Magda with a very relaxed look.

'Oh?' puzzles Sra Fuentes.

'I wish Matías would adopt me as his mother!' says Mamá. 'A true son would treat me with respect, instead of always laughing at me behind my back.'

'Doubtless, sweetie,' says Sra Fuentes, 'you'd find it far more fun to be laughed at to your face.'

Afterwards, I slink away.

Alejandro will be late home from work, true. But I'm now feeling such a strong need for a bit of a kiss and cuddle that I make up my mind to head straight to his apartment and wait for him for as many hours as it takes. On my way I nip into More for Less to pick up some beers. This Abode is Catholic. Long live Christ the King!

He was wearing his white cargo pants that day. God he's gorgeous! Am so fucking lucky! I stand in the shop going over all soppy. Our first date – that date to play the game of tennis – the game that ended with the two of us together in the shower. Yum. The memory makes me smile hornily and serenely in one whack.

Maybe my fuckup with Magda won't prove total. Maybe she'll think it through, and work it out on her own.

Alejandro's apartment is on the ground floor of a new block of minimalist flats off the Avenida Niños Heroes. Only takes me two minutes to hoof it from More for Less. Already feeling a lot less rattled by what went wrong with Magda. Magda knows how to work out the score. She's sure to get it sorted! Think about Alejandro. Yes please! Think about how you're gonna grab him later tonight, the minute he walks inside – knackered from work, poor sod – how you're gonna grab him and kill him with kisses!

Well, anyone but muggins would have nutted out what I scope on opening the door.

A classic scene from a porn pic is what I scope on opening the door. Low lighting, lots of deep shadow and just a few mounds of flesh highlighted erotically. Two mounds of a bare arse pumping up and down. Two more mounds of a bare arse below the pumping arse – a bare arse getting pumped!

He's on a sofa with another boy, course.

'Alejandro – you bastard! You bastard! You fucking bastard!'

Am on top of him, trying to hit him around the head.

He's writhing around under me, pulling his cock out of the bottom boy, twisting to get out of my way. At least the cunt's wearing a condom, thank christ. Two-faced fucking cunt! The boy on the bottom must be getting a bit squashed, poor kid. My whacks – fairly flawed in technique – to his head, to the sharply cut pageboy sported so dashingly by my fucking traitor of a boyfriend, aren't too effective, goes without saying. Cause I don't know the first thing about hitting a guy. Anyway, you tend to punch wild – don't you? – when you're weeping hysterically.

Which course is what I'm doing. Blubbering like a snotty little boy.

'Hey, hey – we're not in a tele soap here, Tito.'

'I love you Alejandro! I love you and you do this!. Do this to me!'

'Point of fact I'm not doing it to you, mate. I'm doing it

to Raúl here – say hey to Raúl?'

Raúl is hiding in the pillows, not looking keen on social chitchat.

'You're doing it to me! I'm yours, and you're mine – I love you, Alejandro!'

Alejandro has now got himself out from under my hapless attempt at a stoush. He's stood himself on his feet and is looking at me kind of ironically. Which as you can imagine makes me feel totally brilliant. Mucus smeared all over my cheeks. Dripping from my lips. And fucked if I can stop myself crying.

'Mate,' he says with an air of calm sweet reason, 'since when did we set up boundaries about monogamy?'

Which bewilders me, course.

'We didn't set up boundaries, Alejandro. We didn't promise monogamy. We just – we're in love with each other for christsake. Aren't we? Weren't we? We didn't set up boundaries cause when you're in love with a guy you just give yourself completely to that guy. Don't you?'

'Who said we were in love?'

'Well, you said – you did say – you said, you said you loved my – '

'Your arse. I love fucking your arse, yep.'

'You don't love – me, myself?'

'Twenty-first century here, little sis.'

'I'm not your fucking sister you filthy fucking fucker! Stop fucking calling me your fucking sister! I suppose you're with this kid cause he's willing to be your girl all the fucking time, is that right?'

'You got it.'

Raúl turns to look at me sheepishly. He's cute. He looks scared. I don't say anything more. Am out the door.

Dogs bark at me from the rooftops of nearby houses. Arf-arf-arf! I'm running away, down the avenue, around the corner into side streets. And the hairy beasts that roam those flat fortified spaces two storeys above the artificially watered earth of our naturally arid suburb will have been feeling restless anyway cause of the hot night and the high humidity.

The silly mutts don't know when they catch my scent and sound that it's only some unhappy sap of a hapless human who's come scarpering past their territory.

Arf-arf-arrrrfff!

They scare me, goes without saying. Also goes without saying I'm safe from their jaws.

The poor curs in fact are just as trapped on their rooftops as I'm trapped by – by bloody him – by his fucking betrayal. Boo hoo! Am still blubbering. Blank concrete walls. Where the fuck – ? Okay, we're outside my sisters's alma mater. Colegio Guadalupe. Closeted nuns will be on their knees praying, or inside their cells wanking furtively, right now. Hard cows whose vocation is to wear white cowls and induce by means of sarcasm and insincerity some desultory sort of misinformation in their pupils. Their pupils yesterday and today, callow nice girls swaddled in uniforms of black and white and grey, shallow nice girls from wallowing white families. A few blocks away stands my own alma mater, Colegio Hidalgo.

Prisons.

Okay, calm down for fuck sake. A lot of the nuns and priests are excellent, and the kids who go to the schools are just the normal range of okay to not quite okay, and it's not the fault of dogs that their instincts tell them to defend their territory. Lighten up, you silly twat.

Alejandro was right, we're doing comedy here, we're not doing melodrama.

Right – rave over!

Predictably, our family home does its own perverse best to look like a prison when I survey it from the street. The massive walls, the iron grilles barring all the windows. Dark, too – only a couple lights burning out the back. Could start to get on your tits, looking at the world like that. You know, kind of dysfunctional. Cause it isn't a prison, is it?

Home – that's what it is – our family home!

Unlock. Slope inside. Stump upstairs to first floor bathroom. Splash face with cold water. Look into mirror.

See a sorry puss! Sorry for itself, brown, swollen, puffy.

Who could blame a guy for wanting to do the dirty on someone with my kind of kisser? Check me out, for fuck sake! Swarthy. Short as a dwarf, nearly. Well – average height in reality. Only, looking at my height, my build, you wouldn't know that a fair few litres of Spaniard run through my veins. You'd think my patrimony was one hundred percent Amerindian.

Black coarse hair. Black peasant eyes. Bloodshot from howling.

I poke out my tongue at myself.

Peering into a sliver of the mirror. A scrappy triangle of glass. The mirror got cracked a couple years ago and this small three-pointed slice is all that's left. You get used to seeing a subset of your own face. All you need do is move a neck muscle or two to slide various segments of your visage into range. You get philosophical. You get philosophical in general, living in this house with this mother and father and maid, coping with the fact that nobody knows how to turn it around, nobody knows how to keep this hulk of a house from drifting onto the reef.

A hulk holed and leaking.

The whole bathroom, like, has seen better days. Check

out the door. Green painted woodwork that's split and peeled. Cracked panels. Handles and lock for the door have been pulled out, too, leaving behind a couple of raw holes. The lock mechanism broke a few years ago. Nobody has managed yet to sort out a new lock. We make do in the meantime by sticking the tip of an index finger into one of the holes to pull the door open when we want to go in or out. You want privacy? Just shove the door shut! An unspoken etiquette of small knocks and diplomatic coughs has been worked out as a way of knowing whether or not someone's behind the shut door, soaking in the bath or squatted on the toilet.

Drying my face, fixing my hair with some fresh gel, helps me to feel a bit more upbeat.

'Yep, you look fit,' I tell myself.

Squaring my shoulders, doing my best to feel fit, I drift back downstairs to the dining room.

Cold, empty. Prints hang in black lacquered frames around three of the four walls. Fruit, lutes, peasant women, dead pheasants. A basalt fireplace abuts the fourth wall. A floor, paved with terrazzo, strewn with carpets that seem on first but not second glance to be Persian. Silver on top of cabinets – showy pieces of plate bought from a department store in Madrid. A chess table, mahogany, topped with squares of ivory and ebony. Orange gladiolus sprouting from a tall vase of cut crystal, bought from a department store in Milan.

Credit card classy, is what.

A big oval portrait of a lady. Heirloom but not worth a lot of money. The lady inside the frame is my mother's great-grandmother. Her hair's frizzed in the style of the eighties of the nineteenth century. And her skin painted to look like the flesh of a magnolia. Her neck slung with a slender string of pearls – the creamy and lustrous old string of family pearls worn during our childhood by Great Aunty Techa.

Tears start to trickle down my cheeks.

Our dead ancestress, not giving any ground, watches while I sit myself at the dining table. The wood in the curved legs of my chair makes its usual protest.

Skre-eeeek!

Why did I go and get besotted with that bastard? Why do I want to fall in love? Why do I want to be in love? Why do I want to find a man and hold him tight and not let him go? What's the emotional logic? What's the logic of wanting your lover to not fuck around with other guys? We all know most men want to fuck around as free and loose as they can fucking well fuck. Only thing that keeps them – theoretically, at least – on anything like the straight and narrow is policing from outside. Policing by mothers, wives, bosses, priests, writers of pop songs, writers of advertising copy. All flogging hell-for-leather the dead horse – the knackered and clueless Rosinante – of the happy heterosexual family.

Why would any sane bent man buy into that farce? We're free, we are. We don't have to buy the matrimonial bedroom suite displayed in the ads.

My longing for a guy to love monogamously – is it just me being a dork?

'Hey,' whispers a low voice. 'You okay?'

A hand on my cheek.

A white woman's hand. Ángela! A weight lifts right away. Not a framed ancestress, this is a thinking breathing young woman. Angelita, thank christ. I reach up and grab her hand. Soft, little, nice. Give it a squeeze.

'Not exactly feeling hardcore perky, is all,' I answer.

'Tell me, Tito sweet.'

Which I do. She sits herself next to me and keeps hold of my hand and listens carefully and frowns at the right places, cries at the right places, and afterwards looks defiant and angry. And says the right thing.

'He's a loser,' she says, 'is Alejandro.'

'Yep – a loser,' say I. 'And a slapper.'

'A loser and a slapper and totally a tosser.'

'A loser and a slapper and totally a tosser and a mutant!'

Now it's like my body, suddenly, surprisingly – excitingly – wants to get straight away out of this glacially decaying dump of an old house and party. Yep! *Fight for your right to party!* Yank pop. Ángela feels my energy. Jumping up, she lets out a slightly wild yell. I jump up and let out a wilder yell. Time to stop acting such a sap. Time for a good time! Ángela stares at me intently.

'What?' she says.

'Clubbing!' I laugh. 'Wanna go clubbing?'

'Sure – let's do it!'

7

Twenty minutes later we're in our glad rags on board a bus pounding its way into the city. Thirty minutes later we're dropping from the bus and alighting in a plaza below the verdigris domes, the fulsome bosom, of Our Lady de los Dolores. The most massive, most opulent, most overblown baroque ecclesiastical masterwork among many others heaving inside the tight geometry of streets and squares around the Plaza Mayor. Olmec. Toltec. Aztec. Hapsburg. Bourbon. Republican. Hapsburg. Republican. Catholic. Money.

'Lovely as always,' says Ángela. 'Only – yawn?'

'Totally, sis.'

We turn away from its greenish highly wrought façade – floodlit in an orange glow – and foot it down a side street. Holding hands, walking lightly on the balls of our feet, we pass a couple of smart little bars. We skirt a second side street where young guys are standing around killing time in provocative clothes, striking provocative poses. Male sex workers who trawl this block. Poor sods, what a job.

A couple more corners and we're outside the club.

'They won't let me in,' says a small glum man standing on its steps. 'A bit strange, don't you think?'

We look at him then look away. Obvious why they won't let him in.

'Maybe they're full,' says Ángela.

'They're not full – it's too early,' pleads the little dude.

A dapper dude dressed in a dark suit. A neat clipped moustache. A trembling lower lip. He looks away from us helplessly and fixes his sad eyes on one of the big blind street doors of the club. One of the big blind doors of old palaces in this historic viceroyal part of Villarreal. Hapsburg. Bourbon. The street doors of viceroyal Villarreal! Vast, cedar, secretive, studded with monstrous knots of iron or brass.

'Maybe somewhere else?' says Ángela.

'I'm going home,' shrugs Dapper Dude.

We wait a bit, watch him wander disconsolately down the street, cause we both feel it'd be offensive to get ourselves admitted to the club right in front of the poor guy. Dapper Dude turns a corner. Smartly, we step up to the cedar door. Ángela presses a buzzer. A little hatch opens with a click and we get scoped silently by the eyes of a heavy.

'*Okey dokey*,' says the heavy, in English.

The little hatch clicks shut. The door swings open. The heavy isn't Yank, course. He's a prole from the wrong side of Villarreal. And runs his thick hands over my hips, my pecs. No weapons. Doesn't deign to take our money, needless to say. No job for a heavy. The job of a heavy is to work out who's okay and who isn't okay. Tidy Dapper Dude was too brown to be okay. He was very brown. Make yourself dapper as you like, your skin's too brown you won't be partying.

As for me, well I sure as hell look too dark.

Only am with Ángela.

Not many girls in this city look whiter than Angelita. Also, tonight she's dressed herself super swish. A little black number worn with the pearls. A bit risky on the bus, but she hid them under an old black mantilla handed down from Ma's Ma, or Ma's Ma's Ma, or some other pious ancestress of ours in ye olde Viceroyalty. Techa handed the string of pearls down, too. On her deathbed, very gravely, slowly, and painfully spelling out – wheezing a lot cause she was suffocating from emphysema – that no daughter of the family owns the pearls for herself but only holds them in trust for following daughters.

Ángela clipped the string around her neck tonight as a way of cheering me up.

'Welcome,' says the cashier cursorily, taking our cover charge of forty pesos.

We step forward, still holding hands, into a dark room stabbed viciously by strobe lights.

A few young pretty women, one or two older guys, in darkness. And lots of young guys. Young guys cause this is the gay club. Ángela insisted we come here. She wants me to enjoy myself drinking and dancing with boys.

'Hey, up for a Corona?' says one lad, catching my eye.

'Sure – you buying?'

He looks a bit abashed.

'*Oops*, sorry mate, thought you were buying. *Anyway*, cheers!'

Oops and anyway are a couple more of those English words flicked constantly off the tongue by matrons or proles or youngsters who want to be thought cool, who hope to be mistaken for highflyers. The boy flops away in his flares. Ángela seats herself on a tiny wooden chair. I take the next. Chairs in the club are all the same, miniaturised pieces of carpentry once used by toddlers at kindergarten now grouped around low wooden tables under the strobes.

We check out the dance floor.

A little polished floor, jam packed with boys dancing to bubble-gum pop. Telescreens sprout from the walls. Cartoons. Tweety. A Madonna concert. A soap about the agonies of a wealthy family in the capital.

Ángela gets invited to shimmy by a gay guy. She's happy to shimmy. I'm joined by some blokes I know from university. We talk a bit desultorily.

'Where's Alejandro?' one of them asks.

'Binned,' I say.

'Bummer.'

'You bin him or he bin you?' asks another guy.

'Well it's always reciprocal in reality, isn't it, even when it doesn't seem reciprocal on the surface?' I say airily.

Three newcomers, wandering into the club, cause ripples. Three glam newcomers. Two boys, one girl. Strikingly white, strikingly tall. The names of the three are quickly whispered around the room. Aurelio Galán and his sister Gladys Galán – from one of the old families of the city.

The other guy is Salvador de la Tijera.

The guy seems preternatural. Not only chillingly blond and frighteningly tall but arrestingly perfect in his body, his features, his blue eyes, his flawless white skin. A white prince.

Wow, what a man!

Wow! I can scarcely keep my eyes away.

My mind nips back to that newspaper on my mother's pillow. Next my mind nips forward to note the Galán boy glancing our way. He and his sister and the de la Tijera dude have sat themselves at a table close by. Galán looks relaxed and happy. Not good-looking. A smiling boy with a face shaped like a heart. Good bod. Dressed stylishly yet casually.

'Check out his suit – it's Versace,' says one of the guys in my group.

'That a Rolex on his wrist?' asks another guy.

'Rolex is cheesy if you come from an old family,' says the first guy.

Which causes me to feel a fleeting pleasure, remembering that Alejandro wears Rolex. Galán looks a lot gentler than Alejandro. Not so sure about his sis. Also got a face shaped like a heart, and as stylish as her brother, but sorta cold. Ditto the boy de la Tijera. Actually, he's still colder. A dead pale face, waxy. Hair pale blond. He looks scarily clean and self-possessed and solvent. Straight, obviously.

'Aurelio Galán – he gay, you reckon?' I ask one of the guys at my elbow.

'Queer as you and me, mate,' says the guy. 'And it's not something I reckon, either, I know it for a fact. He was doing the cousin of a mate of mine last year.'

'How about Salvador de la Tijera?'

'No way he's gay!'

Youngsters from the old families always stick together in public places and never strike up casual acquaintance with outsiders, with people they haven't met already, people they haven't been introduced to properly, people whose families aren't known to their family. A group of them will go as a tight little clique to a bar or a disco and the boys in the clique will never ask strangers to dance. Galán doesn't seem to care about those codes, though. He pops up from their table. He trots across to my group of guys. He comes to me and stops.

He holds out his hand.

'Aurelio.'

'Tito.'

Me! Weird, or what?

'Would you dance with me, please?'

'Cool – sure. Ta!'

We grind together on the dance floor for long enough to work out there's no chemistry. Afterwards, swapping smiles, we slow down and shout at one another the way you do in a club or bar, cause of the sound system. He yells out that he loves partying. I yell back that I love partying. He yells out that he loves techno better than house. I yell back that my fave sound is pop. We grin at each other mindlessly.

'Come and join my friends at our table!' he shouts.

'Yep, okay Aurelio!'

As he steers me back towards his table I note that his sister and Salvador de la Tijera are staring at me insolently. Scary. Fuck. Fuck fuck fuck fuck fuck! Never in my life have I hung with kids of their class. The girl, dressed in black and silver, scowls when presented to me by her brother. I want to shit my pants. Fucked, though, if I show my fear. So get knotted, Gladys! Smilingly, I bow. Afterwards I straighten my spine feeling sick not from bending but from feeling even more overawed by the sight of the guy de la Tijera.

A guy who stands now, takes one step forward, frowns with a sort of gleaming blond glower.

'Hey, how's it going?' I stammer, sticking out a mitt.

The guy, still glowering, lunges at me, grasps. A hard fist. I try to make my own fist hard, but why bother?

'Salvador de la Tijera,' he says precisely.

'Matías López – I mean – nobody calls me Matías – I'm Tito!'

Two young guys, that's what I see, forcing myself to turn away and by mistake catching our reflection in a mirror. Two young guys scowling briefly at one another – a small brown guy, a tall white guy – before dropping each other's hand.

I've fallen instantly in love.

Salvador de la Tijera, so overwhelmingly superior, yet after those first glowers he switches onto his face a look that seems scrupulous, courteous. He speaks with a cool baritone and not a word wasted. I fight hard to take my eyes away or else it'll seem as though some spell has been cast on me to make me look like a dickhead. Or was I born one? Anyway, we seat ourselves at the silly little table.

'Drink, Tito?' says Aurelio.

'Mezcal, ta.'

Gladys sneers sideways at Salvador.

'Excellent choice,' says a smiling Aurelio. 'Anyone else for mezcal?'

'I'm happy to drink mezcal,' says Salvador.

'Call me a cunt if you like but I'm not happy to drink mezcal,' says Gladys. 'I'm unreconstructed enough to think that mezcal is a drink for a man, not a woman.'

'My late grandmother used to take a mezcal in the privacy of her own room at midday, every day,' says Salvador.

'My dad's mother liked to chug a beer,' I laugh. 'Not just at midday!'

Salvador looks at me with surprise. I look at him with what I hope seems like carelessness. I check myself out in the mirror. My eyes – shit, my eyes are emotional and dilated. Salvador looks away.

'Medicinally?' says Gladys.

'For kicks,' says me.

'Fuck!' says Gladys.

A girl from an old family will talk freely and obscenely when she's with friends from her own set but never when with social inferiors. I've heard about this custom. A custom not applying among girls a few steps further down the social ladder. Ángela and her girlfriends would never dream of offending anyone by saying fuck or cunt like Gladys. Why's she using those words in front of me, a guy branded by his brown skin with a big dirty stigma of complete congenital inferiority?

Maybe it's cause she's got something in common with her brother. Aurelio likes to break the rules of their set by being easy-going and upbeat. Gladys, maybe, likes breaking the rules of their set too. Only in her case perhaps it's simply cause she can't be cursed worrying what anyone thinks.

We sit for a few seconds in a silence that grows longer and starts to feel awkward.

'Good thing you guys are watching your words,' I say, not able to stop myself from yammering. 'Always better be careful what you say when you're near me – you might end up in one of my novels.'

Gladys looks at me with a blend of amazement and annoyance, the way she might should a waiter interrupt one of her conversations to tell her about his investment portfolio.

'Your novels?' she says faintly.

'Yep – I plan to be the definitive novelist of this city.'

'May one ask what work you do now? Or are you still at university?'

'Am working, Gladys. Advertising copywriter.'

Gladys sits sneering silently. Can't see signs of any sentiment, negative or positive, on Salvador's drop-dead-gorgeous mug. Aurelio cuts in quickly, starts yakking. The music. The drink. The guys. The clothes worn by the guys. Am feeling ashamed of my own clothes: skintight synthetic tee striped with broad bands of yellow and lime, baggy black jeans, yellow socks, black patent leather shoes. Aurelio in his Versace. Gladys inside her black and silver. Salvador in very fine handsome clothes you don't quite notice, can't quite place yet know to be impeccable.

And then my prince, my blond god, speaks. Quietly.

'I think I heard someone say there's quite the boom in the industry.'

'Industry?' I ask, fervently hoping he's talking to me.

'The advertising industry,' says Salvador.

'Oh, okay.'

You can tell just with a glance that he's straight, unfortunately. His easy indifference to the scene in the club.

His lack of curiosity – in fact, complete lack of awareness – about scores of nearby milling guys trying to catch his eye. At least he's willing to talk to me civilly. Not like bloody Gladys! He and I swap a few remarks about the advertising industry. Aurelio keeps yakking away. Salvador even seems willing to start a dialogue over one of my ordinary offhand off-the-wall remarks about how the house we're sitting inside while necking tequila and listening to techno was built on the site of a temple from the time of the Olmecs.

'Don't you hate it?' I burble. 'Don't you hate the way the Conquistadors laid all that lot waste and created a monocultural desert through so much of our country?'

Salvador looks at me calmly.

'Surely the Olmecs had been laid waste long before the Conquest?'

'Course!' I shrug.

Feeling hot with shame, goes without saying, but working my socks off to look as though I don't give a toss about being a tosser.

'So when you refer to all that lot being laid waste?'

Gotta keep up my end!

'I mean the whole accumulation of twenty or more centuries of structures, artifacts, cultures, concepts – '

'Yes, sorry,' says Salvador. 'Of course that's what you meant, it's just that I'm not as quick-witted as you. I often slow down a debate by wasting time on precise definitions. You've obviously thought about this issue a lot more than I have.'

Gladys takes the chance to slide in a stiletto.

'Matías must have a long list of grievances against families like ours and yours, Salvador. Heirs of those dreadful Conquistadors. I'm glad he's so polite as to sit here with us and not blame us for the way we've stripped him of his history.'

'Yum – stripped him,' giggles Aurelio. 'Hot!'

We all look blank for a bit.

Gladys seems to be the sharpest and shallowest. She's the first to rally. A sweeping critique follows, snipped out in a snooty accent, of the intellectual limitations of those who attribute all ills in our country to its colonisation by Spain.

'Aren't any of your ancestors Indians?' I say, cutting in abruptly.

'What?' snaps Gladys.

'You seem to imply you yourself are certifiably one hundred percent pure-as-the-driven-snow. Almost all the oldest families have a good gloop of indigenous blood, right?'

'Naturally,' says Gladys.

Aurelio, laughing happily, grabs hold of Salvador.

'Not this dude,' he says. 'One upright perfect specimen of walking, talking, blue-eyed Aryan Superman.'

'Yeyo, you're drunk!' cuts in Gladys, grabbing his hand and pulling it away. 'Pity none of us has anything like the generous endowment of indigenous genes that enrich your ethnic heritage, Matías.'

Gladys consistently addresses me with the polite *usted* instead of the intimate *tu* – unlike Aurelio.

'Yep, I'm a real native,' I say.

'Not lacking in native wit,' laughs Aurelio.

Ángela turns up soon afterwards, smiling, and sweaty and pretty from dancing, and takes me away.

'I came on purpose to rescue you from that ice floe,' she laughs when we get into a quiet corner. 'The boy Aurelio looks okay but – brrrr! – that sister and that guy de la Tijera!'

'Gladys is nasty, but Salvador de la Tijera – well, he's – he's not all over anyone, but he's – wow, he's just the most shaggable guy, don't you reckon Angelita?'

She pushes me back and looks at me hard.

'Tito, are you wanting to hit on that conceited snob?'

'Course not – he's straight!'

'Worse than that he's a de la Tijera. Gladys seems very aware that he's a de la Tijera.'

'You've been watching them have you?'

'Is the Pope a Catholic? She's got the hots for him, course.'

'Yep,' I concede gloomily.

I nip out the back for a slash. A tiny security videocam spies as I unzip. Management has ornamented the wall above the urinal with a vast glossy image to perve over contentedly while pissing onto the sheet steel. An image of a woman's arse. An arse cloned along the whole length of the wall. Six arses, vast, glazed. Arses shaped like a pear, course. Not like an apple, like a guy's arse. Pear arses wearing a lycra thong. Emerald green lycra, glittery. Pear arses of a woman kneeling, resting the weight of those big lycra-garrotted bum cheeks on top of a couple of stressed heels and murderously unsteady glossy yellow stilettos.

Twelve slick, sleek, fuck-me stilettos.

Six garrotted lady arses.

In a queer bar.

Men!

After banging the doors back out to the club I see that Salvador and his party are leaving. It's only one in the morning. I've heard people say nobody from an old family will stay at a public place for too long. Aurelio, nice guy that he is, takes the trouble to come across to say goodbye and in his wake he drags Gladys. He says it was fun necking tequila together. He bends forward to peck me with a kiss. I kiss him back. Next, turning out of politeness to his sister, I bend forward and pucker my lips.

Gladys pulls her head back coldly.

'Good night,' she says, hauling her brother away.

'Kissing a woman in a friendly way isn't done in old families,' comments Ángela. 'Not unless you've known the woman really well for years and years.'

'Who'd want to know her really well for one effing week?'

'They think it's horribly common and middle class.'

'We're not middle class, Angelita.'

'Aren't we, Ti? What are we?'

'We're floating free.'

Alejandro – you remember Alejandro? Well it hasn't taken me too long to learn the limits of my pain about Alejandro. Am lying in my bed back at ours, looking up at a bar of blue moonlight on the ceiling. And am not caring a fuck about Alejandro. An ache, sure – yet an ache that seems shallow. No anger, no agony. No lying awake weeping.

I lie awake dreaming, instead.

Dreaming about Salvador.

Swivelling my head on my brown neck I look out through my open window at the moon serenely swimming through the night sky. Silver, indigo. I smile, feeling almost as serene myself.

Straight, white and a de la Tijera!

'Mr Right!' I snort to myself.

8

Sunday dawns hot and sticky. Well, fact of the matter, who knows how it dawned? Ours has been dead to the world for hours and we're now well on the way to midday. I wake up to the sound of songbirds. Sloping in my electric blue boxers across to my open window, I get a glimpse of the foreshortened back of the only other member of our family who seems to be awake. María, while getting up at dawn as always, will however be heading out for her day off.

All the maids of Villarreal take their day off on Sundays.

María's twisted her hair into a long grey pigtail. She grips the handle of a cane basket while she walks away, very slowly. On her way to mass, goes without saying. After mass she'll meet her maid mates and take it easy strolling in the Alameda.

I gaze down at her fondly. The pavement under her plastic sandals looks sultry. Phew – the air's fucking sticky!

María turns the corner.

Nipping across my room, slipping into a pair of shorts, throwing on a loose tee, I dive downstairs. The songbirds are calling me outside. I pad up and down the patio for a bit, checking out my cypresses, peering into pots of flowers, fingering fronds, kneeling to check out insects, stones. Papá glooms through the doorway. He looks tired. These days he always looks tired. We nod at one another and off he shuffles to the driveway where he starts his weekend ritual of washing the car. Turning on a tap myself, I drag a green hose around the garden, spraying water onto the thirsty plants and singing to myself.

'Busy boy, aren't you?' yawns Ángela, next of the

family to come out onto the patio.

'Busy and feeling brilliant, Angelita! Am feeling exceptionally brilliant!'

She laughs, and kisses the side of my head.

We're joined briefly by Mamá. After greeting us with a couple of grunts she clacks back into the house in her old purple mules with cork soles. Her baggy body is wrapped in chartreuse candlewick.

'Coffee!' she cries. 'Coffee or I'll kill somebody, I swear on the Holy Cross!'

Ángela and I head to the kitchen to see to it. And to cook breakfast. It's what we do on Sundays. We have fun. We chat, chop green tomato and purple onion and red chili, we sing, we laugh, we refry brown beans, we scramble eggs. Papá eats a lot as always. And complains about his digestion. And as always is the first to leave the breakfast table. Soon we hear him start his shower. Papá likes to take a very long shower on Sunday. He stands silently under the nozzle. Afterwards he stands noisily on the ceramic tiles and slaps the water away from his body. Slaps himself very hard with the flat of his hands. Very healthy, he always says, keeps a man healthy. Slapping away, he makes loud shivery and huffy noises.

'Brrr, brrrrrrr! Hfff! Hffffff!'

We hear the shivery huffs mixed with the wet smacking of skin against skin while we chew sweet rolls and sip coffee.

'Plans for the day?' asks Ángela.

'Well there's that nuisance of a Paco coming, of course,' peevishly says Mamá, setting down her coffee cup then threshing restlessly through a glossy magazine. 'Heaven knows why.'

'To kiss his aunt like a good nephew, that's why.'

Mamá lets out a snort.

'Well to my mind a good nephew doesn't wait till he's

thirty years old before he turns up to put a face to himself and give his aunt a kiss. He's after something, that's my opinion. He's coming here because he's after something.'

'What could he possibly hope to get from us, Mamá? Our cupboard's bare.'

'Thanks partly to you, my girl, dawdling your life away at university.'

'Don't quite follow, sorry.'

'Dawdling your life away with study when you could be married by now, and out of my hands, one burden at least lifted from around my neck.'

'Oh sure, you're a martyr to your family, poor old Ma,' says Ángela, grinning. 'And you mixed your metaphor.'

After which she runs upstairs to hit the books. Mamá follows with a slow shuffle, clinging to *Marie Claire*. Ma's mules release weary little flaps and flops against her horny yellow heels as she climbs the staircase laboriously.

I stack the dishes then go out once more to the patio.

Watering pots happily.

A blond god.

Salvador.

Papá, after a bit, comes down dressed carefully in cream coloured shirt and cotton pants ready to drive to the cemetery. He spends two hours every Sunday at the cemetery, visiting my grandmother's grave, where he talks to her and prays. Afterwards his routine is to drive back to ours and settle down for the duration in front of the tele, watching football. Papá when young played a lot of football and volleyball. Not now. Now he stares wordlessly at one bout of footie after another, falling asleep in front of the screen and snoring loudly. He always insists that he never snores.

Dinner he eats alone, normally. After dinner, more tele.

'Give my love to Gran,' I say.

'Aha,' says Papá.

He's confronted by a bit of a dilemma, course. On the one hand he knows he should really do the good dad bit and invite me to come along to the cemetery. Not that I want to waste two hours of my life watching him mourning the old lady. At the same time he hates having company. He loves to be alone at the graveside, does Papá.

Off he goes to be melancholy.

Mamá when she comes onto the patio one hour later doesn't doubt she wants my company. The slattern who earlier dragged herself about in a pair of down-at-heel mules now has warped into a stylish matron tucked into a silk suit and gold choker.

'Come with me to midday mass,' she says. 'A nice girl from the capital will be there today – pots of money – youngest daughter of Sra Barrionuevo.'

'Church being the best place to buy brides, Mamá?'

'I pray for your soul daily.'

We waste another minute or two swapping these sorts of courtesy.

'An email's come from Paco,' says Ángela, skimming down the staircase.

'Paco?' mutters Mamá. 'Why won't he leave us alone?'

'He's catching a later flight – he'll be here at six. Here's a printout.'

'Ngh,' snorts Ma.

'In point of composition the email doesn't seem defective,' says Ángela, winking at me. 'The idea of the lap of Saint Cajetan perhaps is not wholly new, yet I think it is well expressed.'

I grab a printout she's holding.

The email tells us how deeply our cousin regrets notifying us in such a tardy manner of the unforeseen change to his flight plans. And how we live in the lap of Saint

Cajetan. And how he hopes we will not be inconvenienced excessively. And how he looks forward with intense pleasure to the prospect of, etc etc. Words to the max, his emails. Always. He's never yet met any of us, having been content to keep in postcard and email contact for years, birthday greetings, name days, new year, Day of the Dead.

'Well that's a relief,' says Mamá. 'That's two hours less of his unwanted company to put up with, thanks to this later flight.'

'Isn't he lucky having such a loving aunt?' laughs Ángela.

'Blessed saints!' cries our mother at six o'clock, peering through the ornamental grille of the balcony and the feathery foliage of jacaranda so she can spy on a pudgy newcomer who's just stepped out of a shiny car and pressed an ignition fob, locking his doors.

'Come away, he'll see you staring Mamá,' whispers Ángela.

'Oh shush, Ángela!'

The car doors have locked with the usual little electronic sound.

Gleep!

A sound somehow underwater, like Tweety dropped into a bowl of water and left drowning.

'He must be rich,' I say. 'The car's a Mercedes.'

'Rich and conceited,' snorts Mamá.

'Mamá, please,' says Ángela. 'We don't know anything about him yet, except his prose style and now the make of his rental car.'

'Which no doubt he can't afford but has hired on purpose to make an impression on the poor relations,' says Mamá. 'He looks impertinent, that boy – run downstairs to welcome him, Ángela, and tell him I'll be with him in a minute. I'm not hurrying myself for any young nephew who fancies himself.'

Ángela darts away. Ma struts in a stately sort of style to the landing, takes up her position, lets out another snort.

As for me, day's been great so far! Swimming at the sports centre and talking with some girls I know. And reading a couple chapters of Borges. My mood has stayed way buoyant. Maybe cause I keep hitting the replay switch in my mind to run one more time through a fantasy vid of surrendering myself to Salvador.

Lame, I know!

Whatever – it does the trick.

Am feeling great. Am feeling on the ball. Am feeling in the mood for any sort of novelty, even this not too promising cousin. Paco manages a maquiladora at Tijuana. A factory churning out shoddy synthetic shit for sale to bargain basements in department stores in the United States. Owner of the outfit is a corporation in New Jersey.

So, bounding off the balcony and loping across the landing, I look alertly down the stairwell into the front lobby.

Ángela, standing on the scuffed parquet below, swings open our heavy front door.

'Casa López?' says a fruity, pompous sort of voice.

'Hi Paco!' says Ángela.

Coz takes a proprietary step forward onto the parquet.

Mamá makes up her mind that the moment is now right to stream in silk and gold down the faux marble treads of the staircase beaming with fulsome insincerity.

'Welcome, welcome to our home – your home, Paco!' she trills playing the matron, the society hostess, the guileful holder of a secretly faulty hand at contract bridge. 'And here so punctually too – six o'clock on the dot!'

Paco beams back at his aunt.

'A positive outcome will only come from keeping strictly to the correct timeframe,' he says after a couple of hearty kisses. 'Schedules are crucial to success, and maintaining a schedule by turning up on time for any appointment is one of the points well understood by our colleagues across the border but sadly not yet taken to heart within our own business community.'

'Well, you appear to be a model of businesslike demeanour yourself, Paco,' says a slightly sarcastic Mamá.

Sarcasm looks to be wasted on our cousin. He wolfs it down credulously.

'Aunt, one of my aims as a businessman is to bring not only the best systems of management but also the mindset behind those systems from the cutting edge of United States commerce into our own disconcertingly laidback land of mañana. So this is the family house? Nice piece of real estate! Looking tired though, distinctly tired if I may say so, Aunt. Needs a new décor.'

Now time for me to make my bow.

'Hey, coz!' I say, running down the stairs and crossing the parquet of the lobby in a few fast strides.

'Matías?' he says sonorously.

'Tito!'

We slowly pump our hands up and down. Paco is a small brown man whose physical movements, in spite of the insistent energy of his words, seem slightly sluggish.

'Your sister's a real babe,' he whispers to me a bit later.

'Hey, Paco – !' I start, angrily.

Stop myself short, though, remembering that the silly prat is after all a cousin and a guest.

'Does she party?' he leers.

I say nothing.

'Dear nephew, it's a lovely sight to see you seated in my salon with your cousins and with myself, one happy family,' Mamá says later that evening, smiling, sighing, folding, and unfolding a good but threadbare linen napkin. 'Wouldn't it be marvellous to know that our future as a family might be as happy – that we might be prosperous instead of poor – that we might end our days inside our own beloved home rather than out on the street with nothing in front of us but the begging bowl?'

'Aunt, anyone's at risk of losing their assets,' points out a helpful Paco. 'Unless they learn how to boost their outputs.'

'Well, no doubt, Paco – if you say so – although how does one boost – ?'

'Outputs in many cases can be boosted best by disinvestment, Aunt. Liquidating low productive plant will spinoff as augmented output no less than operating a high productive plant.'

'You mean we should sell our house?' I say.

'Paco, no!' cries Mamá.

'Calm yourself, Aunt. Tito has misunderstood. The family house as an asset can only appreciate. No, I was speaking more generally about disinvestment as a strategy for maximising productivity in our national economy.'

'You mean, then,' smiles Ángela, 'more money can be made by closing down rather than keeping open a factory or some other business?'

'Precisely, cousin. Not only private sector spending but maybe more crucially spending by the state sector. The central problem confronting our national economy is the government's ongoing inability to restrain state spending.'

'Goodness, is that so Paco?' gamely says Mamá.

Her eyes are starting to fix on him with a look of deference, even worship.

'High levels of public debt raise the risk premium that is part of all interest rates, thereby raising the cost of capital.'

Mamá nods and smiles bobbing and bobbing.

'Dear me, Paco – dear me!'

Ángela takes charge now, trying to elicit at least a few facts if not much sense from our cousin. The maquiladora, for a start – what are the hours and wages of workers in Paco's factory? And what's the margin of profit for the owner? Paco looks at her askance, taken aback by her frank curiosity. He glances down longingly at a newspaper he clutches in one little fist. *Wall Street Journal.* Ángela wants to know about his women workers and also wants to know what percentage of profit goes outside our country.

'Also, what scale are we talking about?' she says. 'How many people are employed by your factory?'

'Employment is a relative term, as it happens, cousin. The factory employs full-time, half-time, quarter-time and we also contract to outworkers, which means that for accounting purposes we refer not so much to men or women as to employee equivalence units – '

'Well then, Paco,' prompts Ángela. 'How many units work for your factory?'

'Four thousand and ninety units are employed by my plant.'

'A large factory. How many units are women?'

'Sixty-seven percent, dear cousin.'

Mamá, floundering far from her depth, grabs hold of the liferaft of hospitality. She sweeps food and drinks towards her nephew. We're now seated, swamped, on the oxblood red sofas. Throats are crammed with sweet snacks and scalded with hot coffee. Papá has hidden himself with his tele inside the library.

'How do you like Villarreal, nephew?' flutes Mamá.

'Slow old place, isn't it, Aunt?'

'My late father said that in Villarreal the best families speak the best Spanish in the Americas,' almost timidly ventures Mamá. 'Dear me, though, I do think it would be delightful if we were a bit closer geographically to the Mediterranean. We're so awfully far away. One can't help but feel we're a backwater here, hidden in our valley. And really, you know it costs a dreadful amount simply to buy a ticket to Madrid, let alone the costs of taxis and hotels and new clothes and so forth – '

'Why would you need to waste resources by buying new clothes, Aunt? A woman with your looks doesn't need any ornament.'

'Oh, Paco – '

He flatters her shamelessly. She gobbles it down.

'He's proved to be such a nice boy,' she says afterwards in the kitchen. 'Always a soft word to toss my way, and a woman wants to hear soft words.'

'Me, I prefer tin tacks,' says María, now back from the Alameda.

'Men were so lovely to me when I was younger,' says Mamá wonderingly. 'I haven't always been the ruin you see before you, a woman old before her day.'

9

A break from our cousin is needed so badly that after an hour or so I duck upstairs and go online to *villarrealgay.com*. You know, to try to hook a hot guy. Any halfway okay guy, really. Salvador's my true love, course. My Blond Prince. A new millennium will dawn before he'd give a nonentity like me the nod, though, even if he wasn't straight. So makes sense to try to get my end away with some guy a little less godlike.

Who should I try to hook? What role should I play?

How about down-to-earth boy next door?

Or maybe tonight I'll pretend to be a rampant top? Or just an ordinary lonely lad who wants to find true love? Hang about – that's me anyway! Isn't it? Yep! Ordinary lonely lad who wants to find true love –

Not a lot of mileage in that, in a gay cyberchat.

Bottom boy, that's the role I decide to play. A guy can usually get laid if he offers himself as a bottom boy and he's got two arms, two legs and one arsehole. Let me write myself a profile.

Here goes:

Horny bottom boy, age 22, brown eyes, short black hair, brown complexion, looking for sex action with hot top.

Okay, let's go trawling! Dive into the chatroom. Quickly, scrolling down the screen, scan the profiles of other guys.

Astroboy, fit manly top, age 26, 1.78 m, athletic bod, white skin, not ugly, not naff, not fem, looking for similar bottom.

Astroboy won't want me cause I'm too short and cause of my skin colour.

BOY21, educated, friendly, age 21, not looking for sex –
He sounds pretty nice. Bummer that he's not looking for sex!

TwoHotTops: looking for a hot lay younger than 25 for a threeway.

'Hey man, you fancy getting yourself fucked raw?' is the opening gambit of TwoHotTops.

Classy!

'Maybe,' is my diplomatic reply.

'Okay. Our ages: 30 and 37. One of us white, the other one light brown. Height 1.70 and 1.75. Weight 75 kg and 80kg. Hard dicks right now, waiting for you.'

'Cool. You two guys want to fuck me together?'

'One will fuck you and the other will suck you while you're getting fucked. Okay?'

'Well to tell the truth – scares me! Sorry.'

'Fuck off then, time waster!'

'Happy birthday to you too, dude. Ciao.'

Okay, now let's look for someone more vanilla.

Erick-xx: cute top, nice hard cock shoots buckets of cum, 54 years old –

Oops! Not looking for a daddy!

Down the list I scroll my slutty way.

D'train: 'You're the one for me' – romance, candlelight, fidelity.

Stick that heteronormative candle up my arse, man!

Come on guys!

CoolDude33: if you're older than 24 and younger than 40, not shorter than 1.70 metres in height, and slim – welcome. Are you the man I'm searching for? My man will be honest and healthy. He won't use drugs. He won't be a liar. He'll enjoy sex but also he'll be looking for love. He'll want to find a man who prefers to start a relationship with friendly evenings spent together talking, sharing opinions, perhaps taking in a movie or a concert, and he'll wait to find whether or not there's a real mutual attraction. He'll be a professional man, like me. He'll be white, or at least his complexion will be light brown and not dark. He'll send me his photo –

Well am not looking for a dude who writes a minor work of literature when what we need right here, right now, is no more and no less than a fast fuck.

HotRod: top, gym bod, manly, 1.83 m, 78 kilos, light complexion, great smile, intelligent and hot! 18 years old, 20 cm of throbbing dick –

Cool! Let's try!

'Hey dude,' I say to HotRod.

'Hey,' says HotRod. 'What you up to?'

'Looking for a hot top to fuck me senseless!'

'One hot top here ready to service you, man! I've got a place. Where are you?'

'A couple blocks from Niños Heroes. Where are you?'

'Central city.'

'Cool! My complexion brown – that okay? I love being fucked.'

'Brown is okay. You love being fucked? I love fucking!'

'Wow! What's your cock like, dude?'

'Very nice and thick, big head.'

'Wow!!!!!!!!!'

'Hehehe.'

'Please dude, please fuck me tonight?'

'Sure will fuck you! Will give your mouth a good fucking first, and cum all over your face. Afterwards will fuck your arse. Can you get into city central?'

'Yep, sure can. Midnight okay?'

'Midnight is sweet.'

'Cool, here's where we can meet, man – '

At ten our whole family party's at Sanborns. As usual without Pa. Also as usual with the family Fuentes. Mamá's now so keen about Paco she wants to share her happiness with her best friend, Sra Fuentes. My nephew's such a steady sort of boy, boasts Mamá. As though she had something to do with it. He's done so well for himself with his degrees in accountancy. As though she ditto. He wears nice sensible suits. Ditto. He's climbed the career ladder so quickly.

Ditto! Ditto!

Paco, encouraged, now serves up invaluable yet free advice to our family, Madga and Sra Fuentes.

'First, life's a rat race,' he says, gripping my elbow when he sees my gaze straying. 'So you got to learn how to handle horde after horde of dirty toothy bastards – I mean rats – you got to make sure you're the biter not the bitten.'

'True – if you want to be a rat,' is my answer.

'Actually the rat is a highly sociable species,' says Magda kinda archly.

'What in the name of heaven are you children talking about?' gurgles Mamá.

'Ching ching, Ma,' I whisper as she calls for another marguerita. 'Go easy.'

'Is the rat really a sociable species?' says Paco. 'Later will search the net and find out.'

'I can help you,' says Magda. 'An engaging species in every respect, the rat.'

'Mamá!' I hiss. 'Please, not one more marguerita!'

'Of course you'll allow me to be host for tonight?' booms Paco.

Ma, scowling at me triumphantly, asks that her marguerita be a double and scarcely takes time to catch her breath before carrying on with industrious praise of her nephew. He listens. He pontificates. Paco drinks many beers quickly, though, so suddenly he's off to the toilets.

'You see how your nephew just tripped over that waitress?' croons Sra Fuentes to Mamá. 'It's because he was looking at the busty brunette by the bar. Seems to have an eye for a good-looking girl.'

'Men always have an eye for a good-looking girl,' says Magda. 'What a shame for the girls who don't look so good.'

Fuck, poor kid.

Magda thinks herself plain. Nor is she wrong, which is one reasons why I'm a failure for not telling her I'm gay. She could well be thinking the reason I'm not interested in her sexually is cause she's not pretty.

Not that anyone could call me catch of the week!

Wish I could say to her that – that if I did go for girls then – well, maybe the girl I'd go for would be her, Magda. Wouldn't that be cold sodding comfort? Shit – wish I could think of something to say to make her feel okay about her looks.

A wish not especially shared by Mamá.

'Magda darling,' she says with a show of goodwill, 'you'll be pleased to hear that he's got an eye for you – my nephew has already noticed your pretty pale skin – he said to me earlier when you were walking towards us that he thinks your skin strikingly pallid.'

'I'm charmed,' says Magda. 'He seems to prefer a prettier skin a bit closer to home.'

'Oh, you mean Ángela, I suppose?' smirks Mamá.

'Got him sitting up to beg,' says Sra Fuentes.

Ángela glances at the two older women, shrugs.

'Yes, I suppose it may seem that he likes Ángela,' says Mamá. 'Well, not to beat about the bush, since we're among friends, I really do think he very much admires Ángela.'

A dangerous smile swims across the foxy face of Sra Fuentes.

'Lovely, sweetheart,' she says smiling so widely that she

shows her two full rows of rather yellow incisors to Mamá. 'In that case, Angelita darling, what's your opinion about coitus between cousins?'

A short silence allows us to blink at one another with dismay at the thought of any erotic life led, or not led, by Paco. Magda starts stirring spilled sugar into a small pattern of stars. A melody about lost love comes oozing out of an overhead sound system. The slim rims of cocktail glasses sipped by Mamá and Sra Fuentes are sticky red with smeared lipstick. Mamá fidgets with an amber necklace strung around the thick folds of her chins. Sra Fuentes inhales pensively the poisons of one of her costly little cigarettes. Ángela, silver necklace falling onto her breasts, sits mildly with her mind in her books while keeping a lively eye out for anything that might pop up.

'He really can be good for a giggle,' says Magda.

'He – he who?' cries Mamá.

'Your nephew.'

Mamá pouts.

'Magdalena, what are you going on about now?'

Ángela laughs, silver necklace shining, and leans forward.

'And not only good for a giggle, a man of character.'

'Wha – character?' I laugh back.

'So sincere!' she says. 'So sincerely convinced of his own rightness. Cardinal virtue isn't it, sincerity?'

Magda lets out a quick little laugh.

'Sincere conceit doesn't upset me necessarily,' she says. 'Not when it pays its way with platinum American Express.'

'If you really believed that, Magda,' I say, smiling, 'it'd be my cue to bow out of your life forever.'

'I don't think you're in my life, are you?'

Well – course I flinch, conscious once more of our bungled talk the other day.

Paco comes pontificating back to the table, plants his big bum back down, starts drinking more beer. Orders taken for dessert. We talk. We drink. Me, a glass of wine. Dessert dished up. We eat, and talk. Magda tells me quietly how worried she's been lately about money. She confesses she really doesn't see how she and her mother can keep their household going for many more months unless somehow they get some new source of income or some lump sum of capital.

Ángela in the meantime starts to have problems with Paco.

Our cousin's quaffing and quaffing. The more he quaffs the braver he grows. And all of a sudden he lurches towards my sis.

'Angelita, my sweet little cozzie, give us a kiss – just one kiss, won't you cozzie?'

He clasps her around the waist with two meaty mitts.

'Paco dear – let me go, please,' whispers Ángela.

Only she can't quite break his grip. Paco squeezes harder. Ángela frowns. Paco breathes onto her face with words of emotion and halitosis.

'Just one kiss Angelita – one itty bitty kissy wissy, just for Paco – '

'Let me go, Paco.'

'Who's my sweety – ?'

A sharp shove from his sweety sends the plump mauler toppling back against his chair.

'Well my dear Ángela,' says Sra Fuentes, 'now one knows your opinion about coitus between cousins.'

Coitus is on my mind. HotRod at midnight. My mind keeps fixating on the fuck. Cock aching over coffee cause it's been stiff and throbbing off and on since the soup. Mamá protests a bit when I tell her I'll stay behind in the central city and get home my own way. She wants to keep playing happy family to impress Paco.

'Sorry, Ma. I feel like a walk. Gonna head down to the Plaza Mayor.'

'It'll be dead, darling. Nobody out and about there this hour on a Sunday.'

'S'okay. Just feel like a walk.'

Mamá gives me a discontented peck on my cheek. Afterwards, other kisses, farewells. Off they all straggle to the carpark.

Not long now!

One arse ready to be shafted!

Loads of cute dudes of eighteen or twenty are scampering along the pavement, some alone, some with their mates, some with girlfriends, in the Plaza Mayor. All proles. Or in other words what Mamá meant by nobody. A few boys wear the ultra baggy look – huge flapping pants with drop-crotch as low almost as the knees, hair gelled flat and held in place with a hairnet. Most guys, though, are dressed in designer style.

Knockoffs in other words.

On their feet they sport knockoff Nikes. On their scrawny backs, knockoff Ralph Lauren. Or knockoff Calvin Klein. Or knockoff Tommy Hilfiger marketed under numerous permutations of the name: Tommy Helfiger, Tony Hilfinger, Terry Holdfinger. Only when you strip these boys down to their knickers will you find all pretence abandoned and their balls and bums bobbing around inside nameless little scraps of nylon or lycra.

No sign yet of HotRod.

Twenty past twelve.

Did we get our wires crossed? Wander up, down, glancing at, being glanced at, by prole lads. Will give my dude another twenty. Not looking too hopeful now. Yet feeling stoic. A fuck's only a fuck, is all. A fuck's here today, gone tomorrow.

And looks like it's not here anyway.

Forty minutes slog past as slowly as a junkie in bovver boots.

Early in my life as a grown bloke – few weeks ago – I'd have felt deeply shirty. Not now. All you got to do is turn on your heels and stride away. Sod some sad cunt posing as heroic HotRod. Poor wanker getting off on setting up false assignations. *Anyway, who cares?* English. Not this gullible prat. Who needs a fuck in real life when you can hug your fantasy of Salvador de la Tijera?

10

'Smug toad,' mutters María. 'And talks like a Yank!'

A week has passed and we're about to be freed from the happy burden of hosting our cousin Paco.

'Please keep your opinions to yourself, María,' moans Mamá.

'Suits me! I'm not paid to have a mind? Suits me down to the ground!'

María works slowly, very slowly. All day long she shuffles painfully yet steadily through her tasks. On six days of every week, year in, year out, she gets up before anyone else and turns on the gas stove to refry the beans and brew the coffee for breakfast. Once the house is awake she makes all the beds. Afterwards she washes the dishes, straightens the kitchen, fills the washing machine with a first load of soiled laundry, starts the sweeping. She sweeps every room beginning with the kitchen and ends laboriously, mutteringly, by working her way backwards down each stone tread of the staircase. We pay three hundred pesos a week, full board, which is the going rate for a maid in our suburb.

She's working hard today cause it's time for yet another supper party.

'The lace from Normandy,' says Mamá. 'We'll spread the Norman lace on top of the supper table.'

'We or me?' says María.

'Oh very well – I'll spread it myself.'

The supper party is our farewell to Paco. He leaves tomorrow. At last! Guests will turn up to stand in the salon and eat delicacies we can't afford, drink alcohol we can't afford, and whose suppliers we'll need to pay with our plastic cards. Mamá tosses down the latest issue of the conservative newspaper, heaves herself out of her oxblood sofa, lurches away in the direction of the linen closet.

The paper has fallen open on the society news.

First communion was taken yesterday in the gardens of the Hotel Mesón del Ángel by blah blah, son of blah blah and blah blah, the sacrament received from the hands of His Grace the Bishop of Villarreal. Godparents were Aurelio Francisco Galán Montoto and Gladys Gabriela Galán Montoto together with family friend Salvador Juan de la Tijera de Lago.

'Tito, come and be useful instead of dawdling the day away over the rag,' says Mamá.

'Sure, Ma. What can I do?'

'You can carry the dining chairs in here for a start. Set them against the walls.'

'Yep.'

'Oh, and Tito – '

'Mamá?'

'Do help me out with the finer aspects of the party. I mean the social interactions, the mingling. I want you to take care of the second rate guests, the ugly ones, you know. Keep them well away from Paco. I mean people like Magda.'

'Are we lionising our cousin and looking down on one of the closest friends of the family?'

'Don't be tiresome and moralistic, darling – leave it to the priests, there's a good boy.'

One hour later the guests, first or second rate, ugly or gorgeous, crowd the salon swallowing pastries and champagne. Magda seems not to notice that we're operating a policy of steering her away from Paco. Seems no need to steer her away. She keeps other company. She keeps company with me, for a while, climbing the stairs so we can look at the stars from the balcony.

Looking, we swap ironic comments about friends and family.

'It's so easy to laugh at Paco,' I say laughing myself.

'Why?' says Magda.

'Because he never understands he's being laughed at.'

'He's certainly naïve,' smiles Magda, swinging her hips against the grille, snatching at a scrap of bougainvillea.

'He's an arse licker towards his gross mercenary bosses in New Jersey,' I say.

'Do we actually know that they're gross and mercenary?'

'Only by a sort of reverse inference from his glowing reports about their avarice.'

Magda laughs lightly.

'He does like to talk, doesn't he?' she says.

'He's a craven little sucker, is Paco.'

'Still, better for your cousin to be a craven sucker holding down a good job – isn't it? – than a craven sucker with a poor job or no job.'

'Not too sure. A craven sucker with no job isn't exploiting a factory full of workers – sorry, units.'

'The workers will be exploited whether it's your cousin or some substitute who sits at the managerial desk.'

'He's just a jerk.'

'He's your cousin, he can be useful to you Tito.'

'Paco? No way, Magda!'

'You might make an effort to be friendly. You're so cavalier the way you behave. You don't let him feel important and happy. You tease him, and you make him feel edgy. He's worth making happy.'

'Why?'

'He's got so horribly much money! Why not turn him into a friend? Invest a bit of time in trying to make him your friend? Looking upon it as a sort of considered career move? You could charm him, you know, if you chose to make the effort. Do it for the benefit of your own career. All that awfully useful money!'

'Magda, you'll never make it as Machiavelli.'

'Suppose I'd better get downstairs and play my more customary role of wallflower.'

'Now you're clear when it comes to the futures market, Aunt?' says Paco. 'We can exploit the futures market as a type of insurance against losses resulting from currency devaluation, but we must understand at the same time that gains in the futures markets tend almost always to be greater or less than losses on the spot market – and also that the opposite holds true.'

'Spot market – certainly, Paco.'

Our cousin is offering us timely last advice concerning our non-existent money before he sets off this morning for Tijuana. Mamá thanks him and says how happy she'll always be to have him to stay.

'Aunt your invitation is received gratefully indeed. In point of fact it's what I've been hoping to hear. And you can feel sure that I'll take up the offer in the very near future.'

Ángela and I look at him with horror.

'Cool, coz,' says sis really quickly. 'But won't you run the risk of upsetting your bosses by coming back here so soon and leaving your desk empty?'

'Ángela, I'm touched. Needn't worry yourself. Can't spell out the facts, but – '

'We'd hate you to put yourself in your bosses' bad books just for our sake.'

'Angelita, no need to worry!'

My turn to try.

'Coz you gotta be on your guard,' I say. 'You know what big wheels are like. Keeping in good with your bosses is your first duty.'

'Admittedly – '

'And your underlings, too. Don't forget about your underlings. They need you! So don't worry about us – our feelings won't be hurt even if your duty to your bosses and your peons keep you so tied to your desk that you can't come to stay with us for years.'

Paco beams complacently.

'My bosses know the score, Tito. Can't say any more, sorry!'

A taxi carries him away.

Papá comes out of hiding – our cousin didn't know his uncle was skulking secretly inside the library – crawls into the car, gets ready to steer towards a suburb where he's to meet one or other of his cronies from old engineering days. Ángela hitches a lift. She's off to the university to start her new academic year. Myself, got to get to work. A slow day at the agency. My mates inside the studio are a lively lot like always, though, so like always we talk and laugh our way through the slack workload.

A whole week passes quickly.

What kind of week? Well, not a great week, you might say.

The agency has been coasting on low gear cause we haven't yet won any new contracts since losing that top commission from the tequila company. Now we get more bad news. The tequila company has made up its mind to terminate all contracts with our agency. Axe our agency. Our spies soon find out that the contracts are to be handed across to a rival agency – the agency that walked away with that first tequila account.

'We must all be clear about this, it's absolutely no reflection on the quality of our work,' frowns Diana, biting a nail. 'What it means no more and no less is that our rivals have been systematically and unscrupulously bribing Mother Superior.'

My workmates sit silent, looking at each other helplessly.

Diana, standing in front of our desks, starts chewing that nail quite ferociously. Miguel, who hasn't said a word till now, rolls his eyes.

'We tried, mates,' he says. 'Went so far as to send me to try out my charms on Mother Superior.'

Diana gets stuck into a second nail.

'Your charms?' says Rosita.

'Rosita my flower what we did is this, we sent me along to her office to offer her a bribe of our own. We made up our minds we'd offer the sainted dragon lady a personal cut on everything if she renewed our contracts. Ten percent, was our offer.'

We whistle with surprise.

'Shit!' says Rosita.

'Yep, that's the word love,' says Miguel.

Miguel has a knack for telling a yarn. He does his best to spell out this story as black comedy. We hear how he crept cap in hand into a coldly gleaming office to stand humbly in front of Mother Superior. We hear how he fixed his face to look meek while she scowled at him severely. We hear how he tried to sweeten his offer of a bribe with a smile of mild innocence. We hear how his offer was followed by a long silence, icy. We hear how Mother Superior rose in her majesty. We hear how she told him she believed he knew where to find the door.

'Meaning she was pissed off that we were only offering her ten percent not twelve,' shrugs Miguel.

Diana looks around at the room mournfully.

'I shall start work straightaway on a shortlist of companies that may be willing to transfer their accounts to our studio,' she says.

So that was Monday.

Tuesday, we work on what we've got to hand. Wednesday, our spirits are perky. Thursday, we learn that the biggest creditor of our agency has suddenly called in a debt cause his spies have told him about the loss of our contracts with the tequila company. Friday, turning up for work, I find the door of our studio still locked. Buzzing the buzzer, hammering the street door, yields nothing more than a hollow echo. What the – ? Trot back down the stairs to the foyer and ask the guard. He shrugs.

'Sorry squire, don't know anything about your agency.'

Step outside to the street. Stand on pavement – slabs of concrete littered with forgotten fag ends and spat-out scraps of chewed gum – looking up at the nondescript concrete structure. No sign of life on the first floor.

Fuck – !

Sit myself on the steps. Wait, wonder. At last, tugging out my phone, I text Rosita.

'What's up with agency? Where you?'

She texts back straight away.

'At mine. Agency bankrupt. Diana kneecapped. No jobs.'

'You and me topped?'

'Topped, yep. Have a nice day!'

11

Peasant women from the countryside are walking along the street. Women artisans and tillers of the soil, that's who they are, come into the city to sell their wares at the weekend market. Old women whose heads are draped with black linen shawls. Younger women who've twisted their own black linen shawls around the top of their head to help support the heavy load of big baskets.

Women of all ages wearing all sorts of costumes depending on where they come from – what province of the state.

Nahua women from one province wear white cotton blouses stitched with dazzlingly coloured embroidery. Long bunched skirts rustle around their legs as they walk. They cinch the skirts at the waist with a wide coloured sash. Women from another province wear black skirts. And women from another wear skirts striped vermilion and scarlet, tied with red sashes. A quite different costume, a sleeveless tunic highly embroidered and dropping to the ankle, marks women from a fourth province. A tunic dyed green or yellow.

What am I doing looking at peasant women?

Well, what I'm doing is walking away from the empty agency and roaming aimlessly. No point going straight back home right now. Gotta think this through –

'A gift for your mother, handsome boy?' sings out a tribeswoman. 'A little gift for your loving little mother?'

My mother, loving and little!

Not wanting to look snooty I stop to take a look at some

wares. A circle of young tribeswomen have spread a display
of ceramics and woven work on blankets under a viceroyal
portico. Others have arrayed dry herbs and aromatic barks.
Nearby a group of old ladies cowering under black shawls
are nodding off over a shambles of chopped portions of
poultry.

Flies!

Villarreal in summer is a city of flies.

Flies hovering over fruit and meat and bread in the
markets. Flies inside cafés crawling into sugar bowls. Maids
and mothers and market stallholders wave bits of cardboard,
rattan fans, swats moulded from plastic, baseball caps,
hopelessly trying to rid themselves of the whole race of fly.

'Thank you, good morning,' I say, wandering away.

'God go with you, my boy.'

A dark skinny guy my own age stands on a street corner
at one of the colonnaded entrances to the Plaza Mayor. He's
pressing an armful of paper flyers against his weak chest,
peeling them off one by one and poking them at any passerby
who's not quick enough to shy away. What a thankless job!
Well that's my first thought anyway. My second thought
follows on fast. How much does the thankless job pay?
Cause a job's a job. And me, right now, well meet Mr
Jobless.

A flyer ends up in my fist cause I feel sorry for the boy.

'Ta, mate,' I say.

'Cheers dude.'

The flyer on its glossy front shows a photo. A good-
looking young guy. A guy dressed in a nice white shirt and
spruce tie sat trim at a desk. A row of white words yell out
above the glossy grooming of the guy. *Win a better job and
earn more!* Saplike, like someone who's never been a
copywriter in the ad industry, I feel a little jump of
excitement. Cool! Maybe this flyer will be the answer! Let's

check out the contents!

Peel open the flyer.

Scan the text with my trusting eyes.

Optimal employers today require optimal Computer Literacy. We offer optimal opportunities for study to equip you for a job. Additionally we offer optimal facilities for financing your studies at our private, exclusive, optimally accredited, Computer Science Academy. Optimal financing facilities, when you take a closer look, seems to mean paying the school a hunk of money.

Quite a hunk of money.

Which is what you find in at least half the ads in the so-called employment columns of the newspapers of the city. Muggins knows cause he worked his weary way up and down those columns a couple months ago before landing the job at the agency. Jobs don't seem to be had for the asking, weirdly enough, when you're a young graduate in literature with lacklustre marks and no strings to pull trying to make ends meet in the fine old viceroyal city of Villarreal.

Wander into the Plaza Mayor, stop for a bit to watch chess players.

'Care to take my place, young man?' asks a coot.

'No thank you, Grandpapa.'

Chess and dominoes are always being played in the open spaces of the town by men, sometimes the odd woman. The punters seat themselves at rickety little tables under big awnings. Me, I can't stand chess cause it's so constructed, so abstract. Which makes me feel sort of guilty. Supposed to be a mark of intelligence, course, playing a good game of chess. You got to consider each move seriously.

Just what I hate!

I hate it when you got to be right on top not only of the move you're playing now but your next move too, and the move after that, and all your other moves, not to mention all the moves of your enemy. That's the logic of the game – that the other player is your enemy.

Well life's not like that!

Is it?

Hate it when the only reason for playing a game is to total the other player. Hate it when the only way to total someone is to be cold and calculating and to conceal all your plans and use a lot of low cunning, and not to trust anything to luck, to chance, to serendipity, to comedy.

Sod that!

Sod low cunning, is what I say.

Yet all the old gaffers seated here at the tables with their earnest frowns and their well worn polyester shirts, most of them looking like they're clerks or shopkeepers, together with the few shrewd and intense women who I reckon are schoolteachers or retired secretaries, they seem sorta admirable. Crouched over their chessboards, they're in the grip of a passion. A passion that clearly connects just about every bit of them from their minds right down to their stomach. While as for me – well, look at me! Hanging about waiting for – for what? Not knowing what, and feeling – well, a bit downbeat, is what.

I need a coffee, so set off across the plaza.

The Plaza Mayor during the centuries of the Viceroyalty was the setting for all sorts of scenes. Markets were held here and foodstuffs and handiwork and woven serapes were sold from stalls. Criminals were hanged here, watched by silent crowds. Cockfights spurted blood and raised dust. Religious processions spurted more blood – from the backs of flagellants – and raised a lot more dust. Along comes the mad Empress Carlota! All stalls and gallows cleared away. The imperial authorities, wanting the place to look continental, lay out a park.

Willows and poplars and pines from France and Italy and

Spain. Gravel walks. Box hedges strutting in geometrical patterns towards and away from fountains and statuary.

Topiary.

Lots of topiary!

Box and pyrocanthus clipped into crowns, balls, spirals, corkscrews, dogs, ducks.

A slightly gritty park arcaded on all four sides by colonial palaces, the herreresque cathedral, the porfirian theatre. My fave café's tucked under the portico of the Teatro Villarreal. Sorta smart but also sorta arty. Skipping up a flight of shallow stone steps, nipping across slabs of marble, I drop at a table inside an archway. Tall table with tall stools. You can drink beer or tequila here, but mostly you ask for espresso.

'Morning,' says a cute young waiter. 'Drink?'

Iron lamps, each as big as a car, hang high above your head from a ceiling garlanded with wreaths of gilded plaster.

'Cappuccino, ta mate.'

He winks. He walks away. Nice arse!

The style of the place is slightly fake. Fake in a harmless way, which is great! Love the place! On all sides are writers, singers, artists, downing demitasses, spouting oratory. Right now you can check out a guy with a huge Indian nose who's wearing a bright floral shirt, open at the neck. He's no clone working for a company. He's wearing sandals. He's wearing ripped jeans, jeans that gape at the knees. He's about thirty years old and he's writing. A poet? Opposite you can check out another guy also about thirty. He's wearing glossy ringlets, a curly chestnut beard. He's white, with green eyes, dressed in a denim jacket and reading a thick book. Academic, I'd say. The two guys in their two different ways look totally cool, totally men who know who they are and where they are and what they are.

Wonder if my life's going to be so good when I

eventually turn thirty?

Hope so. Know so!

Gotta make sure it's good!

First find yourself a job, mate –

An old man comes to the table, busking. Only a couple of teeth in the front of his scrawny jaw. Rags hanging from his back. He bows at us deeply, like an ambassador. Gripping a guitar – stuck together with strips of sticky tape – he starts to strum, to sing, quaveringly, about a medieval court in Spain. Poor old bastard. A spear of terror lances right through my body.

Fuck!

Maybe we're fucked.

Maybe our family's fucked.

Maybe we're going straight down the spout. Maybe what's waiting for me by the time I get to thirty isn't an espresso in the café Teatro Villarreal but a spot in the gutter out in the squatter settlements on the edge beyond the suburbs. Maybe what's waiting for me by the time I get to seventy will be what's come to this old cove?

Yank tourists are strutting past with cameras and cold looks.

I frown upwards, up at the domes of the cathedral, glorious bulging domes glittering with brilliant coloured tiles. Our Lady de los Dolores.

'Waiderr! quacks a Yank. 'Waiderrrr!'

My spunky little waiter trots across with alacrity, knowing he's up for an optimal tip if he keeps on the ball.

'Margueridas,' says the foreign voice.

'Honeycomb, sweet honeycomb!' calls a squat brown man weighed down with two armfuls of plastic bags and swaying across the flagstones. 'Honey, sweet from the comb!'

Two nuns in long brown habits and white cowls, both

wearing spectacles and looking sour, stop the vendor.

'How much?' they ask.

He mutters a price.

'Scandalous,' they snap.

Shrugging, he sways away. He wears synthetic black trackpants and a torn white tee. His plastic bags are crammed with glass jars.

'Honeycomb, sweet honey – '

Okay, so maybe I'm fucked. Maybe what's flapping its way towards me on scurfy wings from the future is a career not as novelist or even salaryman but busking old cove. Better to busk than get fucked by some capitalist!

Paco proves himself as good as his word – a word none of us wants to be proved good – and after a fortnight waddles out of another rental Mercedes. Greetings are swapped. Followed, oddly, by his waddling off straight away to spend the evening with Sra Fuentes.

Magda drops in next day soon after breakfast.

'Tito, I need to talk to you,' she says cornering me while I'm watering my cypresses.

'Oh – okay Magda.'

'I've got something serious to say.'

Clipping her words carefully. How do I feel when I hear those carefully clipped words? Slightly sick, is how. Cause clearly my cover has been blown, somehow. Somehow she's found out about my sex life. Right here and right now she's gonna tackle me about my being gay.

Had to come sooner or later. Take it like a man, mate!

'Sure – cool. All ears here, Magda.'

'It's to do with Paco.'

Once or twice the possibility has crossed my mind that my thick-headed cousin might be angling for Magda. He's come on to her a couple times, I know. Nor has she shoved him away as forthrightly as he was shoved by Ángela that night in Sanborns. No question of my silly cunt of a cousin standing a chance of getting lucky, mind you, with a girl so onto it as Magda.

'We've been sleeping together and now we've decided to marry.'

Course clueless here goes into shock and shouts out sharply.

'Magda, what the hell are you saying!'

'Sex, and next – nuptials.'

'What the fuck – !'

Magda cringes, but only for one tick. She recovers herself quick as a whip and, lifting the corners of her mouth, twists onto her face a look she must reckon cool and ironic and droll. She looks like an actress playing a cameo role – a cameo, cause she's not a babe so thinks she can't ever be a star – standing between the two cypresses in those big blue and white tubs from Puebla.

'Well he's certainly neither a sensible man nor good company. His company, in fact, is pretty irksome. Still – he's not so bad when in a horizontal posture.'

The thought of that makes me boggle a bit.

'Far – out – ' is all I say.

'You're not normally so short of words,' she smiles.

'Magda, um – I hope you'll be – happy!'

'Well he'll be my husband and I'll be his wife. I don't know about happy. I've never thought all that highly of marriage you know. Or of men really. Only I've always intended to get a husband. I've got no money. I'm not pretty. I definitely don't want to spend the rest of my best years working for a salary, with some scrap of superannuation to look forward to as my reward for living on into a lonely old age. No – I want someone to pay my way. And that someone may as well be Paco. I'm confident I can manage him pretty well. He's a dimwit but really you know that's a favourable circumstance since it means he'll always be easily outmanoeuvred by any woman with half a clue.'

'Well you've sure got a clue or two, that's true.'

'And my mother and I are sick of eating leftovers. We've been eating leftovers for so long that neither of us can quite recall what was in the original meal.'

Her affected insouciance gets sort of spoiled when I grab her hand and whisper to her really slowly.

'You won't be happy with Paco.'

An awkward pause follows. Her lower lip droops. I can barely trust myself to speak.

'Ti – ti – ' she starts to stammer.

Ángela steps up, without knowing she's walked onto a minefield, and offers coffee. Magda grabs the chance to regroup. Suavely she drops my hand, kisses my sister, nips away down the driveway. Ángela peers at me quizzically.

'What's up?' she says.

Okay, let's stop for a tick to think how to answer.

I've always felt that my way of looking at the world was not quite Magda's. Yet never would I have thought she'd be willing to screw a slob like Paco. Not only screw but marry! Magda – the subtle perceptive friend of so many years becoming a cynical wife to cousin Paco! A sort of nausea at the certainty that she won't be happy starts twisting into a fear that maybe she's worked it out right, done the sums correctly. Maybe she's willing to sell herself cheap cause that's the way things are, that's the way the planet spins on its axis. Maybe it's my inadequacy. Maybe I'm still thinking like that snotty little kid who used to play doctor and nurse with Magda. A twit of a kid with a gormless dream – a fantasy that we've got a right to be happy –

'Not sure whether I've been authorised by Magda to tell you, Angelita.'

'Okay, wait till you're sure one way or the other,' says sis.

'I do need one of those coffees you offered.'

A couple minutes later – the two of us seated with cups and talking in a desultory sort of way about her first essay for the semester – we hear the sound of bare feet slapping across the kitchen floor and turn to find María.

'Angelita, you're wanted sweetheart – and you too, Tito dearie. We're all to join your cousin and mother in the salon, or so he says.'

'Oh? Any idea why, María?' asks Ángela.

'The toad says he's got news to announce to the family.'

I burst into laughter.

'What's the joke?' puzzles Ángela.

'One of those situations where people say they've got to laugh or they'll cry.'

'He's a pig, not a toad,' calmly comments María.

The fragrance of roses blended with coffee fills the air when we step into the salon and find our cousin standing in a dark suit above Mamá. Mamá hunkers down in one of the oxblood sofas. You can see she assumes she's about to be bothered by some tediously intractable bit of family business and she's fixed onto her face her *oh my poor weary brain* look. No doubt she thinks it'll be something to do with money. She shoots a pleading look at Ángela.

Paco squares himself importantly.

'Aunt – and cousins, and – and what a pity my uncle isn't here to hear! I propose to inform you about a matter of utmost importance to the family. A matter of – of – '

'A matter of spot markets, you mean Paco?' mutters Mamá.

Paco looks confused for a second or two.

'Marriage, Aunt.'

'Marriage?'

Paco has had enough of small talk.

'Marriage may be seen in many ways as analogous to a business merger, since it incorporates not only complex personal relationships but also widely ramified social and material matters. My reasons for wishing to initiate such a merger are as follows. Firstly, as a successful businessman I will find my prospects maximised careerwise. A wife will free me from any necessity to attend to domestic trivia and thus will enable me to focus my mindset on the cutting edge of commerce. Secondly, a young woman possessing manners sufficiently poised may serve me as consort and on occasion hostess at the numerous social functions which play such a crucial part in securing a positive outcome for negotiations in the world of industry. Thirdly, my own personal attributes are not derisory. My career success to date, my prospective career successes for the future, make me highly bankable. Fourthly, I have adored a certain young woman since I first stepped across your threshold.'

At last the sweating wally comes to a stop, not certain of the effect of his oratory.

'Who's the happy girl, Paco?' smiles Ángela.

'Magdalena Fuentes,' he says a bit tensely.

'Magda!' screams Mamá.

'We plan to marry straight away,' goes on Paco. 'And will be ready to leave almost immediately for Tijuana.'

'Magda? You're marrying Magda! She's such a sly little – what did I tell you, Ángela? Analogous to a merger? What are you talking about, Paco?'

Mamá, in her freshly dyed perm, thrashing about

bewildered atop the oxblood, looks like she feels used, violated. She's lost her cool a lot, lately. We're looking at a woman whose mind once moved not a lot more smartly than a tumbleweed and whose tongue was about as tart as that honey for sale the other day in the Plaza Mayor. Not now.

'I only need your blessing, Aunt,' says Paco.

She lashes out.

'Paco – you won't get it! I won't have it! You mustn't marry that scheming, plotting, selfish little Magda Fuentes!'

Mamá perhaps has been nursing some nebulous notion that her nephew might be kept tethered to our family as a sort of blundering yet harmless hybrid between a milch cow and a bullock. You know, spending some of his salary on helping out his cousins, helping out his aunt, generally making her life easy. Scrub that if he marries Magda!

'You're speaking of the girl I love, Aunt,' our cousin says primly.

'Love?' hisses Mamá. 'You're even more of a fool than I thought, Paco!'

A job interview downtown means that I can't stay to see the scene work itself out completely. Got to get myself upstairs. Got to get myself into a suit. Unwillingly. Blue linen, my best suit. White shirt. Black silk tie. Scarper down the street and nab a bus. Pound into town. Drop myself off the bus. A piece of paper in my hand tells me the address for the interview.

Elite Ad Agency.

A big blind wall of scabby stucco, serious, painted saffron. Windows barred with fiercely knotted old iron rods. A big cedar doorway, open now to the day.

Gulp.

Help me, somebody!

Stepping through the doorway and checking out my reflection in a window I try to tell myself I look okay. A small brown guy, but tidy. Pat my hair a bit to try to look still tidier. Butterflies busy in my belly. Scared, cause when the bosses look at me inside the offices of Elite they'll just think – well, what'll they think? This boy's got no style. That's what they'll think.

This boy's not an ad man, he's just an Indian.

I shut my eyes for a second or two, try to breathe calmly – slowly – yep, it's okay – yep, you're okay, you're going to get the job –

Come on mate, get cracking!

Sneaking into the patio – feels like sneaking yet am trying my best shot at looking cool – I find a desk of some sort of hard sharp laminate behind which sits a sharp hard young woman. A security guard on one side wearing as much braid as a generalissimo in the Guatemalan Army.

The sharp woman frowns at me, thinking who's this bloody peasant?

'Erm, I'm here for an – erm, interview.'

'Name?'

'Matías López Urbano.'

'Two minutes late. A moment, please.'

A bit of faffing around with an intercom, and this and that – just long enough for me to feel nice and nervous and sweaty – and then I'm through a door and into some sort of special sanctum. A big cedar desk – and behind it a big cedar sorta guy. You know the kind. Wooden. Blankness. A mouth like a slot. Nothing open for viewing.

'Your qualifications look to be in order,' he says after twenty relentless minutes of interrogation. 'Also I'm satisfied with your references.'

'Thank you sir.'

'We'll be in touch. Good day.'

An idea flits through my mind that maybe if I offer to suck his cock he might give me the job –

Don't go there, dude!

Afterwards, wanting to save my bus fare but also wanting to chill a bit after my grilling, I leg it. These days I do a lot of legging it. Viceroyal façades drop behind after a few blocks. I wend my way through alleys in one of the oldest poor parts of the city. Alleys walled at all sorts of crazy angles. Walls painted brightly and overhung with bougainvillea. Dawdling, taking my time, I look at an old woman, a couple little kids, a stray dog, a goat.

Mamá has started, and sustains with impressive persistence, a campaign of nagging at Ángela. She nags Ángela because of a wasted opportunity. Why should our cousin be marrying Magda? Why couldn't we have got some of his money by getting him to marry Ángela? Why couldn't Ángela have hit on her cousin instead of shoving him away?

'Nothing could have been simpler and more satisfactory than for my daughter to marry my nephew,' sums up Mamá. 'Two birds killed with one stone!'

'Mamá, he's Paco,' says Ángela. 'Why would anyone want to marry Paco?'

We're all seated at the dinner table, eating our supper.

'Magda seems not to suffer from such scruples,' says Mamá. 'She'll do anything to sell herself.'

'And that's what you're asking me to do – sell myself?'

'You're wilfully misunderstanding me, Ángela! Talk to your father – your father will tell you!'

Papá silently cuts into a slice of sauteed pork.

'Why would anyone want to marry without love?' I say, wanting to help my sister here but really speaking sort of rhetorically. 'The only thing worth anything is love.'

Papá, chillingly, speaks up now.

'So you want love, do you?'

'Yes, Papá.'

'We may quote the philosopher. A man has one love – the world. A woman has one world – love.'

'So you're saying – you're saying that I think like a woman, Papa?'

'Any inferences are your own, son.'

'María wear your sandals for heaven's sake, we're not in the jungle!'

María has just slapped into the room on her bare feet. The old woman dislikes footwear. Goes without saying she hasn't bothered to slip on her plastic sandals simply to step through from the kitchen to bring the bowl of fruit and then straight away scarper. Why should she bother when her mistress for years has been willing to shrug at the habit? Mamá has struck out at random, that's all – hoping to smack any moving object.

Not wise trying it on with María!

The flat old breasts of the old darling are sliding about beneath the thin synthetic bodice of her frock. She favours bras no more than she favours footwear. Her frock has been printed with a brilliantly bright pattern of parrots. Her grey hair's plaited into a long glossy tail, as always, but twisted up around her head to free herself for work.

'Sorry, Señora,' she says. 'Forgot we're in the sophisticated city and not stuck in poor old backward Tres Madres.'

'I don't like your tone, María.'

'Maybe you're right about my bare feet. Maybe I'm best back in Tres Madres.'

Mamá tries evasive action.

'Ángela stop conniving with María! Yes, miss, you can try looking as though you wonder what I'm talking about but

I saw you shoot her that little grin just now. Have you given serious thought to the fact that when it comes to hooking a husband your only asset is your white skin?'

'What do you mean, Ma?' laughs Ángela. 'One more asset must be my respectful manners towards my mother?'

'Listen, we can't back you with one single peso to tempt a likely husband, you know,' says Mamá. 'All you've got are your looks – white skin, pretty face – that's your lot!'

'Mamá, you know my thoughts about a husband. I'm going upstairs now. I've got to get stuck into that essay.'

'Me, am staying at table for some of the melon,' I say. 'So you can belabour me for a bit, if it'll make you feel better Ma.'

'*Beam me up!*' says Mamá in English.

An electronic squalling starts on the nearest phone. Bounding across the room and scooping it up, I lift its white plastic headpiece.

'Tito?' says a small, distant voice – slightly wary.

Alert instantly, I answer.

'You okay, Magda?'

'Course! I'm phoning to ask a favour. Would you – well – would you be best man for Paco? He hasn't got any friends down here, and – well, from what I can work out he hasn't got any real friends at all, actually – '

'Course I'll be best man, Magda. I'd be honoured to be best man at your wedding.'

'Thanks a lot, you're a sweetie,' she says brightly.

'A bit of a comedown for her,' mutters Mamá after I pass on the news, 'when what she always wanted was you to be her groom.'

Civil ceremony followed by a smart dinner party. Mamá has a headache before the ceremony. Course she has a headache!

María massages the sore head and recites the canticle of Mary. Massage and the Magnificat are a sovereign remedy in Tres Madres. Suffering from witchcraft or the evil eye? Here's what you got to do. Kneel in front of an image of the Virgin. Next, take hold of a rebozo.

Now, start reciting the Magnificat.

My soul doth magnify the Lord, and my spirit hath rejoiced in God my Saviour.

Knot your rebozo after each third word, and keep knotting, and the witchcraft will have been lifted by the time you come to the end of the canticle. Take pains to say it word perfect, mind you. Make a single slip and you got to go right back to the start and say it all the way through again word perfect – or else the witchcraft will be doubled!

For he hath regarded the lowliness of his handmaiden –

'Heartless, that's what she is, a girl with no heart,' wails Mamá.

'Who, Magda?' I say.'

'What? Ángela of course! Oh it would've been so satisfactory! My girl, my own daughter – pretty as a picture – marrying my nephew. All girls are heartless. Tito – we're heading for the poorhouse, what's going to become of us?'

Mamá slouches on top of her oxblood. The chandelier suspends glittering crystal teardrops above our salon floor paved with slabs of sorrowingly cold marble. A more massive chandelier glitters down at us, couple hours later, when we find ourselves sat with bride and groom and mother-in-law inside a smart and nastily expensive restaurant in the city.

A select party, says Sra Fuentes. Nobody outside our immediate circle except two superannuated aunts of the family Fuentes.

'May we pray for silence?' says Paco, tapping at a wineglass.

'Speech, speech!' laughs a very perky Sra Fuentes.

Paco, needless to say, looks with deep gratitude at that lady. He bares his chemically whitened teeth in a satisfied smile. He clears a little phlegm from his throat. He preens with manicured fingers the lapels of a shiny new jacket manufactured from a variety of thermoplastic polymer byproducts of the petroleum industry. Why does he wear such naff suits when he's earning so much money?

He starts speaking – and keeps speaking.

Hours later my sis and I are back at ours talking it over while taking in the warm night air on the balcony.

'Wonder what she really thinks – Magda, I mean,' says Ángela. 'Surely she doesn't like poor pathetic Paco?'

'I kinda wonder right now whether she likes anyone, especially herself.'

'Oh god, poor Magda.'

'Well who knows what anyone likes or doesn't like? I sure as shit don't know when it comes to Magda. I thought I knew. Suppose I never did know, really.'

'At least we can hope it works out for her okay.'

'Maybe it'll work and maybe it won't work, Angelita. One consolation for you – if it ends in divorce you can always go to Paco and beg him to try a merger with you. If you're very lucky he may say okay, and you'll be rewarded with the right to act as his consort at those cool parties, looking ornamental, flattering his business colleagues, bringing happiness to our poor tormented Mamá.'

'Very funny. Or you could try?'

'You reckon it's likely I could get him to go for a guy?'

'Very likely – as likely as that he'll walk out on his desk at the maquiladora and become a mendicant friar.'

'Yep, bummer. That's me lost my golden opportunity to

make myself solvent.'

'I feel so sorry for Magda.'

'She's doing it with her eyes open, Angelita.'

'That's why I feel so sorry. Somehow it seems even more awful that she's doing it on the basis of rational calculation instead of from some misguided emotion about the guy.'

'Maybe it's not really rational. Maybe it's all emotional. She's doing it cause she's in the grip of one of the strongest of all emotions.'

'Come again – what emotion?'

'Fear.'

'Fear?'

'Fear of poverty.'

'Ugh – just thinking about it gives me the creeps.'

'Angelita, I was thinking about this myself just the other day. The day the agency caved. I've identified a panic syndrome in myself. Panic syndrome about poverty. The scenario is me ending up a codger who's homeless and hungry and snuffling about in the gutter. I've decided to call it my busking old coot syndrome.'

She lets out a little hoot of laughter.

'We'll be okay. We won't sell our freedom just because we're scared, will we Tito? We'll stay scared rather than give up our freedom!'

'Yep, you said it.'

'We're not afraid, we're brave.'

'We're not mercenary, we're mercury!'

12

The office where I start work two weeks after the wedding makes money by administering commercial property. They turn over millions of pesos monthly. The office, though, is tiny. Seventeen people rammed into a space about equal in floor area to an ordinary city flat. All day you hear faxes squalling, landlines burbling, the whooshing of air conditioning ducts. Also a mewing electronic bar or two of Beethoven or *Oops! I did it again* by Britney whenever anyone phones someone else in the office, which is always.

'Okay, your desk,' says a fidgety dude showing me the setup. 'Your laptop – you familiar with Toshiba Satellite?'

'Sure!' I say with a nod.

Familiar defined as never seen one of the fuckers in my entire life till now, dude!

Light from outside blears into the office through two square windows. Not a lot of light. The glass is tinted dark. One window in the conference room, other window in the owner's office. Don Pepe. Glass so dark you won't ever know what the weather's like outside. Other than bright dark. Or dark dark.

'Okay, leave you to it then.'

'Ta.'

My space in the office is small, like not even two metres square. One of those typical commercial dividing walls no higher than your nipples when you stand up – which is frowned on cause if you're standing you're probably not working. Pulpy fibrous painted walls splitting the office into these stifling little cells. My dividing walls are blue. Others are pink, citron, grey. My desk some sort of laminate – fuck knows what sort. My laptop's got a soft pliable sort of screen that seems somehow mysterious, only it's not, it's nylon. Soon get the laptop sorted. Prop on top of my desk a pic of Ángela. Stow inside one of my drawers a hoard of bananas and mangoes and some nice juicy apples. Yum! Love fresh fruit! Also a plastic drinking bottle filled with filtered water.

Gotta keep yourself well hydrated in these toxic workplaces!

A digital clock inside my skull lets out little tocks as it tolls its way through the thought of the seconds – minutes – hours – days – weeks – fuck knows – years! – of work waiting for me in this hectic deadly wankbox of a fucker of an office? Scope the place more closely. Fuck! Hustle, sweat. The work pace in the other cells is frenetic, not at all like the ad agency.

Beam me up! to quote Mamá.

'Don Pepe wants you,' says some suit. 'Jump to it!'

'Yep, sure thing.'

Tosser.

Am here to ghostwrite the boss's business correspondence, Don Pepe not being your bog standard middle-aged man of the commercial class. Worked as a building labourer and like every worker learnt on the job that a good day's toil didn't get a fair day's pay. Or so says María. She knows enough about his doings to have given me a fair earbashing about Don Pepe. Anyway, young prole Pepe sorted out that the way to go was to take backhanders. Next, how to give them. And he turned into a rough but deft operator. Don Pepe, now. Grafting and bullying his way into scoring municipal construction contracts. Rich by the age of forty. Now he's dropped the hod and brickbats. Sixty, sat down to skimming rents from city real estate picked up during his rise and rise.

Apparently he lives in a huge new faux-hacienda somewhere beyond Cerro del Calvario.

He welcomes his new boy with a grunt.

Don Pepe's got this massive square head like half a breezeblock. Only dark brown. Oily. A big square mug bristling with a zapata moustache. Black pinstriped pants. Staring red shirt. Belly ballooning over a thickly studded black leather belt slung with macho jewels – a silver chain, a gold phone, a bunch of keys.

'I got to write to the mayor about an accusation,' he says. 'Some bastard lawyers for some bastard outfit are lying to the mayor.'

'Yes, Don Pepe.'

'They're saying there's not enough cement in the block of offices I built twenty years ago for the law courts. Lawyers are all liars! The cunts say the concrete's cracking cause there's not enough cement in the mix. Sons of raped whores! I got to get a letter straight to the mayor.'

'Want me to take notes right now, Don Pepe?'

'Yeah kid – take notes right now. Start my letter with a good arse lick. Your gracious glorious excellency of a mayor whose smelly stools are the font of all radiance and light in the universe – you know the style, you'll know how to flatter the old cunt, kid – '

Don Pepe is only semi-literate, which is why he needs a ghostwriter.

He tells me what he wants to say. And I work his prole idiom up into suavely polished Spanish. Not a great job. But a job.

A job that pays okay.

At the club. Boogying on down with other gay boys early in the small hours of Sunday. Larging it cause I got to get myself a shag! Well truth of the matter got to get a new boyfriend, really. What I'm wanting isn't to get my end away but to discover true love. Yep, got to come clean with myself. That's still the one. The big one. Am scoping all possible talent here at the club.

My heart fails me from time to time, scoping away.

Cause it's true there are plenty of babes buying beer at the bar and bopping on the dance floor, but let's face facts why don't we? Why would any of said babes want to hit on someone like me, a dark brown, ordinary, nonentity?

'I'm not picky, you know Alex,' I say. 'I'm not holding out till I find a man whose dingus when weighed might bend the scales at the meat market, nor am I asking for a brain surgeon or a career diplomat, and I'm not asking for an Adonis.'

'So that's why you picked me, mate?' he laughs. 'Cause you're not picky?'

'I picked you cause you're a prick,' I laugh back.

Alejandro and me have buried the hatchet, goes without saying. No point nursing wounds. He's a cool enough guy and we run into one another constantly. So course it makes sense to be matey. He's deep into a hot threesome right now. The two other guys are away for the weekend in Acapulco. Alejandro keeps his hand in by hitting on me over our second beer, which is kinda flattering but am not going back there, no way. I don't want a fuckbuddy – like I said, I want a soulmate.

'Hey that dude over there keeps giving you the glad eye,' he says.

'You reckon? What dude?'

'That dude – dude keeps looking at your nipples through your tee like you just invented tits.'

'Nah, he's just looking around generally, don't you reckon?'

'You sad twat, he's on for a shag. Trust me.'

I check the guy out more eagerly. A little taller than me, but not tall. Light brown skin – two or three shades lighter than me – nowhere near white. A slim young man, he looks healthy, straightforward.

'Looks good to me.'

'Off you go! He'll love drilling your tight little butt!'

Claudio, that's his name. Nice name. Twenty-seven years old. Our ages we sort pretty quickly. We sort our income and employment status, too, tactfully. Claudio's a salaryman at the State Agricultural Agency. Sounds like he's completely solvent, thank christ. Not that I'm starting to turn into a gold digger. Am not – we won't mince words – Magda. Not an option! Just want to make sure the bloke can pay his own way.

Or am I kidding myself?

'I share an apartment with two friends,' he says. 'Care to – um – come back with me now for a – um – for a drink?'

'Cool, ta.'

His flat looks as straightforward as Claudio. New block of apartments in a nice suburb. Conventionally designed, conventionally furnished. Flatmates are out partying so we settle a bit awkwardly onto a sofa and he starts to tell me his life story.

'My specific division of the State Agricultural Agency is the Commercialisation Component,' he says. 'We try to get across to poor farmers how they can sell with more market knowhow and not only reach a wider range of buyers but get better prices for themselves and their family.'

'Yep? Sounds like worthwhile work.'

Although his way of talking has a hint or two of cousin Paco.

'Very worthwhile, I think. We don't aim to make peasants into capitalists. That'd be invasive of their cultural values. We empower them to cope adaptively in a capitalist society.'

'So how do you do that?'

'I visit villages and give speeches and seminars, talking to people about cooperative marketing, quality control, how to add value to their products. Right now my main job is to work out how to set up a centralised maize storage facility. We want to buy up maize from poor farmers and hold it for sale when prices are optimal. Small grain growers in our state don't sell their products as a group, so they get swindled by the buyers. Oh, another responsibility of mine is to report prices of the region. By prices I mean output figures.'

'Cool! Hey – what's an output figure?'

A mistake, cause he explains much too thoroughly.

We kiss for a first time and it's a shock. He's got this really sharp pointy tongue. Sharp and pointy and all over the place, working hard, poking, and scrubbing away. I want to laugh but it's also sort of scary. It's really sharp! Ow!

'Your lips are sweet, Tito,' he says shyly.

'So are yours, Claudio,' I say.

No point telling him it's like kissing a mousetrap. So we stop talking and start fucking.

Afterwards, lying in bed, he asks me to tell him how I'm feeling. I tell him the truth. Relaxed, I say. Friendly. He listens carefully. Yet when I ask him the same question he knits his brow and says he doesn't know. After a bit we get up and eat some supper – maybe you might want to call it breakfast since we can already see the first light of dawn across the suburb. Afterwards we fuck. We fall asleep. We wake up, fuck, fall asleep.

We wake up and it's past midday.

'I've never felt as strongly when with girls as I feel when

with you, Tito.'

'Hey – that's cool, Claudio.'

Says he's hardly done anything with guys. Was engaged to a girl last year but broke it off cause he decided it wasn't fair to the girl. Thinks he prefers guys. His smile is warm but his eyes are guarded. He's from quite a good family.

'My sign in western astrology is Sagittarius and in eastern astrology it's the Serpent,' he says.

Beam me up!

'You believe in astrology?' I ask carefully.

'Yes,' he says. 'Not that I'm superstitious mind you!'

After our first night together we start meeting every second or third day. He doesn't quite get my jokes. And then, into our third week, he gets cosmetic surgery. I turn up at his late one Friday afternoon and clock a bandage across the bridge of his nose. Nose jobs are very common in Villarreal. Almost every young guy wants to get rid of the bit of bone across the bridge that makes you look Indian. A surgeon will slice it off for you. Admittedly you'll need to wear one of those telltale plasters for a few weeks. Also it'll cost you a few thousand pesos. Can't pay those pesos? No sweat! Commerce and industry sell plastic inserts to stick up your nose. Buy from your nearest pharmacy! A peso or two will iron out your nasty native hook and make your olfactory organ nearly as nice as the snoot of a white man or woman.

'Are you never serious, Tito?' asks Claudio a few days later, speaking in a worried way. 'You're not always frivolous are you?'

'Nope, not always frivolous Claudio. I wish!'

'Only, well – I'm quite a serious guy.'

'You're a good guy.'

'Am I? You think so, Tito? Tell me more?'

Constantly he keeps wanting to make sure he's good, he's okay, and that I'm okay. Constantly he keeps asking me how I feel, what I think. Constantly he can't think of a coherent reply when I flip the questions back his way. He reaches up instead to pat the gelled spikes of his hair. He seems obsessed with the gel in his hair and always patting it to check it's still in shape.

A letter turns up in the post, franked in Tijuana. A letter from Magda. We tear it open eagerly, me and Ángela. Magda writes drily about the way she's suffered a few comic mishaps. And how she's now surrounded not only with comfort but luxury. Her new home is in a guarded compound a little way out of Tijuana. The house, the landscape, the servants – she writes as though she's pleased with everyone and everything, and only once mentions her husband.

'She seems okay,' I say. 'You could even say she seems happy.'

Ángela folds the letter and sets it down.

'Yes, she's working her socks off to make us think she's happy.'

'Tito – um – I've spoken to my parents and told them about – about you and me,' says Claudio. 'They don't show any hostility – they want to meet you, they say.'

'Meet me? Fuck!'

I let out a coarse hoot of laughter.

We've been together six weeks now. Which is cool cause when you're having an affair you get off on the sense of being busy emotionally, don't you? A feeling that life's important, urgent. Flirty texts, emails, assignations, appointments. Quick kisses, deep fucks. A life not tame and lame and ordinary.

Yet at the same time things have already started to turn

cosy and domestic.

He cooks meals for me at his flat.

First time everything done properly. Bread rolls lolling on a napkin of embroidered linen inside a chased silver basket. One tall slim candle lighted at the start of the meal and kept glowing warmly all through our subsequent fucking.

How about now?

Now the bread rolls just get plopped on top of the table inside their brown paper bag straight from the bakery. A candle is still lighted at the start of the meal, but once we've finished eating it'll get blown out briskly. Also, he looks hurt.

'They had to work hard to accept it, you know – it's not easy for them, they – '

'Sorry, mate! I know!'

'Are you okay about a meet, Tito? Tell me if you're not okay.'

'Am okay – it's cool, it's an honour.'

'You don't seem okay.'

'Sorry!'

He's sincere, course. A nice bloke. So anyway we drive to his family home next evening and I'm feeling edgy about what it will be like to be introduced to a mother and a father as the lover of their only son. Claudio's even more edgy, goes without saying, gnawing away at his lower lip as he spins the steering wheel.

Poor guy.

'Mamá's very excited,' he says. 'Papá's a bit more sober.'

'Okay – so it's him I gotta win over?'

'He can be pretty stern, Papá.'

'Shit. Okay – '

Well, his father in fact is civil. He doesn't welcome me

with open arms but he's polite. The mother on the other hand looks terrified, kinda crazy.

'So this is your – your friend?' she says to Claudio.

'Yes, Mamá.'

'He looks like he might have – that he might have caught that – that horrible di – that he might be sick!'

Claudio looks sideways, scowling at himself in a mirror before starting to fix his hair, twiddling anxiously with the gelled spikes. He's yellow with shock. Not too happy myself, needless to say. At the same time am thinking I look by far the healthiest person within yelling range – bar the dark brawny bloke visible through the arches who clearly works as their gardener.

'He's not sick, Mamá.'

'How do you know he's not sick, my sweetheart. He looks sick!'

Claudio has now started to cry.

'Señora, would you like me to bring you a medical certificate of fitness?' I say, smiling.

Her brain, however, seems to have headed into outer space.

'Oh my god, my darling Claudio – oh god in heaven – be careful my boy, last night I dreamed about you and you were wasting away – you had no blood, you were almost a corpse, and you were begging me to forgive you for your sins, and – you were dying of that disease, Claudio!'

Tears have dried on his face, a couple hours later, and we're outside under a jacaranda. We've each got a beer. He looks down at his tidy hands. He looks at his bottle of Corona. He begins spelling out to me the dreary little items of the sort of life he'd like to live with a partner.

'We'd eat our meals together, and we'd watch tele and

vids together,' he drones. 'Tito, we'd do everything together.'

We'd sodding climb the walls together!

We'd fucking strangle each other together!

'Not sure that's quite my style, Claudio.'

'Mamá will come to love you, I know, Tito,' he says earnestly.

'Cool – won't that be great?'

Whoopee, can't wait!

A dog day, today. A scorcher of a day. All shops and offices are shut cause it's the feast day of the patron saint of the city. Claudio is out of town, holding a seminar in some pueblo in the sierra, so am out for a wander in the old city. My feet take me with no intent towards Our Lady de los Dolores. Crowds are swarming. Groomed people from the capital, mostly, come to take a look at the baroque beauties of Villarreal.

'Grasshoppers!' calls a sweating vendor, her hair plaited into two long pigtails. 'Tasty!'

At the end of her pigtails, a red nylon bow. A tartan skirt. A shallow basket of grasshoppers fried in sesame oil balanced on top of her big head.

'Nopals, nuts, Señora?' a stooped old man asks an ambling matron from the big smoke. 'Wholesome and good from the country.'

'Fruit. What have you got today?'

'Melons, Señora. Juicy melons and only two pesos per melon.'

'Too dear. Mango?'

'Juicy mango, Señora, and only – '

She makes up her mind, opens her purse. The old chap doffs his dirty white hat.

Vendors come to the city overnight, toting sacks of fruit

and bags of handicrafts. All day they sit in front of their wares set out on blankets. At night, wares packed away, the vendors sleep on cardboard cartons folded flat beneath the arcades of the plazas. Sunday evening they'll start making their way back to their pueblo, dead tired, to be ready to work hard on the land during the coming week.

Okay, slope inside Our Lady de los Dolores.

Mooch my way past the pews. Glance, kinda awestruck, at filigreed masterwork of ivory and gold.

And stop sharp.

A blond young man. A sideways prospect of a heart-stoppingly handsome young blond man in a wreathed and curlicued pew. A young man bowed in prayer, dressed beautifully, under a blond halo.

Salvador Juan de la Tijera de Lago. Oh – oh – wow, wow!

He looks totally fucking amazing!

Salvador – wow – wow!

Okay mate, steady –

Starstruck, a right berk, can't help creeping into the same pew. A family pew? Anyway, creeping in only a metre or so. Salvador, breathing calmly, kneeling over his prayers, oblivious. I kneel myself, pretend to pray. After, bum back up on the cedar slab. Salvador still kneeling. Downer!

Princely dude, please look my way.

A sacerdotal is chanting some sort of mumbo jumbo.

Salvador still kneeling.

Here – over here!

Optimally berklike, dipstick stays helplessly planted on the pew a couple metres away from his hero. A little old lady in the next pew mumbles from under a mantilla of black lace. Peasant women in other pews are bareheaded, mostly, some wispy with cotton shawls.

Okay, a waiting strategy.

'Excuse me, I'd like to get past,' says a baritone.

I look up. Wha – ? Oh fuck – he's speaking – I was off in fantasyland and now here's the fantasy man, leaning down at me, speaking low.

'Yeah, sure – ' stammers dipstick.

My Prince looks at me harder, which is sorta scary.

'We know one another don't we? López, Matías?'

'Tito,' I say. 'My friends call me Tito.'

'Oh, sorry. Yes, I remember now.'

Afterwards what else can I do other than stand up. Blond God glides past. Stupidly, I follow him out of the pew. Funny enough he stops short, next. He turns smoothly.

'You coming outside, Matías – Tito?'

Am I what?

Couple secs later we're standing – we, like, the two of us! – together outside Our Lady de los Dolores.

'Phew, the heat!' says Salvador.

'It's wicked, the heat,' I say, starting to burble like a deb on speed. 'Me, am feeling so great today, am feeling so totally great today am in love with the heat and the crowds and even with the smog – and the smell of petrol.'

'Oh?' he says, looking sorta perplexed.

Perplexity being a pretty adaptive damn response to my motormouth. I cringe inside my mind. If that's a thing. Anyway, shut the fuck up! He'll think you're the mad little poof you really are!

'So how you doing?' I say.

Tape that mouth tight right now!

Pilgrims on raw knees are crawling across the paving stones of the plaza. Women, old men, kids, youths, scrape their way forwards, hands stretched out in supplication, towards Our Lady de los Dolores. A few of the very devout are carrying wooden crosses.

'I feel an imposter when I look at these simple people,' says Salvador.

Motormouth gets going once more.

'Maybe they're imposters too? Not that I'm saying you're right in your analysis of yourself – not saying you're an imposter. Just asking myself what's really in their minds. Are they really praying? You know, like, really thinking about the spiritual?'

My Prince frowns, causing a cloud to cross the sun and birds to drop like stones from the sky.

'We can't know – we can't enter their minds,' he says slowly.

My next tactic? Keep yammering, course.

'Bet they're trying to work out how much longer they have to put up with the pain before they make it to the altar. They're counting the metres. They've got their minds fixed on the minutes. They can't wait till they get to rattle out the last of the prayers and stow away the rosary beads and dust off their knees and head home to get the weight off and down a beer. To tell the truth, I don't believe in religious fervour.'

'I think these good people live in a world you and I don't know,' says Salvador.

'Maybe,' I say unwillingly.

'You don't think there's anything other than our world?'

'Of course, Salvador – of course I think there's more than what you call our world. My world and your world aren't one world, for starters. One of our two worlds is nearly empty. The other's rammed to the rooftops with wills, testaments, probates, invoices, stocks, shares, government bonds, debentures, real property, portable property – '

Salvador looks at me very slowly.

'You think I'm a wanker,' he says. 'I think it's quite unlikely, though, that you understand money.'

'You understand money, do you?' I yap, a bit peeved.

'No, I don't,' he says calmly.

I sort of gawp at him for a minute or two, my mind feebly flickering with vexation, adoration, lust. Salvador keeps staring at the crawlers. Absently leaning back, bracing himself against a hunk of crumbling old wall, he slides his hand towards a crack.

I grab it. The hand. Wow – his hand! I yank it away from the crack.

Salvador stares at me, astonished.

'Scorpion,' I say quickly. 'You nearly touched that scorpion.'

'Save me Mary!'

I laugh – I feel great! I touched his hand –

'You sound like a little boy when you say that, Salvador.'

'It's a phrase I was taught by a maid. Dolores was her name. She was always saying that. Save me Mary!'

'Dolores? Like this church!'

'What? Yes!'

'Did you love her?'

'Dolores? She was always saying that and lots of other quaint phrases, and – and – yes, I loved her.'

'Where is she now?'

'A wife with little ones, went to another city. I wrote letters to her, but she was barely literate and after a while moved again to another place and forgot to send me her new address. Well, maybe she didn't forget, maybe she just couldn't be bothered.'

'I'm sorry,' I say after a moment.

He looks at me oddly.

'No need to be sorry – it's just a childish story.'

I keep my trap shut and start skipping down the stone steps away from the golden domes. Salvador follows.

'Although I don't believe in religious fervour,' I say. 'I do believe in passion – and luck.'

We walk side by side across the plaza.

'Tito, you said something at the club about wanting to be a novelist,' says Salvador. 'Was that sincere or a conversational gambit?'

I stare at him – no doubt looking idiotically agog.

'You remember that?'

'It was an unexpected thing to hear in that context. Was it only a gambit?'

'No, it was – it was what I want. I want to be a novelist!'

'Tell me more?'

So that's what I do, I stand there for twenty minutes or more and tell him all about how I've always loved reading, always loved writing, always loved trying to turn my real life into story, and the lives of anyone I come across into story, and – and I catch a glimpse of a sudden calculating look coming across his face, followed by a look that seems deadly fucking cold.

'You're getting bored with all this, I can see,' I say.

'No, not at all,' he says.

Saying it in that careful clipped toneless voice he used the first time he opened his mouth to tell me his name that night at the club. Fuck that! He's a wet dream come true – but fuck that! Am not gonna stand here and be patronised!

'Sorry – gotta go now. Cheers mate!'

And I scarper.

13

A glassy façade. Fuck, looks like a factory for making steroids. I stand outside and press a buzzer. I've got an interview for a new job. Don Pepe last week lost his lawsuit and a fair whack of his ill-gotten millions cause the lawyers – sons of raped whores – have conclusively proved that the cement content in the concrete used for constructing the municipal law courts comes to barely forty percent of content demanded by the city code. Don Pepe's made up his mind to go off in a huff with what's left of aforesaid millions and start a new life as retired layabout at a resort down on the coast near Cancún.

'Only two types of people in this world, kid,' is his last word when he tells me I'm sacked. 'Cunts and sons of cunts.'

'Bye, Don Pepe.'

'Good luck kid. You're not a bad kid. When it comes to writing fancy words you sure know how to make black look white!'

A glassy door gets opened almost in my face by a young guy in a suit. A guy who looks uptight. I try a bit of a smile. The guy nods and keeps looking uptight and leads me straight into a suite of offices. He points me to where I can cool my heels with other hopefuls on a couple of standard sofas in a clean, bare, functional waiting room. A water cooler. An electronic clock. A couple glossy posters. A stack of glossy books. The company makes its money by copyediting technical and commercial websites. The hopefuls are mostly pale guys buttoned into dark suits.

'Hey,' I say to the nearest guy.

'Hey,' he says.

'Spose the plan is to psych us up by keeping us waiting for hours?' I say.

He stares at me silently. I try a grin.

He looks away.

I sit.

I start to sweat.

A waddling brown woman, gripping a broom, starts sweeping the parquet. Flowers of emerald and vermilion and orange – dyed in big loose blobs on the loose thin cloth of her shift – are the only strong colour inside the suite of offices. All hopefuls are wearing drab suits. Apart from me, in green cargo pants and tight bodyshirt made from green rayon. Goes without saying I feel kind of shy and wrong. Wearing the wrong clothes and haven't even had an interview yet!

Come to that, we ever gonna have interviews?

The electronic clock keeps ticking out the tedium. Ten minutes, twenty minutes – one sodding hour! Not till nearly two hours later than the time named for my appointment does my time come. My good buddy, the guy who opened the front door and showed me into this noiseless land of the undead, nods. Follow me, apparently. Okay. Stand, follow. My buddy walks me through to the boss. A room perfectly white except for a beautiful marquetry desk.

A man about forty in a costly suit.

A man slick and unsmiling who stays seated behind the desk and indicates to me, with the most economical possible movement of a hand, that I can sit myself opposite.

'Why are you suitable for this job?'

I sweat some more.

'Um, well – I love language. I love working with words. I, um – I'm very, like, fluent. I'm very, you know – literate?'

'We don't require literacy or fluency. What we require is accuracy.'

'Oh, okay. Sure!'

Armpit temperature now suitable for steaming a stuffed tamale.

'Talk me through your curriculum vitae.'

'Okay, sir. Cool!'

He raises an austere eyebrow. We work our way through my personal details, educational qualifications, employment record to date. References, which he says are adequate. Conditions of employment. Hours. Rates of pay. Dress code. Strict, he says, scowling across the marquetry at my green rayon. Next he raps out questions about my goals, my objectives. Muggins does his best to muddle his way through what he hopes are acceptable answers. The boss ticks, crosses, little boxes on the screen of an electronic notebook. He grunts, nods, shakes his head, hands me a written test.

A minion leads me into a small room where I'm to sit down and turn out the right answers.

Okay, let's hit this test!

A test about the rules of grammar. Maddeningly mechanical. A test that confronts you with questions about language and wants you to answer right or wrong – when of course a language isn't like that, a language is provisional, alive.

'We'll be in touch,' says the head honcho, a couple hours later.

'Thank you, sir.'

They never do get in touch, course.

'Tito, maybe when you're doing a job interview you could try harder to defer to the employer?' helpfully says Claudio. 'You come across, sometimes, as not very – well, you know – not very respectful.'

'Dicks don't deserve respect.'

We're lying in bed together in his apartment. He's just fucked my arse and it's a bit sore. Claudio is a guy who believes in being respectful to everybody. A word meaning, apparently, that when you step outside your bedroom you should always behave as though your every move is under observation by some very old and very innocent and very censorious granny. Like one day I plant a smooch on his mouth while inside his car and the guy is annoyed.

'People don't expect to see two men carrying on with that sort of behaviour,' he says.

'That's their problem, not ours.'

'Well my belief is that if you want to be treated properly by others then you have to behave properly towards them and not cause them to feel hurt or upset.'

'I agree about not hurting but I don't agree about not upsetting – not if it's just the sight of two lovers having a nice snog.'

'It's not right to go out of your way to make people feel bad.'

'Am not going out of my way – am just doing what comes naturally.'

'What we do together isn't natural.'

'Come on, Claudio!'

'Well it's not – and anyway, our sexual behaviour might come instinctively but obviously in a social context it needs to be moderated. A responsible man always makes his personal behaviour acceptable to society.'

'What about all the straight couples? They're constantly snogging in public. Nobody says that's offensive! I bet you and your girlfriend used to be all over one another in public.'

'Well you're mistaken.'

'What?'

'My last girlfriend was annoyed because I've never kissed in public. I don't even like holding hands in public. I don't think it looks civil. Private emotions are for private places, not public places.'

At least he's consistent. Can't knock him for having one rule for queers and one for straights. Claudio's an equal opportunity anal retentive.

'Okay, no kisses in public,' I say, shrugging.

'By the way, Tito – Mamá told me yesterday that she thinks you're a very nice boy.'

The crazy lady has got over her fit of fear so quickly that she's now well on the way to clenching me tight to her pointy yet meagre bosom as interim son-in-law. She calls us her *two boys*. English. How are you both today, *boys*? Give your little Mummy a kiss! Fuck, she gets on your tits. She's one of those mothers who announces her every move to the family. Claudio, I'm just going upstairs now. Yes okay, Mamá. I'm going to be working out on the exercycle for the next quarter of an hour, dear. Sure, Mamá. I'm off to take my siesta, darling – so that's where I'll be if I'm wanted. Sweet dreams, Ma.

As if she could ever be wanted for anything except to create white noise and spend money.

'I love my mother so much,' sighs Claudio.

I make up my mind to bin him.

Binning a boyfriend: new territory. Always in the past it was me who was binnee, not binner. How do you bin a guy cleanly? You know. How do you bin a guy without melodrama? Fucked if I know. Always been binned pretty crudely, myself. Anyway, a couple nights later here's me faffing around at home in the upstairs bathroom getting myself ready to go and sack poor Claudio.

I grimace at myself in the foxed triangular shard of broken dim mirror while gingerly patting chemical crap onto a spot on my chin.

Clearasil, to be precise.

It's a Saturday. My baggy old trackpants have flopped onto the bathroom floor and I've tugged on my sharpest pair of jeans. The trackpants are pretty gamey cause I wore them all day while doing some gardening. Now, jar of gel unscrewed, am just getting stuck into the job of getting my hair groovy when it occurs to me that it's maybe weird to be taking so much trouble to try to make myself look good when the whole point of going out tonight is to stand in front of a binnee and say adios!

Mate, think this one through, I tell myself, index finger poised over the jar of viscous white goop.

Maybe I should be doing my best to look ugly? Why not front up in the scuzzy trackpants with the salsa stain on the crotch? Why not flaunt this shiny red zit on my chin?

Claudio might take one look at me and head for the hills. Problem solved!

So for a couple of seconds here's me planted pensively. Can't do it, though. Stick that index finger into the gel, man! Can't not try to make myself look good. Struggle to fix that bad hair! Who on the planet would want not to bin but to be binned? Who on the planet would want to be binned cause he looks cheesy?

'You're right, Tito,' says Claudio after a couple hours weeping. 'We haven't got a future, we're too different.'

'You're a good dude. I'm just too weird for you.'

'I'll always love you.'

'No you won't, mate. You'll forget me quick smart cause soon you'll come across some really cool guy.'

He sighs deeply.

'You know what really makes me feel so totally bad, Tito?'

'No, Claudio? What makes you feel so totally bad?'

'How to explain it to Mamá.'

Conference inside my bedroom back at ours. Ángela crosses the landing from her own room, looking exceptionally cool, looking brilliant, wanting to know the news about how the binning panned out. A few sentences get her up to speed. So – moving on – sis and me swap notes and jokes about past binnings we have known. Afterwards we wonder whether or not to go out clubbing.

'Am in the mood,' I say. 'Maybe better not, though.'

'Why not?'

'Thinking about the cover charge – gotta be more careful about money. My busking old coot syndrome has started to kick in bigtime lately, Angelita. I can just see myself twenty years from now, panhandling punters at some smart café downtown, arthritic fingers plucking the strings of a guitar – singing my poor old heart out in hopes of being palmed a stray peso.'

'Twenty years from now you'll be forty-two. How come the arthritis has set in so early?'

'Poverty does that, sis, living rough on the street.'

'And since when could you play the guitar?'

'Since never – better start taking lessons I spose.'

'Mm – or you could shortcut the process by setting yourself up not as a guitar player but a storyteller. Punters will pay the odd peso to hear a good story.'

'You reckon? What sort of story?'

'Sob story – your specialty.'

'Very funny. You're right though – I do tell it well. Maybe I could get a job writing the downbeat scenes in tele soaps.'

'Plenty of employment opportunity there – ever noticed how nearly all the scenes in soaps are downbeat scenes?

Don't think I've ever seen anyone have a good laugh in a soap.'

A rap on the door.

I open with some surprise. Outside my door stands a glum man. A dumpy man, an older man, not tall, wearing a threadbare smoking jacket. Papá! What's going down? Awkwardly trying out the novel role of host to my own father, I show him into the room and usher him onto a cane chair, the only piece of furniture that could by any stretch be called cosy. My room I've always liked to keep simple – simpler even than my sis keeps her room. Bare floorboards, white walls, no drapery. My window is screened by nothing more weighty than a light bamboo blind, rolled down when wanted and rolled up when not wanted. The bed is a futon. I love clean space, fresh air, sunlight.

Papá makes a sign to my sister. Ángela glances at me quickly, alertly, then slips away.

'High time to face facts, Matías,' he starts slowly.

'Are we about to have a man to man talk, Papá?'

'We are,' he says.

Papá looks not only weary but kind of boundlessly uneasy. Uneasy in his body cause of the fact that his stiff bones can't get comfy in the cane chair. Uneasy in his mind cause of the fact that here he is trying to talk straight to his son – a son he doesn't really know, and doesn't really like, and doesn't want to like or know. As for me – well, I've seated himself tensely on the futon in a cross-legged posture which I've learned from Ángela. I close my eyes briefly. Ángela's the one who brought me up, not my parents. Papá's a stranger. I open my eyes.

'Any particular topic?'

'Yes, the most important topic of all.'

'Marriage?'

Papá has never nagged me about getting myself wed –

not like Mamá! – but he's always made it clear that a wedding will be wanted one day. A wedding with a girl as good as can be got. A girl who's white and wellborn and wealthy. Not that his hopes about her whiteness etcetera are too peremptory. He knows that a boy as poor, brown, obscure as his own small misfit of a son must set his sights moderately. A girl who's passable – that's what he'll be willing to settle for. A girl who'll look and behave like a decent daughter-in-law. Her looks, her behaviour – in fact, the whole deal of matrimony between her and his son – are things he wants not for themselves but cause they're the required things, the suitable things, the correct things, the demanded things.

'No, not marriage. Money.'

Okay! Same issue, different angle. I try hard to smile mildly.

'Money? Or the lack of money, Papá?'

My father just looks gloomy.

'You're not stupid, Tito. Drop all that dilettantism of yours and get going. Get into, into – industry. Contact your cousin Paco. He can help you. He's an imbecile of course but he does appear to understand about money. I wouldn't know, not understanding money myself.'

Which makes me think of me and Blond God.

'Yeah, but Pa – '

'Tito, get yourself up to Tijuana. Ask your cousin to find you some job. Don't you want to make things hum?'

'I haven't really learned yet how to let things be, Papá.'

'What? No doubt that's meant to be deep.'

'Maybe it's meant to be an evasion.'

'Well life doesn't sit around and wait for young boys who fancy themselves intellectual. Life's got to be grabbed by the throat.'

He says this with a sort of tired groan.

'Life might get throttled, mightn't it – if it's grabbed by the throat?'

He gets galvanised to a bit of low-grade energy, at last, by anger at my cheek.

'Cut the smart talk! Do what I say!'

Gripping the arms of the cane chair – arms that obviously he finds unnervingly pliable – arms that give, with piteous little squeaks, under his weight –the bossy old bastard hauls himself onto his feet and prowls towards the door. Now it's my turn to feel angry.

'Sorry, but I'm not gonna go and lick my cousin's arse in Tijuana, Papá.'

He looks at me darkly yet sluggishly.

'You watch your arse, boy! When are you getting yourself a girlfriend?'

We stay home all evening, in the end, me and Ángela. A sober sorta Saturday. No partying. Only sitting side-by-side reading. Sis, Machiavelli, *The Prince*. Me, Galdós, *Miau*. And after a bit we decide to do one quiet hit of weed. Which I seldom do, as I've said already. Angelita, on the other hand, often puffs peacefully late in the evening.

Course, while weed makes my sis nicely still it makes me silly.

'Ricky Martin is so gay,' I say. 'Apropos of fuck knows.'

'Quite.'

'He's so, so gay.'

'Quite, quite. Changing the theme, I need to say something to you that I've consciously been not saying for a fair few weeks. I've been not saying because it could hurt you. Nonetheless, I'm now about to say it. It's the truth. At least as far as I can work out so far, given my lack of formal qualifications in paediatric psychology. You and I always expect the truth of one another. And rightly so. Okay. Ready? *Fasten your seat belt, it's going to be a bumpy night.*'

The last bit's in English. Ángela and I both love Bette Davis.

'*Fastened and fascinated, sis,*' also in English.

'Cool, here we go. Tito, lately I've been finding it hard to sleep. It's because I'm worrying about you. Your happiness. I've been thinking about it a lot. I believe that I may not have helped you by behaving the way I did when you were a little boy. My theory is that as a baby myself I only survived the uselessness of our revered olds thanks to María. Who had enough on her plate in all conscience, coping with those two. Yet of course she was always kind and loving. And abrasive! She's María. My next survival step was to become autonomous. Which I did quickly. And well. Too well, too precociously. Not healthy. However, there we were. And then came a third step. I was three years old. I was longing to love someone unquestioningly. Someone who'd love me unquestioningly. And along came – ta da!'

She opens the palm of her left hand, motions towards me, then curtseys.

'*Yo, sis!*' I say, again in English.

'A baby bro! Cute as a button! Smothered by me with cuddles from the magic day you were first in my arms, brought to me by María. Cute as a button to this day. Sadly, sweetheart, it was all a bit pathological. A little girl of three was mothering her own mother, her own father, the family maid, herself – and on top of that, suddenly, a baby brother – and should she have been?'

'She should not, sis,' I say, slightly awed.

'And does she regret it?'

'She should.'

'She doesn't. It's been terribly interesting. And we all have our pathologies big and small. And I do love you unquestioningly.'

A little kiss on my forehead.

'I know,' I say, still awed. 'And you know I love you unquestioningly, Angelita.'

We grin at each other for a bit.

'Anyway, while looking on as you swing excitingly and sickeningly up and down the erotic-emotional roller coaster it becomes more and more obvious to me that, no thanks, that's not me. Not guys. Nor women, as you know. That's not my life. Not my passion. No, not mating. I don't get the hots for the contents of a chick's or man's pants. I get the hots for the contents of books. And periodicals. And manuscripts. My passion's learning. Tito, I'm a nun. Not a nun who comes in powder and lipstick to play canasta and swap slander with Ma. Not an ascetic religious sister devoutly closed up in a convent.'

'And wanking,' I cut in, saying what I always say about nuns.

'And wanking. And most certainly I'm not a Mother Teresa. I want to be a Sor Juana. A woman of learning. And reading, always reading, and thinking, observing, understanding, reading more, thinking more, observing more, understanding more – I mean, bro, I want to find out about the whole of it – everything! I mean, why? I mean – the universe!

Cannabinoids kicking in and sis going for broke.

Love it.

'Totally, Angelita!' I say. 'That's you – you've done nothing with chicks, nothing much with dudes, nearly nothing.'

'About to perhaps transgress a boundary here, bro, but truth to say never done anything with any dude below his or my nipples – mine mostly.'

I gape.

And start laughing.

And she starts laughing, too.

Angelita and me, we're writhing weedily around on the floor and we're giggling and giggling and giggling.

Morning and am sat in the patio. Not too cheery. A sober Sunday. Sat between my two cypresses in their beautiful tubs and leafing through situations vacant. Am looking for a job – still looking for a job, and my standards of what might be suitable or not for said job are dropping steadily.

Seeking product demonstrators with white complexion and minimum height 1.7 metres. $150.00 daily.

Flag that, then. No chance for a shortarse whose face is as tawny as a tumbler of Coke.

Bar Tropical 33 seeks security personnel. Applicants considered from 3-6 pm Boulevard Norte 1003.

Security guards, $1,500 weekly.

No point looking at that sort of ad, course, since apart from the fact they won't want guys with degrees – and that the olds would have a fit – am way too little and light to be a heavy. So stop looking fecklessly at everything in the situations vacant. Focus on what's doable. Let's get real! What am I fit for? Am sorta asking the cypresses, since they're so beautiful and erect and confident, and am getting a lot of pleasure from their scent, and from the beautiful gorgeous glazing on their big swollen, secure, stably weighted tubs, those mighty blue and white tubs from Puebla.

Okay, let's check out another ad.

Are you talented at sales? We need personable salesmen to sell encyclopedias –

Well, that's gotta be utter fucking cack. Door-to-door selling! Sad or what?

How about a department store?

Storeman with responsibility for delivering wares to clients. Young man with minimum secondary education –

Can do better than that, surely?

Leading business seeks personnel area of sales wanting to earn $8,000.00 monthly. Superannuation scheme, paid holidays. Experience required –

Clerk, computer qualifications necessary –

Sales assistant, white complexion –

Fuck, isn't there anything in the whole pissy paper that looks halfway okay?

Office boy $950.00 weekly tel. 242-78-09 Lic. Chávez.

Licenciado Chávez turns out to be an ugly thuggish sort of guy who smiles a lot, toothily. A poor man's Don Pepe. Seems to take an instant liking to me – so that's cool. Pats my cheek in a fatherly way while shaking my hand.

'You'll be under me at all times,' he says. 'Other than me you answer to nobody.'

The workplace is basic. A small close room not too brightened by fizzing and popping strip lights. Two steel desks facing one another. One for me, one for the Licenciado.

Perch myself on top of a swaying and intermittently padded steel chair that probably pretended to be ergonomic at some remote point last century. Peer into the screen of a dodgy cloned computer crammed with pirated software.

Tap tap away at keyboard.

The job is easy – in fact dead boring.

Word processing. Writing form letters. Filing documents, manually not electronically, into big tired steel cabinets whose drawers roll in and out with the sound of thunder and slam to a shut with a loud clang. You trot back to your desk. You balance yourself on your ex-ergonomic chair. You look up. You scope the opposite desk and the beaming mug of the Licenciado.

'Soon sort this, Licenciado,' I say doing my best to seem fucking grateful and spry and sprightly.

'Good boy,' he says with a wink.

How gross is that guy? Well, he's harmless and he's on my side.

Our office belongs to a debt collection agency owned by some corporate entity in the capital and managed here in the provinces by some faceless suit. You never see the suit, turns out. Too busy whacking golf balls around the links at his country club. You see the assistant suit instead, a sweaty whitish dude who paces worriedly up and down corridors and keeps poking his furrowed head into doorways. Our offices aren't open plan but a series of airless little cells cause we operate out of some creaky old brick and iron block built not long after the Revolution.

Villarreal was on the wrong side during the Revolution.

The side of landowners, factory owners, banks, nobs, de la Tijera. A revolutionary army rewarded us by blowing up this part of the city. Afterwards speculators slammed down, in a hurry, cubes of brick and mortar and plaster and concrete – mostly scaled down versions of the style you could call, if you want to be kind, Art Deco.

'You'll fit in nicely here, I can tell,' says the Licenciado.

'Hope so!' I chirp back,

The Licenciado struts about, pontificating, taking that fatherly interest, leaning over me, gripping my shoulder, breathing chili and onion onto my face. One day he's planted on his big brown shoes by the filing cabinet when I scoot across from my desk to get rid of a manila folder. A quick grimace from the Licenciado. I sort of simper back, and bend down to slide my manila folder into a steel drawer, and while am bent down feel something drop onto one of my arse cheeks. Something sort of firm and warm.

A hand. The palm of a hand.

Hm.

What to do? Straightening myself up, not saying a word, not looking anywhere, I scoot straight back across to my desk and start working like a dutiful office boy. The Licenciado stays planted next to the filing cabinet, hums a song tunelessly and jingles his keys. He's one of those guys who carry as many keys as can possibly be jammed onto a key ring. You know the kind of guy. He loves his keys cause they're proof to an admiring world of how he's such a big guy – a big guy who's got the keys. A guy who when he stands in the street waiting will run all those sharp little steel teeth between the tips of his fingers, like a rosary, listening to the happy jangle.

Okay, you can cope with the odd grope of your bum on the job, can't you? Course! A job's a job. And now that a salary's come my way again seems a good idea to spend weekends seeing about a bit of a love life. Price of a beer or two. A dude in the right bars can hang for hours at a time over a couple Coronas looking for some beautiful gorgeous intelligent and solvent guy. A guy, preferably, who's hot in the sack and loves reading literary classics and – oh yep, and who's got his own car.

'Sorry mate,' says a skinny brown boy, bumping into me one night in an ordinary cantina and making me spill my beer down the front of my skintight tee.

'Hey, careful – fuck, look at my shirt!'

He shrugs, but sorta sweetly.

'Shit happens mate – wotcher gonna do?'

'Could kneecap the bloke that did it, couldn't I? Might make me feel better for half a sec. Fuck man – my tee's sopping wet. Yuck!'

'Why not take the tee off, mate?' he laughs. 'Maybe we can work out some way to make you feel better for more than half a sec – maybe for a couple hours.'

'Wot?' I say intelligently.

'Name's Álvaro,' he says, sticking out his hand – a nice hand, slender but strong.

Okay! Time to check this boy out more carefully. About eighteen years old, sort of wiry. Wiry, full of energy – with a hell of a hooked nose! An enormous Mayan nose, high and narrow. Acne scars, too. Shallow craters all over his face, which is no big deal cause it's common to see acne scars on young men from the working class in Villarreal – it's a clear index of class, in fact, since prole families can't afford to pay for tetracyclines.

Quite cute, the scars. Make him look kinda vulnerable.

'Hey Álvaro. Tito.'

He gives me that sweet look again and squeezes my hand. I squeeze back. Álvaro doesn't exactly fit the bill of beautiful gorgeous intelligent and solvent, let alone loves reading literary classics and got his own car. Got a job, mind. And a flat of his own. Only a teen but he's been around and is quite a bold sort of lad and pretty clearly likes to take on the world.

So that's near enough for now.

Our first fuck takes place an hour or so later in the darkest corner of the Alameda. A couple other pairs of blokes are sucking or fucking one another nearby. Álvaro and I enjoy ourselves so much we make a date to meet again for more beer and more sex a couple nights later, and then the next night too, and we're getting on great.

'Thing about life is,' says Álvaro, 'life's shit, that's what life is, but I can't be arsed caring.'

'You reckon? I care, I think.'

'No, mate. You gotta not care. You gotta not care about the crap and just care about the – you know, about the yummy food, and – and friendship, and – and the flowers. Yeah, the flowers!'

'And family?'

'Fuck family, mate!'

Álvaro is the youngest of four sons. His mum's dead. His dad's a caretaker in a government office. Álvaro's brothers got him on his knees for them from when he was seven. The boys shared a bed, course, since brothers in prole families almost always share a bed. Brothers who share a bed, when they find themselves growing into horny young teens, start feeling one another up and fooling around and before you know it they're training the youngest to suck the others dry. As far as the father was concerned that was more or less okay cause it didn't go outside the family.

Not the case when Álvaro started having it off with a boy from outside the family.

'I was fifteen and he was the first dude to fill my arsehole,' says Álvaro. 'Which was pretty cool!'

'Was he your age, or what?'

'He was thirty – he was a man, mate. He was a truck driver – a really strong, hot truck driver!'

The fact that the truck driver was so many years older than Álvaro meant that when the dad found out what was going down he hit the roof about *my innocent son being seduced by an older man*. Also a regular routine in Villarreal. A dad finds out his boy and an older guy are shagging and he blames the older guy. The older guy has perverted a healthy young lad who otherwise would be interested only in knocking up women.

Anyway, Álvaro stormed out of home followed by the shouts and curses of his dad. The truck driver left his own family. The two guys set up as lovers in some seedy little flat somewhere and fucked constantly. After a few weeks, the dad tracked down his youngest son and found him a job driving a taxi.

After a few more weeks he allowed the two guys to come together to meals with the family.

'Okay – so how long were you and Truck Bloke together?'

'We were hot for about six months and after that we stuck it out for a few more months only it was sorta going sour. One day I come home from me shift on the taxi and I find the flat's been stripped.'

'Stripped?'

'The whole lot's walked, is what. Table, bed, chairs, pots and pans, everything that wasn't nailed down. Bastard had done a runner.'

A hard year followed after he moved back home, drank, did lots of dope, was screwed by his brothers, fought with his old man.

'Poor guy,' I say, kissing the nape of his neck, which is really cute where the hair's been shaved.

'Got me shit together, now.'

'Cool.'

He's enrolled at university. Accountancy. He hates accountancy but reckons it's a meal ticket. He pays his way by driving the taxi for its owner most of the week, and cause of that he can also afford the rent for his flat in a district of new housing on the periphery of the city.

Weekend comes and we decide to spend the night together.

'The flat's a tip, but wotcher gonna do?' he says.

'Fuck till we're blind and can't see it's a tip.'

'Wanking, innit, that makes ya blind?' he laughs.

'Won't have any need of wanking when it's the two of us getting into one another!'

Typical prole district, his neighbourhood. My first chance to scope it comes when I find myself squeezed into a smelly bus heading out his way at the end of a long dull day at the debt collection agency. The bus, jolting on cobblestones, farts smoke and racket out the back. The district was a lot of stony open fields owned by a bankrupt development company till a decade or so ago. One night the fields were occupied almost silently by a whole horde of whispering squatters. Next morning a troop of police and lawyers and council inspectors were stood about scratching their heads at the sight of a new shantytown. We watched it on tele when I was a boy. Huts, that's what you saw. Bamboo, cardboard, sheets of corrugated fibreglass. And little spirals of smoke corkscrewing skywards where mums were refrying beans for breakfast, and lines of washing pegged out between the huts, and babies crying and kids playing.

Almost always happens with land lying empty around the city, this sort of mass squat.

Afterwards, listless attempts by big business and city bureaucrats to bully or hound the newcomers off the property. Next, a year or two later, the city making up its mind to recognise in a grudging way the founding of a new suburb. Municipal planners trot along. Surveyors lay out a relentlessly uninteresting grid of streets. Streets with no name: Street 1, Street 2, Street 3. And now it's mostly breezeblock houses open straight onto the street. Often a tiny notch of a shop slotted into a ground floor to sell canned goods and plastic-wrapped packs of Tia Rosa.

Fuck – it's ugly. At first glance the whole district is plug ugly!

Raw walls, knobbly with mortar. Iron bars on narrow windows. Rusty steel rods sticking out of rooftops. Plastic pop bottles dropped upside down on top of the rods. To slow down the rusting. Water tanks of blue or black vinyl. Rooftop cabins of bamboo matting, temporary outworks of breezeblock. Mutts, too, growling, padding back and forth on rooftops. Greenery very scarce, course. Trees planted by the city have been hacked down on the sly for firewood or died from lack of water leaving behind nothing but naked trunks riddled with termites.

I get down from the bus and find my guy waiting, giving me a sexy wink.

'Hey,' I say, brushing his face quickly with my lips.

'Soppy git,' he grins.

A cigarette has been stuck behind his ear – he's wearing it as a sort of badge, like lots of working class boys. He's dressed in that very baggy layered look so common among prole young guys. A pair of cheap clean jeans with a drop crotch, over which hangs a clean tee printed with a portrait of Che Guevara.

What's the life of one man worth, asks a text printed on the shirt, when the future of humanity is at risk?

We saunter through hot dusty streets. Hot, dusty, crudely cobbled streets. And on all sides, little makeshifts. Painted stones set out in a circle. Pot plants fierce with colour. Clear slabs of paint – orange, or indigo, or azure – slapped onto any bare wall when a family has found itself in funds. Almost all householders have thrown open their street door for the sake of a little air and as you walk past you glance inside and see the whole family seated sweatily, in vests and print frocks, staring at the tele screen.

'Here's me street,' says Álvaro.

Street 22.

One of the dirtiest looking streets I've seen anywhere in the city. A mound of rubbish on one corner buzzes with flies and seems to be made up mostly of plastic bags bursting with kitchen scraps. A jingling now and then as a pedicab comes rolling along the cobblestones. Boys earn a pittance by pedalling back and forth carrying old ladies or tired mothers with their shopping bags.

Álvaro yanks out a keyring. A plastic keyring moulded into the shape of a football player, half the size of the young guy's hand.

'Cool, innit?' he says proudly.

We step into a tiny, poorly lighted corridor. The stuccoed walls have been painted a scorching red. My fuckbuddy nips up a narrow staircase and I follow. A landing leads onto another poorly lighted corridor. The stuccoed walls have been painted a flaring saffron. Álvaro nips up a second narrow staircase onto the rooftop. Following him, I find my face dabbed and patted by rows of wet washing pegged onto nylon cables by the mothers of the house to be ready for the sun when it rises first thing tomorrow. We cross to a brick block of rooms sticking up like a penthouse.

Álvaro slips another key into another lock, looks sort of shy.

'Welcome to the love nest, dude,' he says.

Poking around in his pocket, he pulls out something. He hands it to me. Tweety. A lollipop made to look like Tweety. Coloured bright yellow. Blue eyes and an orange beak printed on the plastic wrapper.

'Have you given me this cause you think I need to practise sucking?' I say.

'Smart arse,' he laughs. 'Fuck you're mouthy!'

We step straight into a small room fitted out with a sofa

and a square table. Formica square table. Formica on one side blistered black. A burn? On top of the table a gas burner and couple of saucepans. As for the sofa – broken down, greasy. Dropped on top of torn upholstery a lot of shirts, underpants, books, compact disks, coffee mugs. Grimy stucco walls chipped into so as to make a crude groove into which someone – not a certified electrician – has slipped a couple lengths of white electric cable.

Álvaro, loping obliviously past the sordid scene, scarpers through a doorway.

I follow.

An inner room, not overly clean. Three lumpy mattresses cover the whole gritty floor. A window of iron bars – no glass – shows the night sky. Go to the window, squint down, you see the service patio of the house lighted with a yellow bulb. A concrete lid has split over an open sewer. A rat pokes out its head. A bold rat – pink nose, pink paws, sniffing energetically. Oops! The rat scrabbles suddenly up a pipe, ducks between two walls.

'Mmmm, yeah – try it that way dude,' mumbles Álvaro. 'Lemme see, press with your finger?'

Afterwards we lie on the greasy mattresses talking.

'What's your family like?' he says.

'My mum and dad could be a bit more mellow,' I try gingerly. 'They'd flip if they knew I was into guys.'

A voice outside the flat shrills through the iron bars of our window.

'You watch your sodding step, missus, that's all I can say! You watch your step or else!'

'Hag!' yells another voice. '*You* bloody watch *your* bloody step!'

'I'm going to use my witchcraft!'

'Hag! Dirty hag!'

Álvaro, lying all loose and abandoned on the three

mattresses, his limbs sprawled, laughs quietly.

'What's going down?' I ask, planting a kiss on his brown belly.

'One of my neighbours, dude. One of the women who tells fortunes and swears by the seven essences and reads tarot cards and that.'

'She threatening someone in the courtyard?'

'You watch your step – !'

'Hag – hag!'

'Yeah,' he shrugs. 'One of the other neighbours – couple sad old cows – but wotcher gonna do?'

14

Okay, time to clock out. Thank fuck! Objective number one: get myself on other side of office door without being held back by the Licenciado once more spelling out what a heavy load a married man and father has to carry. He wants flattery. Okay! Bet you're a great husband and dad, Licenciado. Say anything to get myself out that door. Choose your wife wisely, Tito. Sure, Licenciado! Choose your noose blindly. Stash your heist wildly. Sidle doorwards while this sober husband and father goes on about how he thanks god in his prayers every night that he's been blessed with two pearls of daughters and a wife more precious than a ruby.

Yeah, whatever.

'See ya later, Licenciado!'

Objective number two: yum down a tamale or two at the little caf across the street where the old señora with only one eye and a hairy wart on her recessive chin has taken a fancy to me, dunno why. We pass the time of day. She tells me about her grandson, who's got a hare lip.

'God go with you, lad,' she cackles when I head out.

'And with you, Mother.'

Objective number three: get the hell away.

Okay, which way? West towards the ecological park? Or east towards the Plaza Mayor? Squirrels or city? City! Walk smartly out of the commercial district. Slow my pace to a nice leisurely stroll – like a tourist from the capital come to look at the antiquities – when I hit the viceroyal centre of the city. Sloping aimlessly, making the most of my freedom, I climb wide worn steps, I cross a couple sleepy plazas. I come to a grim old mansion.

Palacio de la Tijera.

I've sloped my way to the Palacio de la Tijera.

For fuck sake! And look at its façade! Massive, closed, enigmatic. A typical viceroyal façade you might say. A mighty pair of cedar doors stand bolted. Wrought iron grilles ward away any pleb who might feel tempted to try to peer through the high thick windows. A pleb like this swarthy little dude stood right here, gawping, on the weary old cobblestones.

Am probs smelling of tamale sauce too.

A baroque pediment, a stony scroll, uncurls itself above the doorway. Otherwise the whole front is empty. Nope, not completely empty. A black ribbon suspended below the pediment. A big ribbon, a metre across, silk faded by sunlight yet slightly iridescent like a massive black moth perched on the wall, dying at midday.

Aurelia Lacanzo de la Tijera de Lago.

Comforted by Papal Benediction.

We pray for her.

Santa Aurelia-by-Papal-Benediction. A snooty pompous old lady. Well maybe it's not fair to call Aurelia pompous or snooty cause I know nothing about her other than what I read in the paper last summer when I glimpsed that obituary. Am projecting, very likely. It's convenient, isn't it, to believe that dowagers in the old families are bitches? And the men bastards. Otherwise you might start to get eaten up inside by a sense that you're missing out on something good.

A panel of one of the cedar doors, swinging open, suddenly seems to spill into the street a golden light.

Oh my god!

Salvador!

My Prince stepping out, casting the eye of an owner on the world, and – wow! He just glows, way he glowed that day in the church. He looks fucking amazing. And as always it's hard not to gape adoringly.

Why the fuck is he straight?

It's not fair!

Why the fuck is he straight and a de la Tijera? And why do I want to just throw myself at the guy? Or not so much throw myself at him but grovel at his feet hoping maybe he might give me a pat on the back of my head, in passing, before putting in the boot. And – and now serene Blond God turns my way, surveys me coolly.

Shit, and of course I want to cringe back against the walls. My Prince saunters forward. Comes up, holds out his hand.

'Matías,' he murmurs in his beautiful baritone. 'Sorry – Tito.'

His hand holds mine drily, firmly. Masterfully. Just like the hand of a hero in a bodice-ripper!

'Cool, ta! I'm cool, Salvador.'

He drops my hand calmly.

'How's your novel?'

Oops!

'My novel? Um – too busy with work lately to be able to spare time for the novel.'

'What a pity,' says Salvador. 'Your idea of writing a novel of Villarreal really set my mind working.'

Say what?

'Cool!'

Salvador looks guarded, like always, but his eyes are clear.

'You've got to write it, you know.'

'Got to – ? What makes you say that, Salvador?'

'You've got to because it's not just your story, it's a story that belongs to other people. As a writer you've got a moral obligation. You've got a moral obligation to speak to and for everyone.'

Wow!

'Temporary setback right now, is all, Salvador. Gotta pay my way. Gonna write that book, mate – don't you worry!'

'Tito – that's brilliant!'

'Ta, Salvador.'

'Are you still an advertising copywriter?'

Fuck – think fast!

'No, not now. Working these days in – in finance – in the financial sector.'

Salvador furrows that gleaming brow.

Fuck! Switch the fucking topic quick smart!

'Was looking at the funerary ribbon for your grandmother, Salvador. Sad to lose your gran. You miss her a lot?'

He looks at me very carefully.

'Not really. She wasn't a loving woman.'

Yay me – got it right! Ten out of ten score for forensic skills of wannabe novelist! Right now though, man, stay cool. Keep your eye on the ball.

'Drag.'

'Drag, yep,' he says real deft and almost smiling. 'My grandmother's death has left me alone in the world, since my parents were killed a few years ago.'

'Killed? Fuck! Who by?'

'Car accident. They were on a skiing holiday. In Aspen, Colorado.'

'Oh, okay. So you're an orphan?'

'Yes.'

'Wish I was!'

He looks a bit shocked.

'Dude, I mean it! My father's dead to the world, to all intents and purposes. So really the only parent I've got is my mother. And she's too bloody alive for comfort!'

'You don't mean that, of course.'

Only he looks curious. Not erotically curious, goes without saying – bummer! – since he's straight as the cedar frame around his fucking gigantic doors. Curious intellectually, emotionally. According to my analysis right here and now, at least, while we're stood here together on the cobblestones. Me peering into his eyes, trying to suss him out.

He stares back at me, giving nothing away.

'Care to take a look at our house, Tito?' he says, startlingly leftfield.

'Your – house?'

'I was on my way to mass but maybe you'd be interested in a tour? My family has one or two things you might think worth your trouble viewing.'

My Prince wants me to look inside his palace and hopes it might be worth my fucking trouble! Wow! Wowww! Wowwwwwwwwwwww!

Okay, don't lose it. Don't act like a twink.

'Hey – cool – sure! Ta, Salvador.

'This way.'

Lithely, lightly, the prince turns towards the small cedar door.

Palacio de la Tijera was built in the seventeenth century and commands half a city block. Two storeys enclosing two interior courtyards. The outer courtyard, nobly empty, paved with great big hunks of black basalt. Basalt worn and polished now by centuries of heels, soles, spurs. A central fountain, also carved from basalt, dribbles with brownish water. Huge columns, cut from red basalt, are topped with doric capitals. Weighty terracotta tubs in rows, each forced to grow a ficus or azalea kept clipped severely. A courtyard designed – you could say – to scare the crap out of anyone not entitled to entry.

The inner courtyard's another world, layered with greenery, filled with whirls and swirls of flowers, squares of cypress, balls of box, spirals of yew. A great big magnolia, wide and waxy. Arabesques of dahlia, spiky yet yielding, cushions of colour, yellow and orange and pink.

'This place is perfect,' I say. 'Always thought I wouldn't like this palace. Always thought it a bit – grandiose.'

'Thanks,' laughs Salvador.

Why oh why is he not bent? I want not to know he's not bent. I need to keep making myself know.

Salvador is straight.

Okay?

'No, I don't mean – ' I start. 'I mean – it's perfect!'

All rooms opening from the interior courtyard are set out with costly old things from the days of the Viceroyalty. Chests of slabbed cedar upholstered with red leather embossed by dainty little gold leaves and flowers, buttoned with black ebony and bright brass. Cool! Sofas and chairs, also cedar, or oak. A lot more upholstery, embossed red leather, green leather, golden leaves, silver flowers, hammered onto hardwoods by broad brass nails. Chair legs carved to look like paws and claws of panthers. Or else dolphins jumping from the waves.

We stand looking at one another, smiling.

And he touches my elbow.

Electric shock!

Electricity zapping from elbow up and down entire bod. My Prince, kiss me please! Please kiss me. Please fuck me, Blond God!

'Now,' he says, 'we go from baroque to rococo.'

'Always ready to rock with rococo,' I say with deep and shameful lameness.

My Prince leads me to a suite of salons redecorated in the eighteenth century. Coffered ceilings. Dainty plasterwork. Cupids frolicking, plump, pursing lips, wagging bum cheeks. Medallions sporting portraits of the Three Graces.

'So you're working in finance now?' says Blond God. 'Yet you're a writer – what openings are there for a writer in finance?'

Fuck.

'Openings?' I say feebly.

'For a writer.'

One or two secs of wondering whether to try to bluff my way out of this corner. Only, why bother to try? One of the worst follies of my mother and father, after all, has always been pretending we're higher up on the ladder than we are in reality.

'Clerical work, Salvador. That's what openings there are for a writer.'

'What?' he almost yelps. 'You – what – ?'

'Am an office boy.'

'Surely you can't – ? Sorry to seem rude – but – why work as an office boy?'

'Money, mate. Need the money. Cash is what you could call totally in short supply in my family.'

Salvador looks sober, turns silent. No doubt disgusted to have found himself tricked into showing his heirlooms to an office boy. No doubt he'll now shake me off quick smart. No doubt not too politely. He opens his mouth.

He waits.

He starts speaking slowly.

'Are you really so short of cash in your family?'

'Mate, we're not only short of cash we're short of credit. We're so short that the old bloke who trawls the pavements trying to sell knockoff knickers to servants on our street has made up his mind to scratch our address off his list.'

Salvador stares at me wordlessly.

No doubt making up his mind how best to show me the door.

'Sorry to be so impertinently curious,' he says in the end, which leaves me stumped. 'I've no right to ask.'

'Is okay,' I mutter.

We square off at one another, somehow. I frown at him. He frowns back. He looks away.

'The next room you may like,' he says. 'Myself, well for me it's the best room in the whole house.'

'Okay – cool.'

'Come this way. It's best because of its books. It's the library.'

'You mean the books are collector's items?'

'No, I mean it's best because the books are books. I'm like you, Tito – I love books!'

Parquet creaks and sings subtly underfoot as we pad into the library. All four walls have been wainscoted with cedar to the height of my head. Brocade – caramel and silver – sheaths the walls above the wainscot. Coats of arms set into the glowing woodwork. Griffins, unicorns, roses, trefoils. Arms of ancestors. The bookcases are mighty freestanding cabinets. Chinese dragons made of porcelain, each as big as a mastiff, guard the main doorway. Glazed monsters, fierce, incisors bared.

'You can see we're lovers in our family of things shipped on the Manila galleons,' says Salvador.

'Were you scared of those toothy winged lizards when a boy?'

'Never,' he smiles. 'Dolores took the trouble to introduce them to me as beloved members of the family.'

'What're their names?'

'Yin and Yang. Shipped across the ocean by the galleons then dragged inland by oxcart from Acapulco.'

Note he doesn't say Aca. Nor Acapulquito. Which we say. Our family. Aca, Acapulquito. Mamá often speaks flowingly, fondly, about dear darling breezy Acapulquito. Yet I happen to know from reading a squeaky white page in one of Ma's glossy mags that old families think it not only somewhat off to say Aca but unspeakably naff to stick on a pulquito! Meanwhile we scope oil portraits, me, and My Prince. Mighty daubs of dead members of his family. Generals. Marchionesses. Bishops, judges, landowners, ladies. Scrolls at the foot of the oldest portraits are bannered with titles and honorifics. Sr. B. Don Salvador de Lago, Counsellor of the Holy Office of the Inquisition. Also landscape paintings. An aqueduct in an obscure valley. A prospect of a plain covered with maguey. A lake in a cypress forest ornamented with a colonnaded pavilion.

How does it feel to grow up inside this carapace of fakery?

Wanting to centre myself, I bend down to slide my hand along the satiny curves of some woodwork. Nice, the woodwork feels really nice. And while I'm bent down I feel something drop onto one of my arse cheeks. Something sort of firm and warm.

A hand.

The palm of a hand.

Not the Licenciado – though funnily enough that's my first crazy thought. Bloody old perv of a Licenciado! Next thought – Salvador! Salvador's hand! Fuck – what is it about my arse that every straight bloke in town thinks himself entitled to cop a quick grope?

Salvador? My Prince, for fuck sake!

Straightening up, I twist my torso and take a look. He's

smiling sorta serenely.

'What's going down?' I say sharpish.

Cause somehow I feel annoyed. Somehow it's that serenity. An awareness that all he's gotta do is crook his index finger and anyone will be at his feet worshipping him and – and – and licking his boots. Cause of the money, that why? Cause he now knows how poor we are, our family, he thinks he can now just reach out and help himself to a handful?

'Sorry,' he says, not looking the slightest bit sorry. 'Couldn't help myself – you're very cute you know.'

Come again? Cute? How come he's talking like some queer?

'So cause a guy's cute – not that I am cute, by the way – it's okay for another guy to feel him up more or less at will?'

Salvador stops looking quite so serene, now.

'Well no – naturally not, but – '

'Yeah?'

Blond God seems to rally. He lets out a short rattle of laughter. He looks at me cockily.

'Tito you're a babe and you know it perfectly well, and right now what we really should do is acknowledge we've got the hots for one another, don't you think?'

Okay, let's just schedule a tick or two here for rocking back on my heels, silently.

Afterwards another tick or two.

'Got the hots for one another, have we Salvador?'

'Yes, and we should get ourselves straight upstairs to my bedroom. And once we're away from the servants and safely behind a locked door let me show you how well I can ride a boy.'

Obscure anger grows slightly less obscure.

'Salvador, you seem to think I'm willing to be banged by any moneyed bloke more or less for the asking.'

His face stiffens, looks chilly.

'Matías, the truth of course is that I'm not any moneyed bloke. Let's face facts. I'm – you know who I am, you know perfectly well.'

Already we're coming close to a row than a bonk.

'Yes, I know who you are Salvador. You're a guy who thinks he's got a right to tell me he wants to fuck my arse.'

Blond god looks at me sort of wisely.

'Okay, I see what you're saying,' he murmurs. 'How much?'

'How much – what?'

'We keep quite a lot of cash in the safe next door in the study.'

He stops talking. He stands waiting.

'Well, I suppose there's an etiquette in this sort of situation, isn't there Salvador?' I say slowly.

'Etiquette?'

'I mean, a guy who's been told he's a babe with a fuckable arse could at least thank the guy who tells him the good news. Yet I don't feel thankful, Salvador. I feel pissed off. I don't like to be treated like this, mate. I don't want to be any rich guy's rent boy.'

Salvador steps back towards a marquetry bookcase. A rigid jaw.

Scary.

A long cold silence follows.

'So that's your answer?' he says at last. 'I've shown you courtesy – taken you through the home of my family – and all you say to me is that you feel pissed off.'

Whew! My tendency towards fear turns straight into ferocity.

'I didn't ask you to show me your fine fucking courtesy, Salvador. I don't owe you anything, Salvador. Well, maybe I owe you contempt. You seem to think you can push everyone around – you think you can walk around pulling any poor guy. You think you can walk all over my – my feelings – my – '

I want to hit himself, now, cause thinking about my feelings has made a lot of feeble tears start spouting.

'Your feelings?' says Salvador, with a wondering look.

'Yeah, fucking prick – fucking with my mind like I'm some snotty kid, and – and – '

Boo hoo, boo hoo –

A snotty kid grinding fists into his eyes right now to try to staunch the tears.

'Thanks for your frankness,' he says. 'Typical of the manners I might expect from – '

'Yeah?'

He's pulled himself up short though, the bastard.

'Now you've nearly got me behaving as badly as yourself, Matías López. What more can I say? I'm sorry, that's what I can say. I'm sorry if I haven't sugared my phrases enough – no doubt I could've flattered you by telling you I was madly in love with you, or some similar lie instead of speaking honestly.'

'I'm supposed to be honoured by your honesty?'

'Well now I know you're not honoured.'

We scowl at one another under the waxy grimace of Don Salvador de Lago, Counsellor of the Holy Office of the Inquisition. The whole fucking family is ganging up on me inside that library! Only way not to lose my nerve right now is to stay lippy.

'Can't bear the thought can you Salvador? Can't bear the thought that a guy you want to screw wouldn't be falling over himself to be screwed by you. Maybe you should go and screw yourself, Salvador.'

'Which would seem an appropriate point to say once more that I'm sorry.'

'Sorry about what? What are you talking about?'

'Sorry that I – well, that I fancy you. Sorry that I'm hanging around you right now. Sorry that I haven't got the wits to stay well away from you.'

'Let me do you the favour by getting myself away from you, fuckwit.'

Salvador stands perfectly still, perfectly silent, for what seems like a very long time. A look of hard mortification seems to have set into his fine face. I force myself to keep looking at that face. I want to scarper, but feel scared once more – a sense that something final has just happened, something deeply scary. Salvador sorta shakes himself. He visibly squares his shoulders. He's very strong, this prick. Aryan, tall, white, athletic. He towers above me terribly.

A prick whose look now alters, whose eyes and mouth seem suddenly unhappy.

'Sorry that you dislike me so much, Tito. I hope you have a good life.'

Again he crooks his index finger. A servant scuffles towards me from some nook or cranny and shows me to the door.

15

So, who'd have thunk it? My Prince turns out to be a sex predator. Along with nine out of every ten guys anywhere and everywhere. Yeah, well doing my best to shrug it off but doing the job badly. Dismayed is what I am, an hour or so later, deeply dismayed as I duck off the bus and trot along the streets of our suburb.

Our suburb. Tacky –

Course now am looking through the eyes of a de la Tijera.

Arf-arf-arrrrfff!

Dogs, rooftops. Silly neurotics should know me by now since I've been scooting up and down these streets for longer than any of their short lives, but dogs in our suburb are all a bit off their heads, I reckon. Hardly any of their masters or mistresses take them for walks or runs or play with them in parks. The poor hairy buggers stay stuck on those rooftops with the maids and the water tanks and the washing. And they yap. And they snap. And they bark. Dogs round ours are always kicking up a racket – barking mad!

Tito you're a babe and you know it perfectly well, and right now what we really should do –

He really said that? Really and truly?

Fuck, can't let myself think about his beauty! He might be predatory but he's sure a stud! Can't let myself think about his clear blue eyes, his glowing golden hair, the easy power of his long limbs. Gotta stop thinking about Salvador. Can't live in a fantasy, can I? Gotta think about – about what for want of a better word you could maybe call reality.

'Hey, how was your day Mamá?'

'Tito before you run upstairs would you mind popping out to More for Less? We need – '

'Sorry, Mamá. Can't it wait? Knackered here!'

After a shower and a think, I phone Álvaro and ask him to meet at a cantina. He shows up. I tell him we'd better not hang out with one another any more because neither of us can do the other any good. Meaning money. Hang out with one another and we'll go under as a twosome.

'You're cool, but – ' I stammer.

Álvaro shrugs.

'Sure,' he says. 'Shit happens – wotcher gonna do?'

'Try them on, son,' urges the Licenciado. 'We need to know whether they fit you or not.'

Okay, now what?

Clocked in, stepped into our office, ready to start the working day. Licenciado Chávez with an anxious smile hands me a small flat parcel wrapped in coloured paper. A gift from him as my immediate senior in recognition of my good work. Hmm, weird. Peeling away the coloured paper reveals a pair of white Calvin Kleins. Knickers, like. A pair of clean white knickers which when I shake them out of their wrapping amount to not much more than a skimpy little posing pouch – a heavily stitched cup in front for your balls and not a lot else apart from a string to slip between your arse cheeks.

'Awesome, it's real nice of you Licenciado,' I say, deeply stumped.

'Try them on, Tito,' he repeats.

'Can't try them on in the office, Licenciado! Anyone could walk in, couldn't they?'

'Don't worry about that, son. Let me lock the door.'

Which he does, straight away.

Oops.

Licenciado Chávez in shapeless pants of fawn terylene. A white polyester shirt bulging over his paunch. A brown necktie, of course – obligatory. On top of the lot, a shapeless fawn cardigan. He beams at me across the narrow width of our small close room whose strip lights, as always, are fizzing and popping. Beaming at me, but on edge. He's as nervous as me, I reckon. Fuck – what to do?

'Am kinda shy, Licenciado. You mind not looking?'

'No problem, son!' he booms heartily.

The dirty creep turns his back ostentatiously. I start picking at my shoelaces. Can't really go through with this can I? Can't really take my kit off in the office to try on a pair of fucking Calvin Kleins? Well, maybe I can wing it, get through the game intact if I keep my wits about me and don't take my eye for one second off the shapelessly hunched back of the Licenciado.

Course the old bastard swings around to scope my tackle right at the moment when my arse is bare and am stooped struggling to tug on the new pair of knickers.

'Lucky with the girls, are you son?' he says, shambling forward.

'Probably not as lucky as you, Licenciado.'

Fuck, the dirty fat lech is going to try!

'I'm a faithful husband my boy.'

Yep, he does try. No urbane caress of the arse cheek, today. Today we go for a good strong grip on the office boy's cock. A poor shrinking little cock trying to slip from that meaty grip.

'Fuck off, Licenciado!'

'You know you want it, boy,' he growls, ramming me up against the filing cabinet.

'Fuck off!'

Strong bastard, that's my worry. Well not strong.

Weighty rather than strong, cause it's blubber mostly, but a lot more biomass than I can muster. The grubby old cunt holds me down against the filing cabinet with only one arm while he fishes around in his flies with the spare hand.

'Tito my little one,' he whispers, syrupy. 'Day you started here your daddy saw that you're begging for it.'

Fucked if I'm gonna be raped, though.

'Loser,' I say.

Not too brilliant a remark, true, but I back it up by sinking my teeth into the fleshy part of his hand. You know the part – below the thumb, looks a bit like a chicken drumstick.

'Aaaaaaaaaargh!' shrieks the Licenciado.

Cause when I say sinking my teeth, I don't mean a bit of a nibble, I mean driving my teeth into the muscle tissue as hard as I can in an attempt to get the two sets of incisors to meet in the middle. Knowing that they won't. Also knowing that trying to make them meet will cause him a tidy few seconds of agony.

'So just fuck yourself!' I snarl as he lurches backwards.

Licenciado Chávez goes into mild shock. The dickhead drops his big flabby bum down onto the floor and kinda keens at the sight of his bloody thumb. Keening, rocking back and forth, like he needs his Mamá.

Me, meanwhile, getting my kit back on quick smart.

'Son, find me a bandage,' he whimpers.

'Find your bandage yourself, dirty old tosser. Am outta here!'

'Why are the young so cruel?' moans the Licenciado. 'No mercy, no mercy at all.'

Hotel Palacio seeks staff for its service of valet parking. Requisites: driving licence, excellent personal appearance, from 20 to 28 years. Applicants present themselves at 2 Oriente No 13 between 3.00 pm and 5.00 pm, with curriculum vitae, 2 letters of recommendation, birth certificate, academic certificates, 2 studio photographs.

Midday and am back at ours, sat on the patio, leafing again through the situations vacant.

Restaurant seeks waiters. Applicants to 19 Pte 1319 from 1.00 pm onwards.

Waiting at table could be cool in a way. Maybe? Balancing plates, serving orders, flicking white napkins onto the laps of smart customers, flirting with hot guys. Maybe could consider it. Last resort. Meantime better stick to trying to find office work and at the same time keep checking out retail work, and maybe –

Hang about, what's this one?

Driver: advertising vehicle: Apply now with 2 letters of reference. 5 Sur 3918.

On my way to work next day. Yep, got the job. Need to catch two buses across town to company garaging. One bus to the centre of the city, then a short walk. Dawn is breaking as I head past the Plaza Mayor. Black sky pricked with stars at every point of the compass except to the east, where it's dark blue, empty. Street vendors are shoving their stalls into place – young guys, mostly, hunching their shoulders behind the heavy weight while they push awkwardly. Streetsweepers trundle wheeled bins across cobblestones and, with twig brooms, scrape up litter. Dark, short workmen come plodding along the pavements.

Okay, here we are at Calle Isabel la Católica.

A bus stop. Kick my heels waiting for the right bus. Bus after bus hammering by, rammed with commuters, painted with names chosen by their drivers.

Star Trek. Les Miserables. Pancho Villa –

I climb on board Desert Storm.

A bus trip's always full of little events, isn't it? Keep your eyes wide. Don't let yourself think it's just a drudge. You can learn a lot. Now, for instance, next to me on the slippery vinyl sits a fanciable young bloke wrapped around the neck with a clean white towel and I notice a strong smell of chlorine. On his way from his gym? We're passing through a prole part of town where the roadway is mostly potholes.

Wham, bam!

Tyres trying to cope with broken terrain while pounding past bleak housing mixed with lots of little shops. Butcheries, on this particular street, packed with people and hung with hunks of dead pig, cow. Red and white, the insides of the shops. Red, white, flesh and blood and bone, shifting about against the hard shiny white of tiles – hallucinatory under very strong white lighting – shop after shop, block after block.

A kid climbs on board, a fistful of gum packets, looking weary.

'Señores passengers,' he starts droning, 'chewing gum for sale – '

Our bus wheels a bit wildly into a roundabout. A clump of canary palms and some stiff thornbushes sprout. Circling the roundabout a white concrete wall's been latched onto as a kind of holdfast by food vendors. Anchored on its bulk are tents netted by quick hands out of aluminium tubing, blue tarpaulin. Small dark people flit about under the blue and silver, slapping white soft slippery stuff into pans, or onto griddles, or fiddling with gas bottles, fixing tiny blue flames, humming old songs.

'As alone and sad,' sings a Mixteco boy, 'as a leaf in the wind – '

We bump away from the food stalls, cross a broad avenue lined with dusty palms, come into a commercial precinct. Afterwards, a flyblown old produce market. Next, a gleaming new electronics factory. Now bleak housing, once more, bargain basements for prole family on top of prole family.

A stink hangs over this district. Fumes from a fertiliser works.

Next, a kilometre of bare landscape. Pine forest only a few years back. Clawed away lately by bulldozers for a new engineering works. We climb a concrete flyover, cross a motorway, drop down into a grimy valley. Crude houses built from brick and breezeblock. Women and men scuttling along alleys to bus stops. Always in groups – talking, waving their arms, laughing, whistling. Or stood at the bus stops crimping their hair, or cracking jokes, or eating.

We turn a couple more corners and here we are! My stop.

'Chewing gum, señores – sweet sugarless gum – '

Out I jump.

I've been given the job of driving an advertising vehicle cause of my experience in the advertising industry. Ask yourself! Sounds an easy job. All you got to do, so the boss says, is spend ten hours a day driving the Publimobile. Doing what every young lad wants to do, driving. At the cost of the company. Cool name, don't you reckon? Publimobile meaning publicity mobile. Yep, really cool.

Well anyway could be worse.

'Okay you gotta drive the car and you gotta play the tapes, right?' says the boss. 'You got any questions?'

Beady eyes. Blanks any attempt to be matey.

'None,' I say, spry.

A white Volkswagen, twenty years old, looking barely

ten years older, fitted on its roof with a couple loudspeakers recycled from some defunct dance club or political party. Aforesaid now wired up to an audiocassette deck. You control the deck from inside the car. Job is to slot a cassette into the deck and drive up and down streets while a tape plays. At an ear-splitting pitch. Chorus of the tape track's a frenzied snatch of trumpeting by the municipal orchestra of some sad city still more provincial than Villarreal. A score or two bars from Rossini's *William Tell*. Next, trumpets cut out. After, urgent male voice with prole accent lets you know loud and clear – loud, especially! – that you should rush out now and make the most of a newly discounted line of cooking oil. Next, Rossini. Next, cooking oil. Next –

Once the track's played all the way, pull it out, flip it round, stick it back into the deck.

Hit play.

'So that's how it works, yeah?' says Beady Eye. 'Direct publicity. No middleman. It's the key to making money.'

'Yeah,' I say. 'Awesome.'

'Well hop to it, kid! You're not here to give me blow jobs.'

'Sure, boss.'

After which come ten tedious hours driving up and down through the least well-to-do streets of outer Villarreal. And at the end of that tedium, half an hour washing and polishing the poor dinged old fucking Volkswagen. Afterwards, end day by taking a bus bound northward. A bus packed tight. Stood in the aisle holding a handgrip. Swaying from side to side with everybody. We're like a coral colony. A whole lot of organisms squeezed tight and responding as one. Only we don't want to be coral. We want to be people.

The bus hits a notably gnarly pothole and someone's hips shove heavily against my arse.

The someone is a bloke.

Hm –

Well we're all squashed tight and there's no way you can keep any normal sense of personal space. The bus pounds down a flat stretch and everyone straightens up and restores his or her appropriate boundary. We hit another pothole. We all lurch forward. Once more the hips shove heavily against my arse.

Maybe a bit too heavily?

Okay, am facing the rear vision mirror so it's easy to check out the identity of the shover. He's a young guy. He's yummy! We're headed down another flat stretch so he's stepped back a bit. Bummer. Hang about – wham! – another pothole, sharp jolt. Once more slim hips are bumping my bum and this time, instead of shrinking away, I push back. Not too hard, but firmly.

'Señores passengers,' moans a woman standing at the other end of the bus, 'comic books – '

Annoyingly the bus hits a very long straight, picks up speed, zooms along.

And soon we're near my stop.

'Comic books, señores passengers,' the woman moans on. 'Comic books for sale, comic books to make you smile!'

Mamá is not happy about my new job.

She lets me know her displeasure while resting on her bed once more before a game of cards. Cedar crucifix screwed above the bedhead drooping as always with her personal rosary. Black lacquer fan painted with pink roses in its frame of mahogany. A fan that seems so paltry compared with the glories of the Palacio de la Tijera. A painted fan, brought home dutifully after a trip to the faraway fatherland, sainted Spain – kept as a treasure!

Mamá lifts her eyes for comfort to the statuette of the

Black Virgin.

'Shameful, it's shameful, Matías,' she says. 'How can my own son, with my good blood, think of doing such low work?'

'No shame in honest work, Ma.'

'I say it's shameful!'

Mamá lets her eyes drift towards a mirror. Not sure what she sees, but she shudders, shuts her puffy eyes, sinks back into her pouchy pillows.

'What's to become of us?' she whispers. 'How soon till we're out on the street?'

The mirror hasn't got a lot to say.

I slope off to my room. Do a few press-ups on the floor. Restless, really restless. Throw myself onto my bed. Drop into a short doze. A dream about playing cards with Ángela. Ángela must be studying late at university. Cards getting turned face up, one by one.

Jack of clubs – queen of spades.

Joker –

Afterwards, I awake feeling alert and not wanting to be under the same roof as the nuns, whose arrival is imminent. Slip out of the house. Scoot a few blocks down the streets to the local bathhouse. A bathhouse for men, needless to say. Pay forty pesos and you get a pass for a sort of cell block. Two floors of concrete, linked by a concrete staircase. A central concourse on each floor is fitted with rows of benches upholstered in brown vinyl. Men wrapped in white towels are sat or sprawled on top of the benches. Cells open off each concourse and you call one of the attendants – good-looking young guys in green uniforms, jingling rings of keys – to lock or unlock your own personal cell, or to fetch you a beer or a bottle of soda.

Also maybe you want one of them to come with you into your cell.

Well, you can pay.

A cell contains a brown vinyl mattress dropped onto a bench of bleached pinewood, a brown mat, a pair of rubber flipflops, and a white towel printed in blue with the name of the bathhouse. Also a cake of soap: the cheap mass made brand, Rosa Venus. Stripping off my clothes, folding them on a stool, I knot the white towel around my brown waist and set off.

One steam room is hot. The next steam room is hotter. The last steam room is hottest. Only guys seriously into getting steamed can be found inside the last. Others stick to the first two or wander up and down between the cold showers, the warm showers, the massage room. A pair of beefy masseurs pummel and pound. Tough massage, serious stuff. Men of all sizes and shapes and ages are everywhere. Teenagers, eager and skinny. Old groaning walruses and beached white whales. Hardly anyone is fit. Almost all guys over twenty are sporting a pot belly. A lot of clients come to the bathhouse as a sort of club where they hang, talk, sweat, have a beer or two. Other clients come to suck and fuck.

Me, for one.

A first move is made by a thickset bloke about fifty who circles me, sizing me up out of the corner of his eye.

'You've got good big hands,' he says, closing in.

'Ta,' I say.

'One can tell a lot about a man by the size of his hands.'

One can tell a lot about a man by his lame pickup lines. Not that I say so. Core to bathhouse culture is that all are equal and treat one another with courtesy.

'Sorry, nice to chat but am booked for a massage.'

A polite nod, and I scarper.

Oil, water, vapour, aromas, limp cocks, bouncy arses.

Guys scoping your every move while you slope up and down, scoping their every move. A tiny teenager whose waist you can almost encircle with your two hands has squatted on his hams while a thickset man of thirty squats behind him kissing his arse cheeks. A gangly teenager stood in front of Tiny's lips is sliding his cock in and out.

'Come on dude,' says Gangly, grinning at me boldly. 'Help yourself!'

'Not my scene really, mate.'

'Cheers,' says Gangly, closing his eyes and driving himself deep as he can into Tiny.

Slope off to the sauna.

A young prole guy, sat on the bench, looks up and tips me a wink. Okay. Plonk myself down on the bench. The boy with supple brown fingers cops a feel of my tackle under the while towel. One of those prole dudes with a long talon tapering out. Nail of his little finger. Working dudes, course, keep their nails as a rule pared back to the quick. A few, though, especially youngsters like this bro, cultivate one little finger and allow its nail to grow long. Don't know why. Some say it's to do with magic. Or that it's a custom carried down from the Moors. Anyway, this boy has got long pointed nails on his little fingers and when we head back to my cell together, the things he does with those talons – wow!

'Harder, please!' he whimpers while I do my best to make him happy. 'Harder, harder – harder!'

Whew, you have to work like a navvy.

Afterwards we yarn together on the brown vinyl while necking a couple bottles of beer.

'You're great,' I say in a polite sort of way.

'You're great,' he says much much too eagerly. 'What's your name?'

'My – ? – um, Julio. Name's Julio.'

Talon Boy reaches out awkwardly to shake my hand.

Awkwardly cause he tries at all times to keep his cock hidden under a towel. A fine thick cock which any guy would be proud to own but right from the start, as soon as we came into my cell after making our way down from the sauna, he kept turning away from me nervously. A glimpse told me why. His cock is piebald. Know what I mean? A hefty swag but patterned with irregular shapes of black and pink, kind of like a piebald pig. Poor guy! Very adroit at moving his body so as to keep his cock from sight, deeply ashamed of its colour, clearly.

'What kind of work do you do, mate?' I ask.

'I'm a student.'

Okay – out of work. Wonder how he can afford forty pesos for the bathhouse? Don't want to know! Glug down my beer.

Talon Boy tells me his life story.

'My problem is that I can't stop thinking about men. Men who're like you. Passionate and healthy. And love to fuck. And know how to fuck.'

'I'm just ordinary.'

'Getting fucked – that's all I can think about! Awake or asleep, my mind goes round and round the thought of cock. Cock in my mouth, filling me up, feeding me cum. Cock up my arse, filling my whole body, making a baby inside my body.'

Day after day, driving up and down the streets of the suburb designated my territory. Taped trumpets trumpet. Urgent male urges. Cooking oil my first week. Bed linen my second week. Afterwards, cut-price kitset furniture, painkillers, synthetic drapery, cut-price kitchenware. And as I drive up and down the streets every householder and stallholder who catches sight of my battered Publimobile – swinging about with a squawk of dodgy axles – blanches, always.

It's the shriek of the loudspeakers, the whistling howling loudspeaker – squawk! – skre-eek! 'skre-eeeek!

'I'm out of here,' I say to Beady Eye.

'Hang about – '

'Hopping it!'

16

Cold grey days, now. Autumn turning into winter, low clouds blanketing the sky. Villarreal during the colder months of the year can be kinda gloomy. Day of the Dead comes around like an old skull you keep finding in your cupboard. So we traipse dutifully to the family vault and light our candles and pray or pretend to pray. Ángela and me being the ones pretending to pray. Although also I have my suspicions about Mamá. Papá profits from the mood of piously respectful boredom by laying down the law once more.

'Tito, tonight you're to contact your cousin. I want you to ask for work from your cousin.'

'Paco?'

'Who else in this benighted family can get you work? Paco knows he has to help you whether he wants to or not, since you're the son of his only aunt. Get him to send you an air ticket and take yourself up to Tijuana.'

We're walking away from the family vault, father and son under a filthy dark sky.

'How can I go down on my knees and beg for help from that idiot?'

Papá looks as grim as the sky.

'Do it, boy. We need money. Our finances are in a worse state than you or your sister know.'

My chest contracts, hard.

Fuck!

'Papá, we need to know. Me and sis. We need to know the whole story. Why don't we all sit down together as a family? Maybe we could go over the accounts and see what we can sort out. Ángela's bound to have a few clues about how we can maybe – you know – rationalise? Do we really need to – like – keep the family house? Can't we sell up and shift somewhere smaller since the place is such a white elephant and eats up money?'

Papá looks grimmer than the sky, now – no easy feat.

'Your mother's family home is not a commodity, Matías. Your mother's family home is our family home. What else stands between us and nonentity?'

'Hard for anyone to be an entity when they can't afford to eat, Papá.'

He turns on me furiously.

'Do you dare to accuse me of failing to provide for my family? Do you – who takes no responsibility, who treats life as a joke – who won't behave like a serious man but carries on like a – a – queer.'

My turn to be furious now, at same time secretly shrinking inside myself. Fuck the old man can be scary!

My tone of voice is cold. Gotta keep control, here, not lose it like Papá.

'How do I carry on like a queer, may I ask?'

'Shallow, frivolous, thoughtless – words and not deeds – living only for the day – '

'Didn't the founder of your religion say something about living only for the day?'

'Stop talking like a bloody Protestant!'

Not a lot of laughs, the Day of the Dead. Course when we get back home he says no more but slams off to the library. Sad old cunt. Poor young me. I want to cry. Ángela looks at me quizzically. Don't want to talk it out right now. I shrug. I grin. I grimace. I hoof it up to my room. Start surfing the net. Bastard! So many fucking bastards who want to fuck me over! Papá. Licenciado Chávez. Salvador.

Blond God, My Prince, come and save me now – okay?

'Are you bi or gay?' I ask a guy in the cyberchat.

'Straight,' he writes back.

'So why are you in a gay chatroom, dude?'

'Am curious about sex with a man. Want to try. Am straight but want to try it with a man.'

Miguel Ángel is his name and he tells me the address of his apartment. An hour later am pressing the buzzer and he's opening the door. Twenty-six years old he says but looks thirty. A handsome face with pale eyes. He comes from a pretty good family. He's got a wife from a pretty good family, too. She's out of the country, shopping in Miami. Miguel Ángel works as a civil engineer for an international construction company and hasn't had sex with anyone since he kissed her goodbye.

'I don't really look at men, only women,' he says. 'I don't find a man's body attractive.'

'Okay, that's cool.'

'I'm just curious – you've got to try it once.'

'Yep.'

We're alone in the apartment right now. Maid comes only during the day. Miguel Ángel beckons me to follow him into the bedroom, awkwardly. We stand, staring at each other like a couple prats.

'Now what?' he whispers.

'Okay Miguel Ángel, lie back on the bed.'

'Sure.'

I strip myself. I unzip him. I play. He gets very hard very quickly. Too quickly. One or two ticks, he's shooting. Afterwards, shrivelling swiftly. Keeping his hands well away from my body. Only, once, a vague bit of pressure on my shoulder.

'Thanks for that, mate.'

'No worries.'

He hastens back into his trackpants. Asks me what I want

to drink. Won't look me in the eye. We drink a couple beers and talk football. After our third beer he tells me next time he wants me to fuck him from behind, arse up.

'Could be hot,' he says. 'I've seen it in porn and it looks totally hot.'

'Yep, okay!' I say.

Whatever.

'Wouldn't mind doing it regularly with you, guy,' he says when we're stood at the door saying goodnight. 'Not that I like dudes – girls are the real thing, girls are so sweet – yeah, dudes are so fucking dirty!'

'Mate, you wanna get dirty though, right?'

'Girls are totally nice, and – and, yeah, sometimes I get sick of things being nice and I want to be dirty. So maybe that's when I can give you a call?'

Needless to say no word – written or spoken – soliciting any sort of favour will be sent by me this millennium to Paco. Winter can come and a lonely cold stillness sit atop the city sky but I won't crawl to my cousin. Sky might get so grey you can't see your nose on the front of your face but I won't go begging to that silly tit.

Papá says nothing about my failure to obey. Won't even look at me, now.

Nor does he seem to see Ángela.

Day after day he stays withdrawn inside his worry. Dreary old dude has become a sort of ghost inside the family.

Gotta get a job!

Trawl the town for work. My standards re doable and not doable keep dropping. Waiter, barman, sales assistant, courier – yet no matter how low I drop the bosses turn me away. Hundreds of young guys with skills and experience are chasing those jobs. Why would an employer want to take on some literary lad with a degree in Spanish?

'Your mistake was getting a degree only fitted for a wanker,' says Miguel Ángel.

'Thanks for that, man.'

Miguel Ángel and I do the deed a couple more times, but he doesn't get any better in the sack. He still won't touch me, let alone genuinely enjoy my body. I bend him over and fuck him and he grunts with excitement. And afterwards we drink a beer or two.

'Sorry mate,' I say one night. 'Reckon we'd better call it a day.'

He looks hurt, very very briefly.

'Okay, whatever.'

Why would anyone want to hang out with a bloke so uptight?

'Cool – see ya!'

'Yep.'

Make my way back to ours. Cold, dank streets. How the fuck can I find myself a future? All a bloke wants is work. Doesn't need to be okay work, any kind of work. Plus a bloke wants, if poss, a nice warm cuddly lover. Yet right now not only is there no sign of that lover, and sure as shit no sign of work, we also need to fret in a formless sort of way about whether or not our whole household – our home – will soon go bust.

Gotta stop this downward spiral, somehow!

Why not sleep on it?

Out like a light. At least am always a sound sleeper.

'Pop across the street with these, please,' says my mother next day, chucking me a couple packets of aromatic bark. 'I bought them at the sorcery market and promised them to Sra Fuentes.'

'Why me, Mamá?'

'You seem to have nothing better to do than sprawl in that sofa looking as though you've not a worry in the world.'

Mamá has sprawled herself in the sofa opposite, not doing nothing. Quite the contrary, her busy fingers flick through *Vogue*.

'Okay, no problem.'

Casa Fuentes is a modernist house with a sleek façade of strip glass and red stone behind a tiny stripe of fiercely mown lawn and the usual palisade of steel spears. Paco pays the gardener these days. Magda, how could you marry that guy?

Press the gate buzzer.

Bingbongbing.

'Yes?'

'Tito, Señora.'

'Oh, Tito sweetie. I'll be down right away.'

Stand killing time at gate. Right away means some minutes, course. Front door opens finally – handsome double door of faux-cedar slabs offset diagonally – and out steps a suave Sra Fuentes. A dog bounds out, too. A hairy huge Alsatian hurtling past his mistress, barking wildly, baring his fangs, starting to claw at the palisade, fighting to get at me and tear my flesh from my bones. I jump back. Sra Fuentes fans her fingers at the dog in a delicate kinda way.

'Bruno. Stop that. Naughty boy.'

Arf-arf-arrrrffff!

Bruno has known me for the whole of his witless two years, but – remember my theory about the incidence of psychosis among the pooch population of our suburb? – poor dumb fido's seriously schizophrenic, certifiably insane. Knows nobody by smell or sight apart from the inmates of the Casa Fuentes. Now he keeps ravening and gnawing at the palisade, needing desperately to rip me apart, while his mistress claps her hands and stamps her feet and ineffectually squeaks out orders.

'Get down, Bruno! Get back inside the house, naughty dog! Bad boy, Bruno – stop that, come here right now!'

Argh-argh-arrrrgggghhh!

A new ploy. Sra Fuentes tries bargaining with Bruno.

'See – look! – I'm starting to close the door.'

Bruno, ignoring her, slavers away.

'You'll be trapped outside, Bruno. You won't like that, will you? Come inside now, quickly! See, I'm doing it right now Bruno. Bruno, I really am closing the door.'

Grarrf-grrraaarrrff!

'Señora why don't I pretend I'm going away? I'll walk away from the gate. He'll think I've gone for good. You then call him inside. He come. You shut him in.'

'Oh, very clever Tito. All right, you walk away.'

'I'll go a hundred metres, okay?'

When I finally do get safely inside the house young Bruno's been shut away and the only risk remaining is to my nerves – you can hear the claws of one seriously narked canine scraping and scratching on the other side of the door leading out of the salon where I'm received by Sra Fuentes. We swap a few words. Sra Fuentes doesn't like to show any weakness of any sort, social or emotional, but it's evident that she badly misses Magda. She shows me some framed photos of life in Tijuana. I try my best not to look uncool about the fact that at any moment the catch of the salon door could maybe work loose and forty kilos of furry meat-fed muscle might come bounding in to rip me limb from limb.

'Tito, by the way, have you seen the latest letter from Magda?'

'Nope – can I look now?'

'Of course, over there, inside the rolltop desk. Help yourself. You know where to find the key? You'll excuse me now, must just trot upstairs.'

A beautifully written letter on beautifully thick and

creamy paper. Magda, it turns out, addresses her mother in precisely the same literary style as she uses with our family. Sorta simple and lively and empty, not giving anything away. Dear Mummy, the latest comedy concerning my new maid – and while am working my way down the opaque screen of falsely lucid prose a boy lets himself into the room, a boy in overalls.

'Sorry to disturb you,' he mumbles shyly. 'I'm the plumber and need to go upstairs to see the Señora.'

Shy maybe, but I know his face. I've seen him at one or two of the cruising places around town. Cool!

'How are you, dude?'

'Okay, thanks.'

'Tito,' says I, holding my hand out manfully.

'Ah – awesome. Me, am Juan Jerónimo.'

We shake and he looks a bit awkward.

'Can I kiss you, Juan Jerónimo?'

A nervy, excited laugh. He looks at me archly. Takes my measure. Next, taps his cheek with the tip of his index finger. X marks the spot. He smiles at me slowly.

'On the cheek only, please – I'm a good Catholic.'

'Why not on your lips, Juan Jerónimo?'

'We don't know each other.'

'Kissing's a good way to get to know a guy.'

The two of us have just started wrestling our way into a good tight clinch, lips wide open and nicely moist, tongues locking together, when I hear a stirring of fabric – skirts – a woman. And the lightly attentive voice of a soprano.

'How sweet!'

Oops. I twist myself round and see a smirk.

'Sorry – I, er – sorry, Sra Fuentes.'

'Tito my dear, of course this is liberty hall and you're free to carry on with any amount of offensive behaviour under my roof. Clearly you're aware of that already. Vice among young men doesn't worry me a jot. I'm a woman of the world. Sadly, though, I must report it to your mother and father.'

'What? Why must you?'

'Simply must, sweetie – parents belong to an international undercover intelligence sharing operation when it comes to secrets of our youngsters!'

17

'Holy Mother of God, that it should come to this,' moans my mother, swivelling slowly away from me to burrow with one plump hand through a mound of oxblood red leather cushions, looking for – and for a fair while not finding – a box of paper tissues. Afterwards yanking out a fistful of the flimsy floating paper things and dabbing the fistful at random onto her broad, sweaty, white, silly brow. 'Blessed Mary and all the saints, that we should come to this!'

'Come to what, exactly?' I say sulkingly.

'A – a deviant. An – an invert!'

Mamá clearly feels impressed in an obscure way not only by the weight of the words but by the fact that her choice of those words makes her sound like an educated woman.

'People stopped saying deviant and invert about a century ago.'

'Stop being so clever. Why must you always be clever! Why can't a son respect the wishes of his own mother – oh, blessed Mary! – my nerves! Stop being clever!'

'Poor darling,' contentedly murmurs Sra Fuentes.

Shit has hit the fan before I can try any fancy footwork or even catch my breath. Thanks to the friendly offices of our loving neighbour who's so warm a well-wisher of the family that she willed her meagre muscles and stringy tendons to bolt straight out her open front doorway – clittering agitatedly on a pair of stiletto shoes of yellow patent leather – and across the street and into our own open front doorway.

'Would you prefer me to be stupid instead of clever, Mamá?'

'Why must you be so clever when I just want you to be

a – a decent son, a decent – a manly son?'

'He's manly, Mamá,' frowns Ángela. 'He's manly as well as clever.'

'Ángela, what would you know? You're nothing but a girl!'

'Ma,' I cut in, 'I dunno whether I'm manly or not, but one thing I do know – I'm bent as a hairpin.'

Sra Fuentes flushes with happiness for half a sec before slipping back to concerned gravity and twirling the filtertip of her cigarette. Mamá rolls her eyes heavenwards.

'Holy Mary Mother of God – are you telling me you really are – you're really and truly – ?'

'Yes, Mamá.'

'Does this mean you're never going to marry and never going to give me a grandson?'

'Am not making long term plans yet. Maybe could give you a grandchild one day by being a sperm donor.'

'Matías it's not funny – how can you joke – ?'

'Not joking, lots of gay guys have babies that way. Mamá, I won't be marrying a woman and it'll always be men I have as lovers.'

'Men as lovers! How can you talk that way? I brought you up Catholic!'

'I brought myself up, really – with lots of help from Angelita.'

'I want you to give me grandsons!'

'Pity.'

'What's to become of our family if you youngsters won't take responsibility? Ángela won't give me a baby, I know. She won't bat her eyelashes at anything that isn't her own conceited reflection in a mirror. She's as bad as you – the two of you, you're both selfish!'

'Actually there's no shortage of guys getting girls pregnant in this city, Mamá. Thousands more babies are born every year than anyone can feed or care for properly. Why don't you adopt some bastard baby? Thousands of poor little kids being born in this town whose fathers won't own them and who'll end up begging in the streets.'

'Don't exaggerate, Matías,' says Sra Fuentes, calmly cutting in with an air of academic authority. 'Villarreal has relatively few beggars.'

I turn to her and scowl.

'Relative to where?'

'Anywhere.'

No point wasting my words.

'Mamá, all I know is that any girl who happens to find her ovum fertilised by any of the stray sperm of the guys of this or any other town on the globe needn't feel too great about her chances of being happy, or raising a baby to be happy.'

Mamá repeats the rolling-one's-eyes-heavenwards number.

'My god! Kids these days!'

'You were a groovy chick in the seventies weren't you Ma?'

'That was the sixties. I was a good girl who knew how to behave like a lady.'

'Meaning how to hook a husband with an income that on paper looked okay. Pity you got your sums wrong on that one.'

'Tito, when did you learn to be so heartless?'

'My happy childhood years, I suppose.'

Mamá bursts into stormy tears.

I run upstairs to my room and cry. And swear. And fall into a snooze. Afterwards the riot act gets read once more when Papá comes home and hears the story.

'Jesus, Mary and Joseph!' he starts up, crossing himself quickly.

Once he hits his stride he switches from religion to science. Neurology. Psychology. Sociology. Biology. Ology, ology, ology. The logic of evolution opposes homosexuality. Adolescent pathology. At best culturally peripheral. A dead end. A class of narcissism. A case of introversion. A typology of self-destructiveness found only among the infantile.

'Make up your mind, Papá,' I snap unwisely. 'Is it infantile or is it adolescent?'

And he rants away for quite a whack about how he's going to pack me off to a clinic, get me cured by a psychiatrist, pay to have my brain treated by electric shock therapy.

'Papá, I know who I am and I'm never going to change.'

He looks at me sneeringly.

The three of us, me and the olds, are sat at the dining table tinkering with silverware trying to make a feint at eating the evening meal. Only choking, mostly. Ángela has headed away to uni. Papá has known the news for two hours now, but during the whole of those two hours has let up not once.

Mamá shoves back her chair – one of the eight mahogany chairs, the farting chairs – across the cold marble.

Skre-eek!

Silly sap lurches to her feet.

'Prison's too good for boys who behave so filthily!'

She shoves the chair back under the table.

Skre-eeek!

Papá for the next few days keeps talking the talk about dragging me along to a psychiatrist. Am not too surprised.

Lots of families, even prole families too short of funds to afford basic diet or dentistry, upon finding out that their son likes to have sex with guys are eager to shell out for a shrink. I've already heard lots of anecdotes from other boys. The usual story is that a psychiatrist or psychologist will be tracked down with the help of the school or the church or the state agency called Integrated Development of the Family.

'Doctors have reported high rates of success in treating cases like yours and frequently they achieve one hundred percent cures,' says Papá.

'How do they manage that, Papá?'

'By injecting homosexuals with shots of male hormones.'

The two of us are sat alone together in the library.

'Well that's pseudoscience, Papá. Not only is it not true that a guy sexually attracted to other guys is suffering from a lack of male hormones, the main effect of shooting him up with testosterone would be to send him out hunting for even more guys to fuck.'

'Matías!' he thunders.

I've gone too far, it's true – but I can't take this shit. I burst into tears. I bolt upstairs.

My life is pretty crap, let's face facts. Work, for a start. Half a year on the labour market and what have I got to show? Two written references from employers saying my work was okay. One employer being Diana, whose advertising agency was already bankrupt when she wrote the reference. The other employer being Don Pepe, who's notorious in the city as a crook. No papers saying I'm worth my pay – let alone remotely close to glowing recommendations – have been slotted into my employment portfolio letting potential bosses know about my happy career working under Licenciado

Chávez or spinning the wheel of the Publimobile.

'Dude maybe you'll think I look like shite. I'll knock on your front door, and you'll open the door, you'll take one look at me and probably you'll slam the door shut.'

'Got a pic to send, mate?'

'Sorry dude. U?'

'Same.'

Online for some cyberchat and faffing away with some guy name of Lobo. Not only my little life is in strife, our whole family really is going down the gurgler financially. Least that's what we've worked out, me and Ángela, from the occasional muttered utterance about poorhouse uttered darkly by Papá. The old burro still won't take us into his confidence about money. He keeps clutching the cards close to his chest like always. And we can be pretty sure that not only are they not aces they're very likely all blanks. No new contracts have come his way lately. Papá still heads out of the house most mornings, dressed in a silk suit and doing his best to look businesslike, but he's on his way to his fave café near Our Lady de los Dolores – where he sits himself down with a couple old engineering cronies from early in his career, to sip too-sweet coffees and smoke and complain about the declining state of the world.

'Come round to ours now,' I say. 'We can glug a beer and see how we get on, okay?'

'You sure?' he says. 'Maybe you'll think I look like a real dog.'

'Sokay, mate. Am into k9.'

'What? Oh, haha.'

'Hehe.'

He bowls me over when I open the door half an hour later and find myself faced with a smiling young guy wearing flared pants and a body shirt. I can see the two little points of his tits. The shirt's cut from highly starched coarse linen, dyed pure black, with long collars. He looks at me kinda askance – eyelashes a little lowered, head slightly turned, looking at me sideways. Green eyes, like a pixie. Cute! Green eyes and skin the colour of coffee with milk.

'Hey dude,' he growls. 'Tito?'

A deep gruff voice, which throws me even more and makes me want to drop down to my knees and wrap my arms around his hips. I love deep voices. My own voice is such an ordinary boring sort of voice in the middle range.

'Yep. Hey, Lobo.'

'Sorry dude,' he says. 'No offence – you're not my type.'

'Okay, that's cool,' says me.

'See ya dude.'

'Laters.'

Shut the door quietly. Walk away. Scoot back up the stairs. Throw myself back down on my bed. You're not my type. Know what he means by those few choice words?

Here's what he means:

Fuck! You're black as a fucking Indian!

Okay, time for a kip. Night. Wake up feeling weary. Breakfast with a sullen Mamá. Head out the door early. Trawl the streets for work. No luck. Home for an evening of low key domestic melodrama. Namely, more noisy moist scenes about my vice. Papá and Mamá equally noisy. Mamá moist. Afterwards, another night. Kip.

Days pass, real slow.

A change in the melodrama, at least. Mamá's ploy by the end of the week is optimistic garrulousness. She talks about how I'll grow out of it. She talks about how I'm not really like that – about how I've simply been toyed with so often by other boys that their twisted ways have warped me temporarily. She begs me to find a nice girl – any nice girl! – and try. She pleads with me to talk to the parish priest.

Papá by contrast goes silent, stony.

Salvador – my mind keeps drifting back to Salvador. Was it the right thing to do, to turn him down, or was it quixotic? Turn down Salvador, for fuck sake! Gorgeous, rolling in dosh, god's gift to man! Maybe my best ploy right now would be to go back to him on my bended knees and beg. My Prince. Blond God.

I decide to go blond. So here we are inside the cosmetics sector of the supermarket Gigante. Scope boxes of dyes. Sunflower. Flame. Rum. Red oak. Red fiction. Colours of a kind favoured by young guys sick of their own black hair yet not bold enough to go for blond.

As for me – I'm a bold guy, aren't I?

Sure!

Work my way down the blonds. Spring Honey. Daybreak. Moonhaze. Okay, let's go for Daybreak. A pair of rubber gloves comes with the kit. A sachet of gluey stuff you mix up with water in a bowl, shampoo into your hair. Afterwards while it soaks in for half an hour you stay sat on your bum like a dummy. Wash it out. Look at yourself in the mirror. Fuck! Daybreak turns out to mean sorta dirty orange.

'Thick black healthy hair like yours won't go blond in the blink of an eye,' explains Ángela.

'Doesn't want a blink, wants a blitz.'

She laughs.

'You mean you want your skull strafed with bleach by some sort of – of white wizard?'

'Beats getting hit on by an old lizard.'

'What? Now you're too lateral.'

'Yesterday, trying to talk my way into a job at a menswear store. Boss took me out the back to look at my references. Grizzled sort of dude, older than Papá. Turned out the references he wanted were in my jeans not my backpack. Licenciado Chávez, rewind.'

'Gross! You think going blond will stop men like that hitting on you?'

'Reckon so, yep. Worth a try.'

Sis looks perplexed.

'I don't get it.'

'Well, when a boss looks up from counting his bucks and sees me with black hair and brown skin he doesn't see an educated young man with tastes tending to the literary. He sees an Indian boy. A dark kid with black hanks trotting into his shop. A brown boy, easy meat.'

'Sad or what. Why are men always on a power trip?'

'Not all men, Angelita. Not me!'

'Okay, so you grow out the Daybreak. Don't think going blond would stop you getting hit on by lizards anyway. You're way too good-looking, bro.'

'As if. Way I look now will stop me getting hit on by any dude from here to Honduras.'

18

Plaza Mayor, half an hour after a haircut. Can't afford it but badly need a coffee so am sat inside a warm café looking out at green iron benches and red iron bandstand and grey naked tree trunks becalmed in ochre smog. Cold, bleak. Peasants planted about as always. Poor sods hoping to sell their scrappy wares. A sarape hauled over every squat brown body, cause of the cold. Squatted on cobblestones, very static. Proles, meanwhile, straggling to the bus stops. A whole lot of proles. Weary proles, shivering with the cold, on their way home after overnight vigil outside one or other of the churches here in the central city.

Villarreal last night observed Feast of Virgin of Guadalupe.

Boy what a noise there's been in town the past couple days. All day, drums. All night, fireworks, rockets. A lot of proles are weighed down with framed paintings – paintings strung across their humped backs, paintings of the Virgin.

'Ten pesos is what one pack's worth to you – ' sings an old lady trying to flog off some plastic-wrapped disposable diapers.

Glittering tinsel strings twined lovingly around the glass and lacquered frames of the votive paintings lugged by the devout have been knotted with red plastic flowers and coloured baubles which will be recycled in a couple weeks for Christmas.

A young guy comes bounding past the café window.

' – and ten pesos it'll cost you.'

A young guy who catches my eye. My age, wearing a black leather jacket and khaki cargo pants. Okay. He stops.

He glances at his watch. He smiles at me quickly. Cool! I smile back, just as quickly. He looks away. He glances back at his watch, looks back at me, smiles more purposefully.

Twenty secs later he's through the door and standing in front of my table.

'How you doing, dude?' he says holding out his hand. 'Up to lately?'

I grab hold of the hand. We both give a shake.

Black Jacket clearly is faking that we're old mates so others in the café won't think it odd that he's walked off the street and grabbed my hand and, now, sat himself down my table.

'Not a lot,' I say. 'How's it been with you?'

'Cruisy, dude!'

He starts talking ninety to the dozen. Yammers away about the drinking bouts we've had in the cantina with the other guys. About the time Lino fell out with Javi over a game of cards. How they ended up going at it with their fists. Next he launches into the time we all got caned on tequila down by the river. And he's giving me eye contact, rolling big brown eyes at me, sorta luscious and shiny. Wow! Why, though, is he going to such lengths to keep faking that we're already friends? Any slight curiosity aroused by his arrival has gone and everyone else is focused on private gossip.

Maybe he's the sort of guy who's really very shy?

Maybe he's too shy to do anything except talk this crap with that slightly loose gob. Nice lips. A gob somewhat disconcertingly loose in a somehow indefinable way.

An elderly beggar works his way down our café tables.

'Ten pesos a pack – ' repeats the diaper vendor.

'Fucking shite, that's all you ever get from Lino! What I says is – '

Works down the tables with a slowness so painful that I want to run over and lend him a hand. A few uni students sat at a nearby table are eating breakfast. The beggar looks not so much like an old man as a dog. A very dirty dog. A dog that can't walk properly. Cramped into a sort of fixed shrug. Lower back bent so badly he can walk only with the help of two canes. So it's like he's walking on four legs. Two legs of bone and meat. Two legs of cane. Nobody can make out his eyes cause he's bent too low.

The diaper vendor on seeing the old bloke's shame slings her hook, pegging off for another corner of the plaza. Christ the old bloke's dirty. He nudges the students wordlessly.

He holds out a hand, palm upwards.

'I says fuck fucking Lino, is what I says! Lino's a fucking shite artist!'

Our waiter gives us a black look.

Black Jacket's mouth seems looser and looser.

'Well dude' I say, 'let's de-stress here a bit, why don't we?'

'Look, tell you this mate, wouldn't mind punching out his fucking lights myself and if he doesn't watch himself that's just what I fucking well will do – '

Okay. Get the picture, now?

Black Jacket isn't hitting on me at all, least not for what I want him to hit on me for. He's out of his head. Or he's on something. And he thinks we really are mates. Whatever, his big brown eyes aren't rolling cause he fancies me but cause he's loco.

Fuck!

'Good talking to you, mate,' I say, pushing my chair back from the table, standing up, 'but gotta get – '

Glaring at me intently, he bends forward.

'Know what I reckon about that fucking Lino?' he spits out. 'He's a fag, that's what I reckon, he's a filthy fucking fag and if he doesn't watch himself he's gonna find a fucking knife in his ribs and the guy whose fist will be on the handle will fucking well be me, and happy to do it, that dirty disgusting cunt, any bloke deserves worse who lets another bloke fuck his fucking arse – '

Our waiter's looking thunderous now.

'Sure, but gotta get going.'

Black Jacket ducks his head. Suddenly looks kinda beaten, somehow. Scowls at the tiled floor. Looks back up at me almost wistfully.

'Mate,' he says in a voice so low I got to stoop to hear, 'spare me a couple pesos for me bus?'

I slip him five pesos and scarper.

A moment of panic after running away. My eyes narrow into slits as I peer at myself mirrored in the glass of a bar next door. Get it all into perspective why don't you? A boy in a black jacket with problems in his brain, that's all. An old man stuck with the aftermath of rickets, or polio, that's all. You're never gonna end up a bent old coot looking like a dog, holding your palm up for handouts while hiding your shame and being pitied by a penniless diaper vendor. Okay? No need to worry. You're not gonna cry!

I cry. I want to howl.

Am scared, that's why. Am shit scared. My family's going down the gurgler, and me – am never going to find a guy.

Telas Parisina is one of those nationwide drapery chain stores where women come to buy lengths cut from the bolt and take them home to make up into clothing for the family. Not the sort of place you'd ever find Mamá. Telas Parisina is for mothers and daughters of modest or thrifty households. Anyway, here's me walking past the downtown branch of the chain in what's now the middle of a hard chilly night. Raining. After the contretemps at the café this morning spent the whole day looking for work. The shop occupies a converted cinema from the thirties of last century. An immense Moderne hulk looking like the superstructure of an interwar transatlantic liner somehow stranded a block or so from the Plaza Mayor.

Okay, stop myself outside. Almost down to my last peso. Time to head home?

Look up at the shop ironically.

Villarreal prides itself on its past as a Catholic City, a city of domed basilicas, yet it could also lay claim to historic status as a capital of monstrous mouldy old movie houses. Telas Parisina tonight looks like it's been busy. Makes sense cause today's the fifteenth of the month and it's also a Friday. White collar workers in our city always get their pay on the first and fifteenth of the month, which is a custom that goes back to the viceroyalty. Arcana. The tidy mind of bureaucracy. Not the needs of workers or shopkeepers. So shops one day a fortnight are always heaving with customers wanting to buy things put off till payday. Worse when the fifteenth falls on a Friday. Shops go into a frenzy. Shop workers arc knackered hours before it's time to clock off.

Lucky for them it's time now.

Senior staff with steel hooks have stepped out onto the pavements to roll down the steel barriers. One portal stays open, a slot in the scrolled steel wall through which stooping customers come popping out awkwardly. You need to stoop to pop out. Staff who've clocked off for the day start stooping and popping, too. Steel Hooks Men stop each sales assistant or window dresser to look inside their bags. All the long wide rows of lights inside the great squat building, meanwhile, are going down slowly like it really is some ocean liner come to the end of a calm crossing.

Okay, time to wander away.

Slope down a couple streets to the Plaza Mayor. Wet weather has kept the crowds of diners and drinkers under the arcades, where they crowd the dressy youngsters and the Yank tourists and the old ladies of family who want to promenade as always around and around the plaza.

Fancy a beer, but can't spare the money.

'Do I know you?' says a bloke.

A bloke who's about forty, sat at a café table, he's nicely groomed, nursing a tequila. A lawyer, looks like. Or civil servant somewhere near the middle of the hierarchy. Sat with his tequila, taking his ease, clearly cruising for a guy. So cause he seems acceptable – cause he seems the sort who might stand me a beer and maybe offer a bit of worthwhile conversation before he takes me somewhere to fuck – I smile at him in a friendly sorta way.

And he frowns, quite sternly. Which throws me, a bit.

'Er – not sure – ' is my gambit.

The bloke's gone sterner, glaring at me blackly.

'I don't know you. What the hell do you think you're staring at me for?'

Oops!

'Sorry mate, thought you, er – someone – er – '

Scarper back the way I came, blushing hotly. Fuck! Looked like he wanted to punch out my lights! Gotta be more careful. Not all blokes in town want to be openly cruised by a boy in full view of the whole of the Plaza Mayor.

Scarper all the way back to Telas Parisina.

All the windows dark now other than a long glazed row on the mezzanine floor. The floor where they sell window treatments. A frilly, frothy, chiffony sorta fantasy of looped and bunched fabric, highlighted from behind, offering passersby a mirage of matrimonial prosperity, heterosexual felicity, blissful domesticity.

'Gizza fag would ya, Dolores?' wheedles a girl shivering in a white blouse and black frock.

'Luz, it's me last,' whines Dolores, puffing on a filter tip, also shivering in white blouse and black frock.

'Trust me luck,' says Luz.

'Yours and mine both, honey. Christ am tired.'

Dolores and Luz are stood under an awning with a row of forty or fifty similar girls in white blouses and black frocks. Nearby stand a row of forty or fifty boys in grey shirts and black pants. All look dead weary. Waiting for the rain to ease up so they can make a run for the buses. Cold, bored, peckish probably. Run my eyes appraisingly along the row of guys. One boy glances at me, glances away, glances back.

We're on!

Skintight body shirt clinging to his skinny chest. A ribbed lycra shirt, gleamingly cheap, dyed a shiny grey. He looks cold. His jacket won't keep him warm. A modish but scrappy jacket of white cotton tugged over the lycra shirt. Cotton trimmed with dark blue stitching, crudely worked. His shoes are black patent leather, shiny and slippery.

'Hey, how are you dude?' I say, stepping up.

'Cool – how's it with you?'

'Excellent, man.'

Playing the same game, the game that went so well at the café this morning, of faking that we know one another already.

Héctor, his name turns out. And right now the rain lets up. We walk to a bus stop. We hardly say a word. He's not an intellectual, course. Nor does he seem to want or need to waste words anyway. We smile at one another a lot. He seems a gentle guy. A bit fem, wrists a bit limp. No doubt he's a bottom boy. His eyes are crescent shaped, which is sort of mysterious and romantic, though mind you he's also a bit popeyed. A melancholy look.

'Here's my bus,' he says after we've stood a couple minutes at the stop.

He buys a pack of sweets from a street vendor when we come to his stop in a prole suburb. Avidly he pops one hard little sugary pellet, filled with synthetic colour and sweetener, into his mouth. He starts sucking intently.

'Want one?' he says, remembering his manners.

'Want you,' I reply.

'Wha – ?' he stammers. 'Sorry, I'm stupid – '

Now his stammering makes me think I'm a prick.

'Nah, Héctor.'

We head down the street, pass a church. Héctor crosses himself. Most blokes our age don't cross themselves, course. A few do sketch a hasty cruciform pattern on their chests with the tip of a finger and look slightly shamefaced for being so uncool. Héctor by contrast – it's the whole deal. He crosses his face. He crosses his chest. He kisses his hand. We turn a corner and trot down a couple streets to the room he rents nearby. As soon as we're in the room he switches on the tele. Straightaway, without a word, he cruises channels till he finds a station screening nonstop pop.

We start to kiss.

He's a nice kisser, very sweet.

Our eyes while we kiss keep flickering away, checking out the telescreen. You can't help yourself when a screen's in scoping distance, can you? No matter what crap's going down you check it out. Pop videos are crap enough in all conscience. All the girls skinny, heaped up with huge hair, lips bulging, full gloss lipstick. All the boys so androgynously gorgeous you want sex with every tight bum. Yet all you get is stylised heterosex. A choreography of fast non-fucks. Girls shimmy anorectic hips, ogle with wide mascaraed empty eyes. Boys thrust their own bony hips. Rigid choreography. Jerks, lunges, of arms, legs, heads.

Synchronised, stratified, straight lines, ranks, triangles, authoritarian geometry.

Pop music's a fascist dictatorship!

Héctor's very dark brown when naked. And scrawny.

'You don't eat enough, mate,' I murmur.

'Sorry – don't you like my body?'

Fuck! Acting like a prick, not thinking straight.

'You've got a really nice body, Héctor. Just you could maybe – you know – maybe you could eat more?'

Cause he makes me feel protective, is why. Poor kid. Too many of those synthetic sweets, not a lot else, by the looks of him. Maybe he can't spare the money? How much do they pay him at Telas Parisina? We keep kissing. He trembles when I start nuzzling him at the throat. Work my way down. His nipples are small. His limbs are thin, his skin sensitive. Cock almost black. We've found our way to his bed and now he's lying on his belly. Tactfully he's offering me his arse. A skinny arse. An arsehole – oops!

An arsehole guarded by a big shiny haemorrhoid.

Not enough good food and exercise, course. Well anyway, we do the deed. Wonder what it feels like with a woman? How much easier life must be for a man who likes going with women. A man whose whole life with a wife will be a window treatment of chiffony loops highlighted from behind through the night.

Afterwards we sit on the dinky bed. Héctor smokes a Marlboro Light. His thin body, skinny shoulders rounded, head thrust forward, seen from the side looks like a C.

'Can we see one another again?' he asks.

Not a good idea, I think. He makes me feel sorry for him instead of horny.

'Cool,' I say.

The wrapper on his fag pack tells you that inside's tiny tubes of toxin are relatively low in nicotine and tar. Which makes me think of Sra Fuentes. And relatively low rates of beggary. Curious as always – you could say nosy – wanting to know a bit more about Héctor, I pick up his wallet and have a poke around its contents. He watches me quietly. He lets out a little stream of violet smoke. Two prayer cards. Saint Peter. Saint Sebastian. An amulet to ward away envy. His plastic identity card. He looks sad in the card pic. Which makes me want to give him a cuddle. Which I do, straight away.

'Mmmm,' he says.

'You're a nice guy, I really like you Héctor,' I say feeling hypocritical cause I'm just being a social worker.

'Tito,' he whispers back, 'you're the one who's a nice guy.'

Course now I feel not only hypocritical but panicky. Hope he's not gonna fall in love with me, is he, poor kid? We fuck again, course. He keeps checking out the tele screen. Our fuck finished, we lie in one another's arms and fall asleep. I dream about money. Well, lack of money. Closing scene consists of me, still young, busking for stray pesos while getting yelled at as a bum boy, a cocksucker, by that nicely groomed man of forty sat with his tequila in the Plaza Mayor. Also, women of good family are jeering at me, and Yank tourists.

Faggot, they're screaming, spittle spraying.

Awakening from that fun experience, stickily opening my eyes, wondering whether what made me feel most shame in the dream was that I was queer or that I was skint, I scope a couple of curved closed eyelids, colour of coffee, very close – centimetres away. Héctor breathing deeply, trustingly, in my arms. One of my arms is getting pins and needles but I feel very tender, looking at that sleeping face.

After a while I stand up, gently spread a blanket over him, and head to the basin to clean myself.

'I haven't got a phone here but can I phone you tomorrow from the payphone?' he says to me when we're saying goodbye.

'Cool, here's my number.'

A mistake, but what else can I do? So one week later we get together again after he finishes work. He works from ten in the morning to half past eight in the evening, six days a week. A beggar, collaring us while we're waiting to cross a street, asks for alms in flowery language straight from Cervantes. Héctor slips him a coin softly.

The beggar kisses the coin and holds it up for the saints to witness the act of charity.

'Heaven bless this Christian young gentleman!' says the beggar.

Well warranted as a benediction yet by the time I'm on a bus back out to ours in the suburbs my goal for the evening has been scored.

Héctor binned.

Sigh.

No point taking anyone else down with me as I sink.

19

María has caught flu and is stuck in bed so I visit her in her room, bringing a warm drink. Chamomile tea, which she swears by. Sitting up on her pillows she takes a noisy slurp. Our servant quarters are out the back at the top of a spiral iron staircase. Roomy quarters meant for a whole staff not just one old lone woman. Roomy and ugly. Walls slapped with cheap paint. Flaking away in hunks. María took an old broken-bummed easy chair we were about to throw out and made it look cosy by draping seat and back with an embroidered blanket from Tres Madres.

As so often before she's my only source of warmth from the senior generation of the family.

'You think I'm a sinner, María?' I whisper sorta hoarsely. 'Me being gay?'

'You're my lovely boy.'

'What would people think about me in Tres Madres?'

At which point she laughs a bit roughly.

'All families have a boy or two like you in Tres Madres. Always been boys who want boys. And girls who want girls. And special ones, with special powers, who're not girls and not boys. Or are both girl and boy. And more, too. Always knew you were a boy who wants boys.'

I pulled back a bit, needing to look her in the eye. She met my gaze levelly.

'How did you know, María?'

She shrugged.

'Eh, I don't know how I knew. I just knew, that's all.'

'How long have you known?'

She shrugged again.

'I've always known, my baby.'

So thank christ for that bit of – well, of love, really. Cause there doesn't seem to be a lot on offer, right now.

'María, do you dislike Mamá and Papá?' I now try quietly.

She sets down her cup of yellow chamomile brew.

'Dislike them?' she says.

She looks at me hard, shrewdly. A big brown and pink paper saint pinned above her bed. Santa Ana of Nazareth, grandmother of God. Not late lamented Sra Aurelia Lacanzo de la Tijera Comforted by Papal Benediction We pray for her Casa de la Tijera de Lago Palacio de la Tijera viceroyal Villarreal, grandmother of Blond God. The servant quarters have been used for years to shove or stow stuff we no longer need but think too good to chuck out. Boxes of books. Crates of outmoded crockery. A stack of three big old televisions, screens grey and vacant. Cartons of records – you know, those big flat disks of black plastic. Italian opera. Spanish classical guitar. Broadway. Stacks of knackered kitchenware. An electric blender of cracked plexiglass. A stainless steel frying pan, lacking its lid.

'Dislike them, the way I do,' I say.

'No, child,' she says after a sigh that ends in her coughing up phlegm in a green plug. 'I feel sad for your Papá who's struggling with the ghost of his own croaked Papá.'

'Well he should stick to the struggle with the ghost and lay off my living bod.'

'True, my boy. Only we're in a real world not one of the dream worlds. And as for your Mamá, she keeps me keen because she's a phenomenon!'

'A phenomenon? Or a phantom?'

'What do you mean, baby?'

'Mamá looks like a vampire. Mamá looks like she drinks blood.'

'Tito she's your mother, it ain't right – '

'When I was walking up our street just now I saw a worker of some sort – gardener, delivery boy? – pressing a buzzer. Stocky little bloke. A plain kinda guy. Yet he looked strong and healthy. Looked like he owned his own body. A working dad. A pair of generic jeans. A red tee shirt. A white baseball cap. Stood calmly on the street waiting. Then the house door opens – '

'Don't worry, my boy,' mumbles María.

'The creature that takes a step out that door makes me think of Mamá. Why do those women put on those masks? She looks sickly, the woman. Hair whirled upwards into a kinda halo. A wiry ferocious halo of fake gold. Body scrawny, half starved. Starved not from lack of money, course, but from fanaticism, a need to be slim. Swathed in shiny silk. Scrawny little legs. Vampire women never walk anywhere except to and from their cars, in nylons. Pointed little heels like daggers. A woman aged about sixty, a lady, ordinary, suburban, mistress of servants, presenting herself to the world in the way she knows is the right way.'

María does her best to keep looking at me hard but think she's feeling too lousy to be able to focus all that well. Got a fever, and is shaking.

'Tito, my little boy, your thoughts make me worry.'

Poor darling. She's not well and here's me doing some selfish rant.

'They're just words – no big deal.'

But they're not just words and it is a big deal. A big deal for this very small person, that's to say. A type of terror. Anger, too. Anger linked with childish thoughts about fairness. It's not fair. It's *not* fair! I've worked so hard to get work – to find love – I've taken risks – come out – okay, fair cop, been outed – and – and what do I do next? Am tired of working at it. Why should I have to work so hard?

Sunday morning, out for a walk. Making myself walk.

One kilometre, two kilometres. Proles, peasants, have got the pavements to themselves right now cause people pretending to any sort of tone seldom go out before noon on Sundays. Smog bad today. Sky kinda blank. Streaks of grey and yellow. I go down avenues. I go up avenues. I go in and out of parks. Hours yawn by. Good families start to come out for midday strolls. Not dressed up – not like promenaders when my mother and father were young – but dressed down. Whole well-bred households, having slept in late and skipped holy service, slither into the streets without having showered, sometimes without having combed their hair, everyone wearing trainers, trackpants, sweat tops.

I wander on to the Alameda.

Dark thousands of proles, brown crowds. Parked on cold benches, picnicking on cold grass, promenading along cold gravel walks. Maids, labouring men, factory hands, dads, mums, kids, granny. Teen boys wearing tees printed with logos in English. *Planet Hollywood. American Cowboy. Weekend. Don't Ask for Less – Pepsi. Help! I'm on the phone and can't shut up!* Teen girls, pairs and threesomes, long black hair loose and glossy or caught back in ponytails. Synthetic skirt and blouse, or synthetic slacks. A few bolder spirits wear jeans and a slash of lipstick.

Boys and girls walking slowly, checking one another out. Walking very slowly. Everyone walking very slowly.

Why the fuck can't they hurry up!

And why the fuck am I so fucking angry?

One family wandering along in front of me hardly bothers to lift its flat heels. Frayed clothes, cracked footwear. Mother, father, granddad, a little boy. A little girl. Who carries a basket. A picnic for the family. The little girl walks tidily. She doesn't waste one movement. The basket is heavy and she's a good girl. The boy, free of any burden, runs about. Free cause he's a boy. Coming across a black strip of rubber lying in a flowerbed, he snatches it up, bends the strip, flexes it, wonders how to make use of it. A rubber strip that looks to me like the seal from a car window. Our boy flicks it, whips it. Meanwhile his sister plods along responsibly with her clumsy basket.

I feel angry with the family.

I feel angry with them for being so poor. I feel angry with them for going so slow. I feel angry with the freedom of the little boy. I feel angry with the docility of the little girl. I feel angry with the mother and father and granddad for allowing the boy freedom while asking from the girl servility.

I feel so angry I almost want to be sick.

Stopping for a bit at a fountain, wondering what to do next, I notice that am being scoped by a small boy. A boy about nine years old. He's looking at me dead seriously.

I nod, then look away. The boy pipes up.

'Matías López?'

Who the fuck – ?

A small dark hand with gnawed nails. A baseball cap printed with a phrase in English. *Punk is Dead.* Colour of cap orange and indigo, streaked with black grease.

'How are you, mate?' I say.

'You've forgotten my name,' he says, holding out his right hand for me to shake. 'José Gallego at your service, Señor.'

It's the nipper who picked my pocket that morning last summer when I was starting work at the advertising studio.

We shake hands gravely.

'So what's been going down, José Gallego?'

He wants to sit with me on one of the benches, turns out. He wants to talk. So we sit opposite the fountain. And we talk. He talks, mostly. He talks cause I make the mistake of asking – wanting like always to work out the story of the person who's with me – I make the mistake of asking a few too many questions about his childhood. The little lad turns out not really to have had a childhood. He never knew his dad. His mum works as a laundress, or did last he knew. He hasn't seen her for a couple years cause she went away to the capital looking for work and left him with an uncle and aunt.

'Treat you okay, did they?' I ask worriedly.

'My aunt was okay, but she didn't know my uncle was fucking me – he kept fucking me, and it hurt, so I ran away.'

'Jesus!'

'Wasn't so bad. My uncle's cock wasn't too big. Getting fucked is okay. Lots of guys like to fuck me. I ask them if they want to. And they pay. You want to fuck me, Matías? You wouldn't have to pay cause I'd like you to fuck me. Cause I like you. You're a nice guy. You treat me nice. Can I be your boyfriend? Can I come and live with you? I'm nice, really. I could make you happy. You could fuck me as much as you want. All night, every night. Please would you let me be your boyfriend? I'd love you, Matías. I'd love you forever.'

Wordlessly, I pull out my last few pesos.

'Here, mate. Take these. Gotta go.'

'Don't, Matías!'

'Sorry little dude, gotta.'

Totter away. Don't look back. Get myself out of the Alameda. Don't look back! Walk down the Avenida Hidalgo. Walk into Calle Colón. Walk on, and on, and on, and on.

'Tito, you're not looking too happy,' says Ángela. 'What's going down?'

'Nothing's going down, sis – am just going to ground.'

'Going to ground? Or getting ground down?'

Makes me grin, so I look up. We're in her room talking over my state of play. Talking is a bit of an event these days. Sis is so busy with assignments and exams that she can only catch me on the run while she's rushing in or out the door on her way to or from uni. Her sights still fixed unerringly on qualifying to do a doctorate. Anyway, here she sits cross-legged on her bed, checking me out. Am stood by her bookshelves, pulling out volumes. As always, room's quiet and orderly. Walls, porcelain blue. Charcoal sketch of her face, drawn by me the year before last. Eye of a deer handed her many years ago by María.

'Am okay,' I say with a bit of a shrug. 'Getting by.'

'Hey! We're having a reality check here.'

'Yep, I know. Am talking reality.'

'Since when are you content just to get by?'

'Since now, sis. Getting by's good enough for now. Can't always be a party bunny.'

She looks at me levelly. Wants to know the whole story and for some reason I don't want her to know. How these days am feeling so low in the food chain. How these days am feeling like someone whose life is tat, whose world has turned into a khazi, someone whose fucking close to being totally fucked. Someone who –

Truth of the matter, lately I've started to think about topping myself.

Which scares the shit out of me.

How can I think about topping myself? What would that do to Angelita? How would that feel for María?

'Come on,' she says. 'Tell.'

'Winter, that's what!' I blurt, cause that's easy. 'Cold, and me trawling the streets – and I want to see the sun, sis – I don't want to be cold – I want to be hot!'

Ángela lets out a slow little breath, jumps to her feet, gives me a kiss.

'Keep talking,' she says.

Next, while am trying to dwell on the cold, everything else comes elbowing its way out of my mind, tripping off my tongue. I keen out a kinda blues rhapsody. Jobless. Poor. Lonely. Hopeless. Holding back, which I shouldn't, course, but I do. Holding back about wanting to kick my own bucket.

'Feel better?' she says after my rant.

'A bit, yep. Ta, Ángela.'

'Okay, let's go over some of it again and see if we can work out any answers, why don't we? Job options, for one. Maybe we can nut out something right now – '

'Sure, sis. Yep.'

Blah blah blah.

Ángela keeps talking for an hour or more trying to coax me to feel better about the world. Course we can't and don't nut out any answers. Somehow, waiting for her to hit on an answer – having winced once it becomes clear there won't be any answer – I start wanting to blame her for her useless words, or lack of the right words. Course totally irrational and ungenerous. Only – well, Ángela without any answers!

My sis not catching me when I fall.

Totally unfair of me to think this way. I think it in spite of myself.

'Okay, we're out of ideas right now but we're not leaving it here,' she says a lot later, almost desperately. 'We're coming back to it when I've broken the back of my next assignment.'

'Sure.'

'We'll work it through and we'll sort out some answers.'

'Yep.'

She looks like she wants to cry.

'Bro, you don't look quite right in yourself, you know.

You've gone a bit – introverted.'

'Well ask yourself, for christsake. Winter. No work.'

'Sweetheart, please – '

What do I do? I turn on my heels and walk out the door. Somehow my character is kinda warping, these days. Somehow it's a meaner me, a colder me, these days. What the fuck do I think I'm doing? First time in my life I've ever turned my back on Ángela.

'You need to be admitted by voice recognition,' drawls the voice of a young woman.

'Okay – how exactly, Magda?'

'Record a couple of sentences through your phone right now, Tito. And they'll then be digitally stored downline here, in our admittance memory.'

'Any special couple of sentences?'

'Just speak normally.'

'Magda, are you happy? Magda, you deserve to be happy.'

'Okay – got it, Tito. See you soon.'

'I want an answer, Magda.'

'Mind your own business, sweetheart. Apropos, I'm planning to ask you lots of questions of my own, so get yourself ready for systematic interrogation.'

El Marqués is the newest of the new wealthy suburbs of the city. A suburb where clipped lawns and terracotta courtyards of some of the very rich hide behind high walls scanned by lasers and topped with barbed wire or steel spikes or broken glass. A suburb where the only people who come riding in by bus, other than muggins, are little brown maids. Magda sent an email the other day telling us that her hubby's been ordered by his bosses to fly down for an industry conference in Villarreal. Paco sent a follow-up email telling us that the colleagues he hopes to hang with down here will be what he calls high powered. Magda, therefore, has come along to be his hostess.

Steel bars, well sprung and well oiled, swing aside soundlessly.

Walk up a driveway. Clipped cypress. A row of yews. Above, a glistening and intimidating citadel, a shiny stark structure of techno-architecture. And a widely open front door, cedar.

'Hi, Tito,' says Magda, kissing me quickly.

'Hi, Magda. Quite a house.'

She laughs shortly.

'Am glad not to be one of its maids, Tito.'

'I feel funny stepping inside territory so tainted by money.'

'Don't worry,' she smiles. 'Only a rented taint of money – it was leased for a fortnight by the company, and it's getting paid for by the company.'

'You look great, Magda.'

'Ta.'

Magda not only looks great she looks glossy. Sort of a sheen to her – her hair, her skin, even her nude white elbows sliding out of the highly tailored sleeves of a white suit of tightly woven wool.

Maybe it's a good idea to go for money?

Or – if money means Paco!

Who walks into the salon and welcomes me fulsomely. Slaps my back. Preens himself. Booms at me offering booze. A beer will be cool, I say. Magda wants a tequila. Paco pours ponderously. Keeps booming. I look on with wonder at the way his quick young wife sips her spirits as blithely as though she hasn't wed herself to someone witless.

'My chiefs and I were discussing brand extension, you'll be interested to hear, Tito,' says Paco with a conceit almost endearing in its inanity.

'Yep? You mean your chiefs in New Jersey?'

'Quite so. We're in contact daily.'

'Sorted. Next question – what's brand extension?'

Paco looks at me contentedly.

'Extending a brand, cousin, means trading on an established brand name by applying it to new non-related products. Products new to the customer yet attractive to same due to association with brand name. My chiefs and I have decided to extend our casual and sporting garment brand into state-of-the-art convenience food marketed as low-cal Tex-Mex.'

'Wicked!'

Paco shrugs in a worldly way. He knows not all guys can have the good luck of working at the cutting edge.

'Tex-Mex, low cal, oven-ready,' he adds.

'Will downmarket consumers,' says me, 'want to buy convenience food for no better reason than cause it's got the same brand name as a cheap baseball shirt?'

'You just watch the suckers!' cries a triumphant Paco.

We neck our drinks meditatively.

Next we talk about the employment structure of the company. Am asking questions from a vague feeling – moulded partly by the ambient opulence of the salon – that maybe it makes sense to do what I've been told by Papá. Hit on my cousin for a job. Try to get him to pull a couple strings for the sake of family.

'Coalface gets handled by accountants, lawyers, managers,' says Paco.

'Marketing? You use inhouse ad copywriters?'

'Not cost effective. We tender marketing out to agencies and always choose the cheapest tender.'

'Agencies that tender cheapest – aren't they likely to be screwing their employees to keep costs low?'

Paco looks at me sluggishly.

'Setting up to be a saint, coz?'

'We'll eat lunch now, shall we?' says a pleasantly

noncommittal Magda. 'Oysters for starters.'

'Excellent!' booms Paco, rubbing his brown little fat hands.

Magda, turning, nods adroitly at a small brown woman tied up inside a uniform of black and white. The woman seems to have been teleported from some older and simpler world into the lambent spaces of this techno pleasure dome.

'Oysters up from the coast at daybreak,' adds Magda.

After nibbling our way through light and delightful food, delicately prepared with the best ingredients and presented with a beautiful simplicity, we roam for a while through white rooms looking at what coz calls artworks. And then find ourselves back in the main salon. Paco swallows a couple more drinks then heads away.

'I'm worried about your future, Tito,' says Magda after he's well out the door and she's tossed back one more tequila.

'No need to worry – in the end it'll pan out okay.'

'How will it pan out okay, exactly?'

Grin at her, now, since her question stumps me kinda.

'Cos it's got to, that's why!'

'What can I do to help you? Here – have some – he gives me plenty!'

Grabbing her handbag, yanking out a fistful of banknotes. Thousands of pesos. A handbag made from the lightest and suavest sort of snakeskin. A filament of silver, slim, narrow, woven with a wire of gold to form a sort of frieze around the seam of the shiny scales. Banknotes popping from the handbag like a jack-in-the-box. Or moths – or bats – flapping from what looks like the scaly jaw of a tiny Quetzalcoatl.

'Hey, you can't give me money, Magda.'

'What can I give you if not money? I want to give you

something, Tito.'

She looks at me intently.

Fuck she's clever, and she's strong. Knows now that I'm bent, too, thanks to the kind offices of her mother – so at least I don't need to keep any secrets any more.

'Okay, you can give me some advice.'

'Well that's easy. You don't need to ask any woman twice if she'll give you advice!'

She bends forward, eager.

'A guy – it's a guy – a guy name of Salvador.'

'Tell!' she says, pouncing on a silver cigarette lighter and setting fire to some sort of fragrant costly fag.

And that's what I do. I tell my childhood pal the whole story. Only leaving out the same stuff that got left out when I last talked with sis. Topping myself. Magda listens without comment. Her only occasional input is to prompt, almost brusquely. Outsiders might think she doesn't like my story. Or that she's hostile to what I say. I know Magda. She's getting the info as efficiently as she can and processing it at warp speed.

'I don't get it,' she says finally.

'What don't you get, Magda?'

'Salvador. How could you have had any doubt? He was offering you everything you want, wasn't he? He's got the lot. He's got looks. He's got banknotes. And more important, he's got ivory embossed gold-plated pure white blood from half the families in the stud book. A bonk buddy in the top drawer. And if you were to play your cards right he might turn out to be more than a bonk buddy. How can you go wrong?'

Her clarity is kinda dismaying so for a couple secs I do my best to fudge.

'Well it's academic cause I turned him down and the offer won't be open now.'

'Crawl on your knees to him, Tito.'

'What? You joking Magda?'

'Nope, serious. Go after him. Try. Do anything you can to get him hot for you again. He's a de la Tijera. I know all about Salvador de la Tijera! He's the optimal option. He's – look, let's not screw things up. My husband's a dolt but marrying him has been by far the best thing that I've ever taken on. The whole deal pays its way nicely. I've got resources, I've got space, I've got freedom. I've got a life, in other words. My old life was a sort of shadow.'

I feel really sad.

'You were happy when we were kids, Magda.'

'We're not kids now. Only bummer about the hand I'm holding is that I've got to spend a certain amount of time dealing with the dud cards your loser of a cousin keeps dropping into the play. Yet he's easily managed. Am not my mother's daughter for nothing. Paco gives me what I want in the sack, too. I make him. Surely it'd be an even better deal to shack up with someone as totally fit as Salvador?'

'You really want me to be some pampered dude's kept boy?'

'Look it's not my fault that you're so mixed up about money.'

'Mixed up?'

'Well, speaking candidly here – fucked up.'

'Hey, why are you treating me so waspishly, Magda?'

'Cause I'm your second sister, remember? You told me that day at Sanborns. Sisters are allowed to be waspish to their brothers aren't they?'

'Magda, sorry – '

'Sorry doesn't cut it with me, Tito. Just go after the guy. Hook the bastard.'

'But – '

'And more importantly make sure you hook a good big

hunk of his money!'

'Whew!'

Paco drives me back to ours at the end of the day. Mamá insists that he come in for coffee. His mother-in-law, who happens already to be sat at the coffee table, smokes ardently and smiles dangerously. Ángela looks inside a slim green book. Mamá does gracious white lady. Cake and cheese on the table, with the coffee, so coz starts chowing. Scarfing happy as a kid let loose in a pastry shop, he schools us four others in politics and money.

Sra Fuentes, whenever her son-in-law opens his lips to speak, rolls her eyes satirically.

'I do miss my darling girl,' she whispers to Mamá, 'but my comfort is that I haven't so much lost a daughter as gained a high fidelity loudspeaker.'

'And a credit account,' snaps Mamá.

Not that my mother doesn't want to make the most of the credit account. A couple days later, coz having flown back north with wifey, we learn that good dutiful nephew has secretly slipped loot from his wallet into the purse of parlous aunt. Secretly cause word of it must on no account get to Papá. A private loan, spells out Mamá. A simple matter of a small sum within her own family, not Papá's family.

'Okay, so how much has he given you?' asks Ángela.

'Don't be vulgar, darling,' simpers Ma. 'A quite adequate sufficiency for now – enough to keep the household afloat for the next few months without my needing to worry your Papá.'

Ángela is not happy.

'Ma, we can't live like this. We've got to admit to ourselves we can't keep up this house. We've got to sell it. We've got to live more thriftily.'

'I don't want to be alive at all if I can't live like a lady.'

'I don't care about being a lady. I'm a woman.'

'What on earth are you saying, silly child?' raps out Mamá, twisting a big silver ring on her right hand. 'And changing the theme, María, I'll thank you not to harrow my poor head quite so hard with those claws of yours.'

Which she's been saying for at least twenty years.

María massages just as hard. Bony digits, blunt, digging deep into a thick skull.

'Brings the blood up and feeds the follicles,' she grunts.

'Feeding the follicles may be desirable, but I don't want my scalp lacerated!'

'Sorry Señora,' again grunts María, still digging.

'Sorry?' goes on Mamá. 'Why does everyone say they're sorry when they're not sorry?'

'Cause they seek to oil the happy wheels of human intercourse, Mamá,' says me.

'You know nothing about humanity!' she snaps, suddenly rabid. 'A boy who carries on with other boys in so loathsome a way – a boy who deserves to be confined to a psychiatric ward – a boy who should never have been born!'

Okay, it sorta hits me. Tears prick my eyes. Turn away for a tick.

A couple sentences come next from Ángela.

'Mamá you've gone too far,' sis raps. 'You owe Tito an apology.'

Our lame mother leaps to a random conclusion.

'Oh! Oh – oh! Of course! Now I know why you wouldn't marry poor Paco! You're – you – you're one of those too!'

'One of whom, Mamá?' puzzles Ángela.

'The same as your sinful, unfilial, dirty, depraved, wrongheaded brother – '

'Ma?' says Ángela in so bewildered a way it makes me start laughing.

'Don't you see, sis? She thinks you're a dyke!'

Ángela lets out a hoot.

'Matías, hush!' hisses my mother. 'How dare you use such words in the presence of the mother who brought you into the world, amidst her sufferings, from her own womb?'

'Sorry, Mamá,' I say still laughing.

'And let me add, young man, sin is not amusing. And if it weren't for my rivalling the blessed saints for patience – '

'Señora, sit still!' says María.

'María, I swear you're drawing blood! And while we're at it why aren't you wearing your sandals for heaven's sake? We're not in the jungle!'

Which she's also been saying for at least twenty years.

Cold, grey, dreary. Coldest day so far this winter. Bleak, utterly sunless. Am looking for work. I don't go out of my way. All I do is keep doing what I've done for weeks. Walk the streets. Stop here, or there, to try a cold call. Cope with the reply. Keep walking. Anyway, by midday am feeling down. Way down. Downer than I've ever felt before in my life. Trapped. Angry at having to put up with a cold city.

A bloke, about thirty, picks me up.

A young salesman here from the capital to look over a new territory for his company. Nice looking. We strip off in his hotel suite. He flexes his body. Slim and energetic hips. Powerful thighs and buttocks. He's got great staying power when he fucks, which he does for a couple of hours before finally letting it all pour out. Afterwards, he shows me photos of his family.

'She's pretty,' I say, looking at his wife. 'What's her name?'

'Laura,' he says quickly.

A nice looking woman with an open face, peeking at the camera while cradling a little boy.

'And your lad – what's he called?'

'Matías.'

I feel sick.

My gut hurts. A slicing cramp in my gut. Ouch! My gut fucking hurts! A wife, a little boy, smiling while looking at a camera. Why do my guts hurt so much? Not the guy's good looks, good health – not even the good job. The loving wife, that's what – the little boy. A son, Matías. I'm a son who's never going to have his own son. I was speaking bullshit the other day when I spieled to Mamá about being a sperm donor. No dude's ever going to shack up with me let alone make plans for a baby. My life is going to be lived alone, punctuated by the odd fuck.

'Scuse me mate,' I mutter, running to the bathroom.

'What – ?' he starts to say.

No chance for me to answer cause am spewing into the toilet bowl. So fucking sick with loneliness and so scared shitless of the life I see ahead of me – no love, no loyalty. All I can do once the gushing has stopped is straighten myself. Flush the toilet. Wipe my face. Afterwards, having said goodbye to the babe, I pick up a drunken older bloke who's got a terylene paunch and this time I charge money.

'The witches are in the salon still holding their black mass,' grunts María when I step inside ours.

'You go to bed, María. I'll do what needs to be done down here – you're knocking yourself out.'

The old darling, on deck once more after her flu, peers at me closely.

'I can take a fair few knocks. Tito, son, you don't look the best yourself.'

'Bit tired, that's all. Go on, get up to bed María.'

'I'll make you a hot chocolate, that's what I'll do – that'll see you right.'

'Charming,' says a new voice from the doorway.

Mamá – teetering in stiletto heels, squeezed into a lavender suit – stalks into the kitchen. María bridles – planted on her bare feet, bony limbs poking out of a lime green cardigan.

'When you two have quite finished babying one another,' says Mamá, 'would it be too much to ask for someone to serve the supper?'

She stalks away.

María rolls her eyes and starts setting things out on silver trays. I help. The cold wind outside has started gusting stronger and stronger. Creaks and squeaks can be heard from the courtyard. Hoots, shrieks from the salon, as always on canasta nights.

Midnight, get myself up to my room and stare at the bare boards, the cane chair, the bamboo blind rolled up at the window. No comfort tonight in my clean simplicity. I feel lost. Wander away from my room, wondering why. Out to the balcony. Black night, cold, windy. The wind has turned sorta wild, tonight. Flop back inside, onto the landing. Look down at the vestibule where my mother is having a confidential, hissing gossip with a lady.

'What's she really like, the new neighbour?' the lady asks Mamá.

'*Quite nice*,' says Mamá in English.

Wander back to my room, to the computer. Flick the switch. Stare at the screen. Online for cyberchat in *villarrealgay.com*. Stay for a couple hours making unrequited love to my modem, trying to hook a hot guy.

Or maybe a nice guy.

Or any guy?

Next day. Cold. Poor. Trapped. Why is life such a bloody battle all the bloody time? Why can't I just live? Wander downstairs to find the rooms empty of family. Mamá must still be sleeping after her night of debauchery over the bridge cards. Papá no doubt will be masquerading as a man of affairs in the city or else visiting my grandmother at the cemetery. María must be out at the shops. Ángela of course will have set out early for university. Okay, slope onto the patio. The wind has dropped, thank christ. Air still cold but at least it's calm, and –

Fuck!

I burst into tears.

My cypresses. My terracotta tubs!

The two big glazed tubs, white and azure, dragged by me onto the patio and planted with the cypresses. My beautiful trees, my beautiful tubs – the wind last night has toppled the lot, dropped them onto the pavement and cracked the pots. Cracked them wide open. Shards of baked clay, shining with a slip of glaze, scattered in an arc across the patio. Soil from the pots flung across the same arc. Cypresses tips are drooping, dying.

Stooping, lifting one of those limp tips, I sniff it for its scent.

Hardly any scent today – too cold.

My face streaked and snotty, I get a spade, a broom, do a bit of a tidy. Sweep up the spilled soil. Stack the cracked shards. At the same time I try to work out why I'm feeling so much grief. Cause the cypresses will cope with this little setback. The health of the roots – that's the main thing. No matter what minor trauma's troubled the boughs, a bit of a tumble in a high wind won't have harmed the roots. So no need to grieve for the cypresses.

What's got to me is the tubs.

Tubs that till yesterday were so lovely. And now, well, the shattering of the tubs means a lot more than cracked clay. Now that the pots are smashed they're lost. When terracotta pots crack, we can no longer buy new pots. Things will break or wear out or be lost, year after year, and our stock will grow smaller and smaller.

If it gets too bad can stop it by killing myself.

A cold world. Cold, cold, cold – out of control. Oughtn't

to let myself start thinking this stuff, really oughtn't, only here it comes, gushing out of my guts. Am a loser, am lost. Nothing I can do about it. Am alone. So alone. Oh god am lonely and am a loser and am lost. Locked in. Beaten! Killed!

How's that for a spot of clearheaded self-analysis?

A knock on the door.

A really tentative knock, a tiny little knock – what you might want to call a knockette.

'Tito?' says a similarly tentative voice.

'Ánge – '

Can't even finish cause I kinda start to choke. I kinda can't speak. Sobbing, instead. Tears not trickling, bursting. Ripping out of my whole feeb small swarthy body. Not that I need to speak, turns out. Ángela comes at a run into the room. Light on those sweet feet of hers, is my sis. She flings her limber arms around me. She presses the back of my brown head with the palms of her white hands.

'Sis, our family's fucked. Who's looking out for us? Who's looking out for you and me? Nobody, that's who. Am getting myself a ticket to – somewhere – am getting out of here. Am topping myself, sis. Am out of here.'

She squeezes me tightly.

'Tito.'

'I won't really do it – will I? Don't they say you don't do it if you talk about it? It's those who don't talk who do it – isn't it? So reckon I must be safe then, right? Cause even when I feel as crap as I feel now I can't seem to stop fucking talking – '

'We'll always keep talking won't we? Always.'

'It's not words, it's not – there's no we, Angelita. It's you. And it's me. We can't help one another now. I'm not crying for you. It's too late to think about you, it's only me now. Am crying for me.'

Ángela cradles me while stroking my hair.

'Things are hard for you, I know,' she says after a bit. 'Don't know that the correct inference to draw, though, is that we should ditch one another outright.'

'Angelita, the family's fucked – '

'Tito, we're not – '

'Our family's fucked. I'm fucked.'

'You're not, and I'm not, and María's not,' says sis. 'I reserve judgement on Ma and Pa.'

22

Dimly, a slow sort of dawn seems to creep up on me over the next week or two. Spring. A sort of lifting. A lightness. One or two ticks of weightlessness. Tiny balls of ballast, lead, somehow have been let drop. Bubbles of – relief – floating up inside my body. Bubbles of some mild vapour less dense than air, wafting up through my body.

Bubbles of buoyancy.

'Wow!' I sing out to María, who's slapping the tiles with a wet mop she twirls in and out of an orange plastic bucket. 'Look at the green and white buds on the jacaranda!'

'A young bud yourself, dearie,' says a grinning María.

So, stood on our balcony, am borne up, don't know why, by jacaranda buds. Buds close to blooming. Sap rising, swollen small nodes, greenery soon to be growing.

Which seems incredibly exciting, suddenly.

Wow – the buds!

And jacaranda bark, smooth and grey, a greyness that only lately seemed grey enough nearly to kill me looks more a grey sheen, now – smooth – dovelike – white and green buds with tiny tips – folded up now but waiting for sure warmth on its way – buds ready to bolt for it, take a leap into the light.

Whatever, wander out after a bit to join Mamá between my cypresses in the patio.

'The sun's too hot,' she mutters, lighting another fag.

And scowls, smokes, flicks through a fashion shoot inside *Harper's Bazaar*. Nearby, a newspaper – the city's conservative paper as always – lying open on society gossip.

An engagement to marry, announced yesterday at the Palacio de la Tijera, binds the hand of the radiant Gladys Gabriela Galán Montoto to the distinguished son of our city, Salvador Juan de la Tijera de Lago. A select gathering of family and friends witnessed –

Am sorta stunned.

Salvador marrying Gladys?

My brain blinks back to the night we first met, me and Salvador. At the gay club. Me stood under strobes scoping three white, tall, glam young newcomers: Aurelio, Gladys, Salvador.

Gladys, face shaped like a heart, wearing black and silver, staring insolently.

Why would a guy want to get himself wedded to anyone so arsey?

Also, does this mean Blond God isn't queer actually? My Prince, is he really straight? Then why was he hitting on me – ? Well obviously he swings, like half the men in town, but still –

María comes out with a silver tray.

A glass of water sits in state on it, next to a blue packet of paracctamol. Mamá, jcrking her big coiffed head cursorily by way of thanks, grabs the packet, pops out two pills, gulps them down with the help of two slugs of water. Afterwards she purses her lips and glares up at the bright sky.

'María, please fetch me my sunglasses.'

'You take too many of those things, Señora,' says María, nodding down at the paracetamol. 'The packet says only every four hours.'

Mamá glares up.

'Old maids like you don't know what a mother suffers, María. Anyone would think me a sainted martyr were they to understand the agonies of worry I must cope with – the headaches that cripple me daily.'

'Darling, your head'd be good in a trice if you let me brew you a nice fresh infusion of bark,' says María flatly.

'We're in the modern world for heaven's sake. We don't use old bits of bark and leaf and – and mould, for all I know! Who knows what kinds of fungus and slime they doctor themselves with up in the sierra?'

'Sorry I spoke, Señora. Forgot we don't know anything, us hicks from Tres Madres.'

Am going out for a wander to see how long I stay perky.

'Mamá, gotta get going into the city.'

Another glare from Ma.

'Matías, can one hope that these roamings of yours up and down the streets of the town might lead one day, in the not too distant future, to some form of gainful employment?'

'More likely to lead to some form of painful redeployment.'

'And what's that enigmatic utterance supposed to mean, may one ask?'

'Playing with words is all, Mamá.'

As I scoot out to the street I catch sight of a small flash of colour on the nearest jacaranda. A flash of purple! One flower – just one! The sun has coaxed this first little blossom to unfurl.

Yippee! Spring!

Leg it through the shimmering streets striding towards the city.

You know where I fetch up after an hour or so, don't you? Course you do! Palacio de la Tijera. Blank wall. Baroque pediment. Wrought iron grilles warding me away.

Don't know why.

Do know no handsome mysterious male redemptive

agent will emerge for me from this relic of the viceroyalty. Not hoping now to be saved by Blond God. Nope. Not in need of being saved. Don't know what I need, yet.

Only know what I don't need.

Saving.

So why am I here? Why am I stood on these cobblestones looking across at that façade?

Fucked if I know!

Well, scarper – why don't you?

Or some sort of displacement activity? Yeah. Go and get a coffee or beer at the Bar del Borgo. Angelita has slipped me a few pesos. She gets them from Mamá. Who gets them from Paco. Am sauntering away from the Palacio de la Tijera. Nip into a side alley. Clock a yawning receptionist on the inside of the glass door of a dental clinic. Very brown, tiny. As she yawns she holds out newly painted tangerine nails to dry while sitting with her neck twisted so as to scope a telescreen mounted on one side of the lobby.

The screen gleams with a scene from a soap.

'Carlos, watch out for my foot,' snaps a weary brown woman to her toddling brown boy.

'Grasshoppers!' cries a brown vendor. 'Oily and crisp!'

A young brown man from a country pueblo squats on his hams on the pavement, watching the world go by. Chewing a pistachio. Dressed in his very best. Black moccasins, white nylon socks, black nondesigner jeans, big brown leather belt studded with a gigantic buckle of fake silver, brightly patterned rayon shirt open at the neck. City outfit completed with a black vinyl jacket. A bushy black moustache over a mouth chewing gum.

'Good afternoon, Señor,' he says to me gently, apparently thinking that even in an urban alley every encounter must be signalled fittingly.

'Good afternoon, Señor,' I say.

A bridal boutique on the opposite side of the street. Dummy young women pose in the windows with fixed glassy smiles above vast frothy frocks. A whole wacky world, the white wedding. Gifts. Drinks. Toasts. Weepy mother, proud father, good wishes, blessings.

So fake, so weird.

Turn to the right, towards the Bar del Borgo.

An old wooden doorway. Two brown doors. One careless word spraypainted in white on each door.

Queer on the right-hand door.

Fag on the left-hand door.

Turn away.

Bar del Borgo. You walk straight off the street, up a flight of worn stone steps past a pair of massive cedar doors swung wide open and bolted back during the day. The barman is a dad type wearing black pants and white shirt, gel slicking back his glossy black hair. He stands on the steps, when not needed by his clients, leaning back against one of the doors, surveying the street.

We nod at one another.

Slope inside, see maybe ten or twelve wooden square tables, each with its own set of wooden chairs. Seats woven from marsh rushes. Wooden masks hang from the walls. Carved, painted, in a pre-Columbian style. Toltec? A big vibrant oil painting, abstract, using only pure pre-Columbian colours of ochre, white, black, chocolate. Also a compact disk player thumping out mainstream rock.

Clientele: men only. A few coots. Well dressed dads downing whisky while on the lam from business. One or two young men –

Salvador.

A blond white young prince dressed beautifully.

Okay, stay cool man!

'How's it going?' I say quietly.

Takes him a couple secs to work it out while his wide blue eyes and long narrow nose and thin pale lips stay bland. Assess interloper swiftly. Size up. And those big blue eyes – that fine slender nose – those soft pale lips – all seem somehow to flare. The nostrils take in extra air quickly. The eyes – the lips, kissable lips –

Shut up, dickwit! You don't want him, got it!

Two intensely kissable lips start to smile, lightly, delightfully.

Fuck – wow!

Fuck he's gorgeous!

Salvador jumps up. He holds out his hand. I take it, dazed, bleary with excitement, not quite registering that, yeah, here am I with my hand held by his hand, skin with skin, warmth with warmth.

'Good to see you Matías.'

'Tito,' I say kinda abruptly and automatically.

'Sorry, I keep forgetting,' he says in his beautiful baritone. 'How are you – how's your novel, Tito?'

'My novel? I've just been reading *The Useless Life of Pito Pérez*. You know, Josć Rubén Romero. Maybe the novel I'm supposed to be writing – the novel I never have any energy for these days, the novel abandoned on the hard drive of the computer and not properly backed up onto a compact disk or floppy – maybe if that novel ever gets written it could be called *The Useless Life of Tito López*.'

'Oh. Sorry. I'm really sorry to hear that.'

'Well my novel's history, Salvador. Chucked it.'

'Truly? I mean – well, it's obvious to any observer, or listener, that you've got the ability.'

'No big deal. Am moved on from novels, is all.'

Salvador looks away, frowning briefly.

He looks back, smilingly.

'Care to join me? Please? I'm drinking coffee – as you can see.'

He points down at a coffee pot which is sat on the table kinda lumpishly. Bar del Borgo prides itself on serving coffee in old pots the way your grandmama on the hacienda used to serve coffee. A pot shaped like an egg, glazed brown, sitting on little black feet. Propped on the tabletop next to the coffee pot is a well worn, thoroughly thumbed, antique book open on an engraved portrait of the windmills and Don Quixote.

'Ta,' I say, grabbing a chair and getting sat. 'You reading Cervantes?'

'Every year since my teens I've been reading this old family volume all the way through,' dropping back onto his own chair. 'Cervantes is my hero.'

'He's brilliant, Cervantes.'

'Yes.'

'Not that he needs my praise!' I say with a laugh, 'Cause what a cheek!'

Salvador looks at me awkwardly.

'Maybe you'll be the Cervantes of Villarreal.'

'And maybe not.'

'I esteem your modesty.'

'What chapter you up to?' I say, grabbing the book.

'Just got past the scene where Basilio impales himself on his dagger.'

'Okay – the wedding of Camacho and Quitería. Cool! Do you agree that Cervantes wasn't so much writing prose as oratory? Hey – speaking of weddings, gotta give you my congratulations on your good news, Salvador. You and Gladys – '

He blinks.

He opens his eyes again with a look of ordinary candour.

Fuck, he's a cool customer, is Salvador.

'Thanks, that's kind of you Tito.'

'No problem, Salvador.'

Blond God looks me over carefully. Very carefully.

'How's your career going, Tito?'

'Down the drain, thank you for your enquiry, Salvador.'

'Down the – ?'

'Shafted. Stuffed. Fucked. Non-existent.'

He laughs unhappily.

'Sorry – you mean you're out of work right now?'

'Out of work, out of perk, a right berk, yep.'

He looks even more unhappy.

'You're an amazing guy, Tito,' he says, shaking his head. 'You laugh at your situation when most people would be gloomy, and – and – how are you managing financially?'

'Am managing by not managing.'

His white skin goes pink.

'Sorry, don't want to pry. Don't want to seem impertinently curious, but – well, we're friends, I hope? You're managing by – relying on your parents till you find a new job, presumably?'

'Relying on my parents would be marginally less wise than relying on my fairy godmother.'

'You mean your parents are a little – improvident? Or maybe – cavalier?'

'Mate, they're not cavalier – they're cadavers.'

Salvador looks shocked.

'Sorry?' he stammers. 'I think I don't follow you exactly.'

'Cadavers and at the same time kids.'

'How do you mean, Tito?'

'I mean my mother and father are sorta dead in some ways. Sorta unborn in other ways. Well, most people are, aren't they? Aren't we?'

'Phew!'

He shakes his head, making fun of himself.

I laugh, cause suddenly he seems cute – suddenly he seems not just My Icy Prince, Blond God. He seems a nice bloke.

'My turn to say sorry, now,' I say. 'I go into these free word associations, stream of consciousness, dicking about really.'

'A born writer,' he says, bending forward and fixing me with those glacially bright eyes. 'Language is your destiny.'

'Fuck!' I say with a little laugh, feeling scared. 'I can't live up to that, Salvador!'

'No, listen – please – look – I know I behaved badly that day when I asked you to – well, the truth of the matter is that ever since that day I've been wondering about you – your novel, how it was going, how you were – and – well frankly, always thinking about you.'

'Yeah, sure,' I say tautly.

What game is he playing at now?

'Always. Always been thinking about you. You're so alive, Tito. You're so – I don't know the words. You can tell me the words, can't you? You're the novelist!'

'Am not a novelist. Told you just now. Binned it – don't want – '

'Tito, listen to me please. You're gifted. You're vitally alive. Maybe you can do me the honour of – letting me help you out financially. You know – not the way I meant last time – just as your friend. Let me help you out financially. You need to write your novels and not worry about money.

'You serious, Salvador?'

No need to ask, though. Can see the answer in his eyes.

Deadly serious, his eyes!

'Please say yes, okay? Please, Tito. And we can – can we – well, can we – I mean, this isn't related to what I've just offered, please don't get me wrong!'

'Eh?'

'We can be – lovers?'

'Salvador! What the fuck? Can we – what the fuck – ? How the fuck – ?'

All I've ever hoped to be offered by a guy.

'I'd like to be your lover,' he says more firmly.

Fixed look. Leaning forward. High white forehead nearly bumping my low brown forehead. Brilliant bright eyes glittering. Wonderful voice dropped to a whisper. Throwing me – throwing me completely. Why? Why me, for starters? He could have nearly any arse in the city! And why the hurry? Wouldn't it be better tactics – looking at it from the point of view of a guy who for some mysterious indeed seriously weird unknown reason does seem to want my arse – wouldn't it be better tactics to wait till I've taken his money before putting on the hard word? Plus, why's he blurting it out in such an uncool way? Blond Gods seduce more skilfully, don't they? Also, what about the fact that he's just gone and got himself – ?

'Salvador, how does this square with your planned nuptials? You know. Gladys!'

Salvador shrugs, handsomely.

'Gladys?' he says.

'Gladys.'

He opens his mouth a small sexy slot.

'What happens between myself and my soon-to-be wife has nothing to do with what may happen between myself and you.'

'Or may not happen.'

'What?'

'Fuck you, man!' I snap, standing up suddenly, making

a racket by mistakenly knocking down my chair in my haste to get away. 'For one fucking minute I was starting to think that maybe you were fucking okay!'

Salvador looks colder, and harder.

'You say your mother and father are just kids,' he says slowly. 'You're being a kid yourself.'

Fuckwit!

Course now my waterworks open the spigot – am blubbing wetly.

'Get knotted, cunt,' I snarl.

My best shot, sadly.

Salvador surveys my blubbering with a deeply disdainful eye.

'Matías López, why not look at this coffee pot and consider your options carefully?' he says once more opening his mouth a slot and nodding at the tabletop so curtly that without a thought I follow his orders and stare down at the bulbous brown glazed pot on its little black feet. 'Boys of your genetic origin have a lot in common with this coffee pot.'

'We – what?' I yelp, thrown by this clearly insolent, startlingly lateral, leap.

'Indigenous boys like you have a lot in common with this coffee pot from the point of view of physique.'

'Physique? Salvador, gimme a break!'

'Boys of indigenous ancestry when young can be slim and enchanting. Enchanting and slim like you. When they're young. No doubt you know you're enchanting. No doubt you're calculating that you can bank on good looks indefinitely. You'd better essay a new calculus. Regrettably you've only got two or three years left of your beauty. And then your waist will start to thicken, your belly will swell, your bum cheeks – pert now, deliciously fuckable – in a few years those cheeks will be flat khaki pancakes. Your whole body will be ballooning. At thirty you'll have the profile of this coffee pot. Lithe brown boys like you end up like this coffee pot. Always. Short and squat. Ungainly. No grace. You're the cutest kid in town right now, and you know it. Only soon you'll be as ugly as any peasant.'

Strongest emotion during this extended exercise in conceit and nastiness and rhetoric, maybe, is incredulity.

Slim and enchanting? Cutest kid in town?

Come off it! What's he playing at?

Takes me a bit of time to click onto the fact that he means it, that he really thinks it's the truth. Fuck! Me? Cute, enchanting?

Fuck – !

'Sod you, Salvador,' I say, bolting away.

23

A hot morning in early spring. A fortnight since the Bar del Borgo. Spring you can now enjoy, all of it, in great big gulps. Greenness, growth, waves of warm air, flowing light, flowering. Jacaranda just gorgeous. Life is great! Climb solo onto Cerro del Calvario. Look out from its stone terraces across the valley of Villarreal. Our ancient city, historic, hazed with purple. Jacaranda roots, bulky. Rugged trunk. And opening out, slim long boughs like necks of grey swans. Flaring out into filmy filaments.

And mauve blossoms, tiny soft trumpets.

Okay, down from Cerro del Calvario. Cracked concrete slabs. A carpet of fallen jacaranda petals, a bridal display, like confetti tossed for a wedding.

'The ugly girl with the cleft palate, she's the one for coriander,' says María, tying on her shawl. 'Don't let her choose the bunch, mind – '

'Sure, I'll choose it myself. I know the drill, María.'

'Make sure it's fresh, baby. Test the freshness by nipping a stem with your thumbnail – '

'Come on, off you go!'

Noon, nearly. Am in our kitchen. Papá has driven down to the cemetery. Ángela is away studying for final exams. Mamá has headed off to Sanborns. María is about to pop down the street to see a sorceress about her bunions, partly cause I've told her I'll take care of buying the greengroceries and herbs today. María has her doubts about the wisdom of this plan. She prides herself on knowing the ins and outs of how and where to go for good produce.

'And keep your wits about you. She'll charge you more than you should pay. She'll make a play for your pity because of the cleft palate – '

'Go and get those bunions sorted, María!' I say, kissing a scrawny old cheek.

'God bless you my baby.'

Alone at home, now. Open the newspaper to scan situations vacant. Already scoped the ads first thing this morning but you can never be quite sure your eye might not have blinked at the wrong moment and missed some little goody. Hm – *Waiter, experience necessary. Sales assistant, experience necessary. Data entry, experience necessary. Call centre, experience necessary.* No goody missed, clearly.

Fold away newspaper.

Wander into salon. A space filled with flowers, scented peacefully. María's doing. A book left lying open by Mamá. A manual telling the status conscious householder what to stamp out in the home in order to be thought superior to the ordinary middle class. Among many things forbidden by this *Y2K Index of Chic* are the following:

All porcelain figurines by Lladró.

Opium by Yves Saint-Laurent.

Cut crystal.

Smoking cigarettes by Dunhill.

Salmon served with capers and cream cheese.

Okay, greengrocery. Down the street I stroll. Above the pavement of crushed purple, above the pretentious rooftops, soars the sierra as always. Dark, deep. Pine, cedar. Outside a bakery stands a young guy. Cargo pants, white, hanging loose from his backside and tight little tee clinging to his pecs. Brass buttons studded across the cargo pants.

Additionally, he's not happy.

'What's your trouble, mate?' I ask.

The boy says his backpack's been stolen. And all his money. And he's got to pay his landlady. His whole salary was in his backpack. He's so worried his landlady will throw him out that I make up my mind to lend him some money. Seventy pesos. Poke it into his hand. Watch while his fingers close on it uncertainly.

'You sure, dude?' he says. 'You don't know me from Adam.'

'We know each other now, mate,' I say.

The money was given me by María – who got it off Mamá – who in turn peeled the pesos off what's left of the stash sponged from Paco. The boy looks at me with wide open eyes. He holds out his arms and grabs me, pulls me towards him, hugs me tightly. Wow! I can feel his balls inside the thin cotton of his cargo pants – his balls sorta rolling against my thigh!

'Jordi,' he says, breathing into my ear.

'Tito, mate.'

Jordi gives me his phone number.

'Gimme a call, okay?' he says eagerly. 'Wanna pay you back as soon as I get my salary.'

'No sweat, Jordi.'

'Please, dude – gimme a call.'

Phone rings as soon as I step back inside ours, not a lot later, holding one meagre bunch of pumpkin flowers to show for my journey. Who's phoning? Jordi! Yay! He's hot, Jordi. No, don't be wet. Some vapid matron trying to track down Mamá. Or some crony of Papá's. Or – hang about –

My heart bumps. Lunge at phone. Pluck it up.

'Casa Lopéz,' suavely, then a bit breathlessly, 'Jordi?'

'Tito?' inquires a guarded baritone.

Oh.

'Salvador?'

'Tito, can I come and see you?'

Okay, do my best to speak casually.

'How did you get this phone number? You been doing detective work, mate? Why do you wanna come and see me, Salvador?'

'I want to explain things to you. Okay? Can I come to see you and explain?'

'Er, sure – feel free to explain away.'

'Well – um – see you in twenty?'

'Yep, see ya. Hey, hang on! Lemme give you the address.'

'I know the address.'

'Oh, okay.'

Neither of us takes the indicated next step of letting drop the headset of our telephone.

'Tito – um – '

Fuck! Till now I've been keeping the scene at the bar the other day shoved down to my mind's deeps. Not cause I feel confident I acted the right way. Cause I don't want to think. Want just to leave it to my instinct. Cause thinking about it, him, could make me go crazy.

'See ya in twenty!'

Drop the headset as though it's turned white hot. While as for myself, I've gone cold. So cold I've got the shakes, my whole body trembling violently.

Okay, twenty minutes later you find me loitering in our front portico.

Am skulking, thinking that somehow am trying to break out of a locked house, locked house filled with loot – not love – lurking behind wrought iron, painted ornamental grille, crimson blooms of bougainvillea, mauve frills of jacaranda. And spying. Eying a gleamingly handsome young man stepping out of a shiny car. My Prince, who presses an ignition fob.

Gleep!

Glancing sideways, I see that the widow's veil has come into bloom. You know that bush in the front garden? Flowers the colour of lilac, weeping in long limp tendrils.

'Hey dude,' I say.

'Hello, how are you Tito?'

Gravely, we shake hands. Very gravely. I wave him into ours. My gravity sways for a beat when in spite of myself I see the vestibule, the salon, through his eyes. Plaster grapes, tortured brass rods, bits and bobs – teardrop chandeliers –so standard, so precisely suburban as to show that my mother yearns for the opposite, for style. Style that for a fleeting tick I wish she'd scored.

So I wouldn't need to feel what I'm feeling here in front of Blond God.

Shame is what I'm feeling. Salvador can see now that we're an ordinary family on its ordinary way down. Only my next feeling is annoyance. Annoyance that I've given way to shame –

'Want a coffee, Salvador? A beer?'

'No thank you.'

We gawp at one another helplessly.

'Dude, come out to the patio,' I say. 'Come and look at my cypresses.'

Wordlessly, we step out.

'Tito,' he says once he's stood himself next to one of my cypresses, now in cheap new pots picked up at Walmart, 'I've come here to your house for one reason only.'

'Yeah?' I croak hoarsely.

Am stood a couple paces away.

'I've come here because – can't you see it in my eyes? I was hoping you'd be able to see it in my eyes, Tito.'

'What? I'd be able to see – what?'

Salvador comes a step closer. Me, want to take a step back! Only don't. Stare wonderingly, instead, at Blond God. Who's looking at me really hard, really intensely. Seems almost angry.

'Tito, I love you.'

Okay, here's me standing stiffly, fiercely – listening hard – yet for the first time in my adult life I can scarcely make sense of a single word, or say anything myself.

'Huh?' I do manage to mutter.

'I've – fallen – in love – with you.'

'Salvador, are you playing some weird sorta game called fucking with the minds of the peasantry, or are you just on something?'

'You're not a peasant, you're a man of letters. I've been in love with you since summer.'

'Would it make a diff if I was a peasant?'

'Tito, I love you.'

And then, suddenly, I believe him. Yep, he's in love with me, it's true. Blond God is in love with me, Tito. Salvador! Look at the guy. A guy who's lovelorn. You can see it plain as a white plate on top of a mahogany table. Revenge! Yay for me! Victory! And not only that, also – yep, also bewilderingly, suddenly, it becomes clear to me that myself I'm no longer in love with Salvador.

Weird or what? Wonder why?

Cause he was only ever a fantasy?

'Sorry, Salvador. Let's drop the topic. It's quite possible that I scarcely like you.'

Salvador ducks his head quickly.

'I want to give my best to you, Tito. I can't get along without you.'

'Sure you can, mate.'

'I want you in my bed, in my arms, in my life. I don't want any man with me if that man isn't you.'

'Hey – what about a woman? Somehow whenever you and me get together these days it always ends up my job to remind you of someone sweet called Gladys.'

'I don't want Gladys.'

'Hope she knows that, dude.'

'Sod her – I want you!'

The big blond bloke bursts into tears.

Fuuuuuuuuuck!

'Look, you don't even know who I am, mate,' I say much more gently after both of us have done a bit of stertorous breathing. 'You seem to think I'm some sorta hidden genius or something – you know, what you said the other day when talking about the Cervantes of Villarreal.'

'All I know, Tito, is that I love you.'

'Resuming my theme, Salvador. You say extravagant things about me when in reality what do you know? You know nothing about how I'm only now coming out of the worst weeks I've ever lived through till today. About how I've been feeling so lousy that I've even sold my arse a few times to guys.'

He doesn't flinch at all, which is kinda cool, and looks at me very – well –

Very lovingly!

'Uh,' he grunts. 'You poor guy.'

'Yeah, well, am trying my best to work it all out.'

'Tito, I can love you and look after you and help you to heal – I can make you happy.'

'I'll make myself happy, Salvador.'

'Please – do you like me at all? What do you think of

me? Tell me, please. I'm getting eaten up inside from wanting you. You move your body so beautifully. Tito, you've got such a supple, eager way of moving your body. The light in your eyes, too. I just desperately want you, the way I've never wanted anyone before. I'll never get tired of looking at your face, your eyes – '

And now he's the one crying jerkily, violently. Snot smearing his beautiful face.

'Salvador, it's not – it's not gonna happen, mate. I don't feel that way about you.'

'I want to hear you, I want to smell you, kiss you, tell everyone I love you – '

Poor guy.

I unbend my left hand and drop my fingertips lightly on his forearm – a white forearm all aglow with blond hair.

His skin feels sorta creepy.

Funny, that. Theoretically he's a man whose skin I find very attractive. After all, muggins mooned away for months about the guy. Only its whiteness – well greyness really, greyish pink, the true colour of white skin – it makes me flinch, and – yep, creepy is definitely the word. Next, mind you, my brain flips over to incorporate another new bit of sensory input.

Namely, a stiff sound of rasping.

A rasping silk skirt. Again. The skirt of a matron lady. Only this time not Sra Fuentes.

'Matías, what – who's this young man you're – ?'

Twist myself round and see Mamá.

'Christ, Ma! You crept up on me as quietly as a nun on castors.'

'My god, isn't this – ? How do you do, Señor? This is – isn't it? – isn't this Señor Salvador de la Tijera de Lago?'

'Er, yes,' stammers Salvador. 'Yes, that's me Señora.'

'Well my goodness – what an honour! How delightful! Quite an unexpected pleasure, I'm sure! You'll take refreshments, I hope? Do please come into the salon, and – well, what on earth!'

Salvador, casting one look of despair at me, takes his turn to bolt away.

24

Mamá swings her thick hips, bulging inside a costume the colour of mustard, and looks at me with wonder. Matronly jacket buttoned correctly. Matronly black camisole top tucked inside the jacket. Court shoes and matching handbag the colour of cocoa. Permed hair dyed the colour of oak. Skin not quite the colour of cream – we've worked out that she's something like eighty percent white, twenty percent native. Around her neck hangs a fillet of gold. The lobes of her ears are pierced by tiny gold hoops.

'Why didn't you make him stay?' she says.

'How was I supposed to make him stay, Mamá? Tie him to the railing?'

Knitting her brow, looking away at the vanishing sight of the chromed arse of Salvador's Saab, my mother subjects me to acute scrutiny. A brain – a brain below that wiry coronet of permed oak – clearly trying to nut out why Blond God would lower himself to drive into her humdrum suburb and call on her troublesome son. Mamá gnaws at a glossily sticked lower lip. Her obvious doubt about what next to say makes me burst into a fit of silly giggling, like a little kid.

'You seem quite hyper,' she says warily, probably not wanting to provoke me, somehow sensing that I'm in a new position of power.

'Hyper, Mamá?'

'Hyper.'

'Well, if I am it's cause there's a reason – I've just had a proposal of marriage from Salvador.'

'A proposal of – what? You mean he wants you to be his best man? That's what you mean is it, son? He wants you to be groomsman at his wedding? God, how wonderful! He's asked my darling boy to stand by his side when he gets married to that girl Galán! But – why? How odd! Or are you and he friends – ? But how could you know each other – ? And – well, odd! Now what's the name of the girl? Oh yes, Gladys isn't it. Gladys Galán. How long has he known you? My god, this is so – just think! My dear sweet darling boy – best man to the town's most eligible bachelor when he weds Gladys Galán!'

'He wants me to be his best man full stop, Ma.'

'What – ? What?'

Mistake to make it a joke, course. The poor rudderless woman finds herself floundering for a fair while in waters far too deep. Although her hull displaces a hefty draught she's a drfting craft at best and nobody at the wheel has anything like a chart for this sort of voyage. Not that she saves her breath to try to steer herself.

Talks instead – nonstop.

'What in heaven – ? My god, you never leave me in peace do you? You always want to torment your poor mother who's never done anything worse than love you. No respect! Not even common politeness, common consideration – or don't you know the meaning of those phrases? What are you saying? What?'

Poor old cow, I gotta take pity.

'Lemme put it another way, Mamá. Maybe there's more money in your boy being bent than being straight. Salvador wants me to go and live with him as his lover in the Palacio de la Tijera.'

Still takes a tick or two to get it, course. When the penny does finally drop –

'Holy Mary mother of god! Our prayers have been answered! My baby boy! We'll need to get you some nice new clothes, Tito. I saw a gorgeous white suit the other day at the mall. Oh, come here! I'm longing to give you a hug. Come here, my sweetheart! Praise the blessed saints.'

'Ma, it's not going to happen. I've turned him down.'

'Turned him – what?'

Her look of utter dismay makes me laugh out loud.

'Sorry to laugh at you, Mamá – but you'll catch a lot of flies that way!'

Course, doesn't surprise me that she now invokes not only the routine saints but the Virgin. After all, my mother has always been willing to rope in any divine deputy when hoping, moaning, wishing, complaining, blaming. What does surprise me is that she's swallowed the concept of her son getting offered a career in queer concubinage so very enthusiastically. Not the slightest flicker of doubt, evidently.

I take one more hard look.

Nope, she's so dizzy you'd think Ángela had just come with news of being begged for her hand in a proper old-school proposal of holy matrimony plus star-making female lead in a groovy movie about endless tomorrows of haciendas and money and old blood in the seventies, only better even than the true seventies, with vistas of agave in rich thick dark glossy rows surrounding some especially monumental hacienda, plus ocean view apartments in dear darling sweetie Acapulquito – featuring cameo but gorgeous role for stylish still beautiful mother-in-law, witty hostess of Palacio de la Tijera Comforted-by-Papal-Benediction – by Blond God.

Papá, coming home an hour later, is similarly over the moon.

'Good lord!' he says, having had to work quite hard to make my mother slow down enough to spell out the story in a coherent kinda way, though she only gets to the offer from the prince, not my turning him down. 'Congratulations, well done son!'

'Er, Papá – '

A fatherly complaisance coming from a point so completely off my compass that for a couple secs it's me not the olds who's drifting rudderless. Who would've thunk? Papá pleased with me, pleased as punch, for – for seducing a queer!

'Tito my lad,' he says very proudly, very paternally, 'you've obviously played with your cards close to your chest.'

Okay, time for me to grab that tiller!

'Papá, all my life you've been telling me to stay away from gay guys.'

'We're not talking about history, son. We can forget that – dead and buried. Won't hold it against me, will you my boy? Now we're talking about your future and the future of the whole family. You're set up for life. He'll probably tire of you after a few years but they're an honourable family and will take pains to see you right. You'll be mixing with the best people. You'll be making the contacts you need, and more. And it'll be a splendid chance for Ángela.'

'Angelita? How come?'

'Your sister will be welcomed, as your sister, into the Palacio de la Tijera. She meet men from the very top drawer.'

'Papá, remember what you told me when I got my job last summer?'

The old bloke looks kinda perplexed.

'What, my boy?'

'You know, when I got my job in the advertising industry. Stay away from queers. Those were your words Papá. Lots of queers in the advertising industry. Remember what you used to tell me about the dressing rooms at the sports centre when I was a boy? Full of queers, the dressing rooms at the sports centre. You were right, too. Full of queers, the dressing rooms. I've had heaps of sex with guys in the dressing rooms at the sports centre.'

'Boy – shut your mouth!'

'Oops, sorry Papá. Only reminding you of your own words. Remember what you said the other month when you found out I was gay? You said that homosexuality is contrary to nature, that it's socially marginal, that it's narcissistic, that it's self-destructive, and that it's sick. You wanted me to be strapped down and given electric shocks by some quack. You wanted me to be injected with male hormones.'

'Ten out of ten for rhetoric,' he says drily.

Which almost makes me laugh – hadn't expected him to run with the ball quite so quickly.

'What score can we give you, Papá? Eleven out of ten for hypocrisy?'

Once more he startles me by not bursting into a random angry rant.

'Look lad, let's deal with this matter on the basis that we live not in a perfect world but workaday reality. Go after Salvador de la Tijera. Go after him and make sure you get good hold of the chap. And more importantly make sure you get good hold of some of his money.'

'Magda used almost exactly the same words.'

'A girl who knows on which side her bread's buttered. You could do a good deal worse than model yourself on Magdalena.'

'Pa, lemme get this clear, okay? Don't you find it the teeniest bit ironic that you're now goading me to do what a few months ago you would've regarded as the indulgence of a dirty disease?'

He looks at me with frank dislike.

'Words! A spoiled brat playing with words!'

'Anyway, whatever. I've turned him down Pa. You can get the whole story from your wife, who'll be pleased to make sure your ears cop the lot with maximum possible melodrama. And before you start laying into me for that, I've got a phone call to make, okay?'

Lope up the staircase without bothering to look back at what I know will be a face of thunder.

'Boy!' he calls out, just as I dive with the cordless through my doorway.

'Go away and die, Pa,' I mutter to self.

Tip of my index finger punching numbers on the cordless, causing it to make little peeps. Got a good feeling about this guy. Maybe he's back home already. A woman answers the phone very politely.

'Hello, I'm looking for Jordi. Is he free by any chance?'

'Jordi?'

'Yes, Señora. Jordi.'

'I'm afraid no such person is known at this number.'

'You sure, Señora?'

'I'm sure.'

'Weird,' I say. 'You sure he's not your – um – your son?'

'I certainly hope he's not,' says the woman drily. 'This is a convent.'

Paco turns up, sent for by Mamá. She wants him to make me get fucked by Salvador. We sit down to pastry and coffee in the salon. Magda sends her love, he says. Her pregnancy is proceeding optimally. Paco's sentence, course – not mine. Mamá now shoves aside the small talk.

'Look at him sitting there saying not a word, selfishly forking pastry into his face,' she says with a sulk.

'Tch tch,' says Paco.

'Conceited, unthinking, a burden on us all when by lifting one finger he could – '

'Am lifting four fingers, Ma,' I cut in.

'Cut out your cheek, young man!'

'But you've just said it – am lifting four fingers and a thumb to fork pastry into my face selfishly.'

'Very droll,' she snaps. 'And next week we all starve to death on the street!'

After coffee my cousin corrals me in the library.

'Now there are three reasons why you need to accept this bid from Salvador de la Tijera,' says Paco as carefully as though spelling something out to a slightly senescent shareholder. 'Firstly, you set yourself up prudentially for an indefinite, possibly lengthy, period of years.'

'Paco – I'm not gonna do it, man!'

'Secondly, as soon as you accept the bid we can anticipate multiple spinoff financial benefits for the whole family.'

'You mean I'll be able to wheedle money out of him so Mamá can spend it on nuns and canasta?'

'You know you're joking and I know you're joking, Tito. I like a joke as well as the next man. We're talking seriously here, however, and I'd be grateful if you'd hear me out. I understand the world. You've led a sheltered life so far. A degree in literature! You need to listen to what I've got to say because it's meant well. And we're cousins.'

'Sorry, Paco. Okay – lemme hear what you got to say.'

Might as well save my smart remarks since they won't make any odds. He clearly has to be allowed to tick off each of the points on his agenda.

'Thirdly, by accepting the offer you're protecting yourself and the rest of us in the family from scandal.'

This comes from leftfield.

'Scandal?'

I genuinely don't know what he's talking about.

'Your preferences – your deviancy. I'm sure you don't

mind my calling a spade a spade, Tito. We're both men – well, I'm a man and you're a – and – and here we are. Salvador de la Tijera carries so much weight that even if people do talk about you two behind your backs they won't dare say anything to your face. Salvador de la Tijera's name will shield not only your name but also the good name of our whole family.'

Throttling first thoughts of slaughter, I make myself smile in a way Paco will be fool enough to think friendly.

'Well I'm really very grateful for your advice, coz. The last bit, especially, about protecting the good name of the family.'

'Coz, glad you see sense,' he says, puffing up.

'Although maybe an even better plan would be to adopt an alias? I'm a criminal anyway, right? Cause of being queer. So why don't I just start going under an assumed name? And then nobody will know I'm any relation of yours.'

He says nothing.

Afterwards he grunts, stands up, walks out to the patio.

A couple of businessmen come to the house a bit later. Paco, goes without saying, is not the sort of guy to kill one mere bird with his stone – having sped down here on silver wings so expensively – on any trip away from Tijuana.

'Targeting the middle market consumer,' he says to a suits squad, hour or so later, over drinks in the salon. 'My man at the factory will let you know our critical path analysis for the brand extension, and our strategies for damage limitation.'

'Priority at this point in time being a leveraged buyout of an existing franchise for the product?' asks Suit One.

'Affirmative,' nods Paco. 'A franchise about to go into meltdown not for lack of asset base but for want of profile.

Our worst case scenario preliminary asset overvaluation. We propose incidentally to terminate their existing product and activate our own. We won't clone their product.'

'Do you contemplate a demand-led plan for your new product placement?' asks Suit Two.

'Excellent query,' yaps Paco. 'Demand-led for the first two stages of the proposed timeframe, and subsequently – '

'We're not lost, Tito,' says Ángela that night, summing up her thoughts after getting the latest on the state of play. 'We're starting to find ourselves.'

'Gnomic, sis.'

'Apt, bro.'

25

Knocking on her bedroom door, come to say a soothing word or two. Only the poor pathetic acting-school-dropout – she didn't really go to acting school, given that a polite young lady in the seventies did nothing but primp and wait and slop her face with slap and pray – takes a while to hear my knocks. Hairdryer whirring. Squalling! A hot little motor inside a pod of plastic ravening behind her cedar door is one reliable element of our morning routine. Day in, day out, every morning she'll wash her hair while showering and afterwards cook it under the dryer.

'Come!'

I swing the cedar slowly open to see my fat little mother sat at a sultry silken tulle shrine consecrated to motherhood, the Virgin, Villarreal, Our Lady de los Dolores, Christian Lacroix.

'You don't know,' Ma says clutching the hairdryer dully and looking up at one of her painted saints, 'how hard the world is for a woman.'

Hair hanging in wet rattails. Skin mottled and pasty. Two eyes watery as though the task of standing under the warm spray for her morning shower has partly dissolved her pupils. Only after the whirring of the dryer, together with half an hour of paintwork, will she be able to bust through doorways looking like the mother we all know.

Mamá sets down the hairdryer. She takes up the rosary.

Glazed saints look towards heaven beatifically. A pompadour bedhead, quilted with fake damask, whorled with fake rosewood, props up a heap of fake satin pillows.

'Lucky the world's plain sailing for a queer man, Ma.'

'Always laughing at me up your sleeve! What good are you? What good are you to me as a son? Holy saints! You won't help me – you could have made Ángela marry Paco! She'd do anything for you. And nothing for her mother! The more I think of it the more I understand that it was last summer when things began to go awry. Really it was staring us in the face that my only daughter should marry my own rich nephew. My nephew, my surname. So much nicer than your father's nasty commonplace López. Also pots of money. Why did you let that devious scheming little Magdalena get her hooks into Paco? Why couldn't we have got Paco for ourselves?'

'Mamá!' I say, laughing. 'How was I supposed to stop Magda from hitting on Paco?'

'By making out that you were keen on her yourself.'

'Lying to her, in other words?'

'She'd have come running, let me tell you! Oh, oh, oh, my god! None of you cares about me, neither of you kids. You don't love me. You laugh at me. My own children will kill me! I'm dead already. Dead and in purgatory. Blessed Mother Mary, what are we going to do? We're poor, we're going nowhere. Don't grin that way, Tito! You give me the creeps when you grin. You look like a malevolent imp. I've got the most murderous headache, you wouldn't believe. Of course you don't care, you won't offer to run down to the pharmacy to buy me some pills. My nerves are shot to pieces! I need a tequila. I've had a couple already. I told you, Tito – would you listen? As for Ángela – selfish, selfish – '

Yanking fistful after fistful of flimsy tissues from a box printed with chrysanthemums.

'Tito, where's María?' says Ángela, slipping into the room.

'Don't know, Angelita. Why?'

'Hitchhiking to some pueblo, that's where!' snaps

Mamá. 'She knows we're a sinking ship.'

'What do you mean hitchhiking?' frowns Ángela.

'María was being perfectly impossible! She just kept going on and on about how it was all my fault. My fault – I ask you! She told me that if I'd been a halfway decent mother – and so on and so forth. All her usual primitive rubbish. Stumped off upstairs and ten minutes later stumped back downstairs with a case and said she was off for a holiday. She said she was going to the bus station first, to say goodbye to you two. She said she'd then hitchhike up into the sierra. Damn fool of an old crow. Pegged straight out the door with that suitcase – no word – and good riddance, I say!'

I swap a quick look with Ángela.

'I'll go after her,' I say.

'Yep,' she says.

Bound down the staircase in sets of three treads. Dive into the salon. Snatch up the car keys. A few more bounds and am out the door. Not feeling any real worry about María. The old girl can look out for herself pretty cannily. Also, when among peasants and proles, she's a respected old lady. Key into ignition. Backing. Out into the street. Knocking noise under the bonnet a lot worse lately. Poor banger's thirteen years old now.

Checking out a nearby street, following a hunch rather than turning towards the bus station, I spot her sat on a bench. A green bench, worn by weary bums and weather, under the weltering mauve boughs of a jacaranda. An old woman sitting, tossing breadcrumbs to dusty sparrows.

I feel a lurch of love for María.

Quietly, gliding the car to a stop, I scope the only person who's ever given me the steady love you look for and hope to find in a mum or dad or granddad or grandma. Someone small, wiry, sat there on that blistered green bench under that soft mauve welter. Wrinkled dark skin. Sweaty. Glistening. Grey hair in its two pigtails hanging down her bony back.

Braking, getting out of gear, slipping out of the front seat, I pad across. Course she senses me coming. After all, she's from the sierra!

'I'm sick of your flighty bloody mother,' she snaps.

'She's sick of herself, darling.'

'Hmf!'

A short silence filled only with the flitter of mauve petals falling.

'Coming with me?' I ask.

María lets out a little dry cackle.

'Course I'm coming with you. My two hoary hooves aren't up to slogging the whole way to your bus station!'

'I mean coming with sis and me,' I add, helping her to her feet. 'Coming with us all the way from ours to La Libertad.'

Ángela and I talked it through last night. We want María to come with us, get her away from Mamá and Papá. Not a top plan but better than leaving the old love trapped in the suburb.

She grasps the concept surprisingly swiftly.

'I'm too old,' she says, quick smart.

'You're not old, María.'

'I'm old all right, dearie. My babies don't want my flyblown carcase dragging along when they set out to see the wide world.'

'Don't we?'

'You don't,' she nods. 'No, love – I'm seeing you two on your way then that's my lot – I'm off home to Tres Madres.'

'Off home for good, or only a holiday?'

'For good or bad, to stay.'

Ángela nods after being brought up to speed. We agree we'll head to the sierra every season or so and keep an eye on how things go in Tres Madres. Afterwards we talk about uni. Grades not awarded yet but examiners have let Ángela know on the downlow that she's top graduate in her year. Sis, in other words, has scored her goal. One examiner has sorted a doctoral scholarship for her at a new university.

'La Libertad isn't a proven institution – has to prove itself,' says sis. 'Which suits me just fine!'

'Sweet doing a doctorate at a holiday resort,' says me.

Cause it's not an old city, La Libertad. Only a fishing village, not even an incorporated town until the seventies of last century when the state decided to pump money into developing a tourist industry along that coast and a whole new metropolis of white slabs of concrete and glass sprang up among the banana plantations. Now it's a city twice the size of Villarreal. Plenty of work for me in its tourist industry – surely? Sure! Plenty of work for a literate lad with his wits about him, I'd say.

Well anyway, we've bought two bus tickets to La Libertad.

Soon we'll be off!

Papá has confined himself to the library. Mamá's come down and sat herself in the patio, sulking, sucking on a fag, slouching on one of the recliners. Ángela and myself, waiting for a taxi, have just quietly joined her when Sra Fuentes comes stalking.

'Hullo darling!' she says, grimacing at Mamá.

'Always know where to find trouble, don't you Dora?' grunts Mamá.

'*Nice!*' says our neighbour in English. 'María – extraordinary woman, not quite playing with the full deck I dare say? – told me you could be found here, my poor sweet, though not before favouring me with a brief lecture on the wrongs done to her as servant of this house for half a century.'

'Have you hunted me down just to be generally offensive, Dora? Or have with some more specific insult in mind?'

'*Oh my god, sorry!*' says Sra Fuentes, again speaking English. 'I'm here to commiserate with you about losing your son and daughter.'

'I never had a son and daughter,' moans Mamá. 'They're foundlings.'

'Or orphans?' brightly says Sra Fuentes.

'We've never been a family – we're wandering Jews!'

'Quite a common theory, once,' says Sra Fuentes. 'Mormons still believe it, evidently – a theory that the natives in this part of the world are the lost tribe of Israel.'

'What, Dora?'

'Mind you, I'll happily eat pork any time of the day.'

'My only son and only daughter are abandoning me to a lonely old age. Heaven alone knows why we do it! Why do we do it, Dora? All the love and suffering we spend on our children, and then – adios! A pack of ungrateful bloody kids! A mother is born to suffer!'

'Not this mother,' says Sra Fuentes.

María crosses herself and waves goodbye as the wheels of the bus bump a couple potholes on our way out of the concrete station concourse at the start of our journey. After watching our oldest friend shrink away, we sit back. Ángela smiles absently. Thinking her own thoughts. Me? Well, always the would-be writer, am gawping out the window. Scoping the people on the streets of the city. Vendors, workers, mothers, clerks, kids. Stucco façades, stone façades. Skimming above rooftops the golden domes of Our Lady de los Dolores. Above domes, scoring our skyline, the haggard yellow peak of Cerro del Calvario.

We swerve across a flyover, swing onto the ring road.

Prole suburbs, now. Grid after grid of streets with no name, no history. Raw brick, raw mortar – and those rusty steel rods sticking out of rooftops. Only look closer – look, and like always you scope all kinds of tiny signs that there's some sort of history. Pink and orange and turquoise paint slapped onto surfaces here and there, yellow and green and red parrots in cages popped onto pegs, pots of flowers dropped onto ledges, by folk doing their best to make the rawness less ugly.

We swing off the ring road onto the western expressway.

'You've shown real bravery turning down Salvador,' says Ángela.

'Hope it's not just bravado.'

'Least it's not bravura,' she says with a laugh.

'How do you mean?'

'I mean you've done it quietly, you've done it simply. No scenes, no drama. Sorry Salvador. It's not me, it's you. Hope not to catch you later Salvador. Quite the achievement when one considers how likely it is that the two of us have been lumbered from both sides of our family with a genetic predisposition to self-pitying melodrama.'

'Well it's only a comedy, isn't it? We're not doing tragedy.'

'Certainly we're not!'

'Plus, now and then, some burlesque.'

Countryside opens out on either side of the expressway. Young maize. Bamboo. A peasant walking behind a plough drawn by two burros. Villas. Walls topped with broken glass. Shacks knocked together from flattened tins and lengths of bamboo. Stalls where women wearing cotton frocks are selling tamales, toys, bottled water. Thorny fingers of mesquite scrabbling up a steep slope.

A long straight stretch of flat land, next, where we seem to travel forever towards a mighty multicoloured billboard gleaming under a sere blue sky.

A billboard on which two handsome young white men are grinning.

Ad for fags, it turns out.

Nearby in a bare field old brown men bend over their hoes. Straw hats, once white, now reddish with dust. Dusty pants of faded denim, buff terylene, hanging from their hips. Tucked into a leather holster at the waist of each old man is a machete.

We stop at every pueblo.

Peasants get out, peasants climb in.

'El Niño Santo,' croaks the driver, crying the next pueblo.

Not that peasants need to be told. All of them know their way up and down this valley. A lot of blokes on board have accessorised their town outfits with armadillo boots and baseball caps. Wares, lugged on the bus, stowed in the gangway. A carton of baby maize next to Ángela. One row back, a hemp bag of green mangos. Baskets, boxes, sacks. An underfed very dark young man, upper lip delicate with a little wispy moustache, sits in front of us embracing an enormous watermelon.

'God is good,' sighs a woman pleased by the sight of rows of maguey glowing in the sunlight, strong and olive and silvery.

'Know it's pathetic to hope for too much from buying two bus tickets,' laughs Ángela. 'Know it's not wise to hold to a vision of freedom – but I'm so happy.'

'Same, sis. We're on the bus. We're busting out.'

Fieldstone walls stray across the land. Sparse sickle leaves of eucalypt, drooping, resinous, offer a sketchy sorta shade here and there. Spikes and spears mark spots where yucca has driven its fleshy root more deeply than any fencepost.

'Dead right, buster. We're busting out, we're bursting out!'

'Who gives a toss if we have to end up busking?'

Ángela lets out a light little laugh.

'We'll busk together,' she says. 'We'll have each other.'

'Way to go! I'll be a busking old coot. You'll be a busking old crone.'

Ángela grabs my hand and we sit smiling, staring into the hot empty sky.

Globes of nopal, great green lungs, sprout blooms of vermilion and scarlet. Joconoxtli swells, showy, shameless. Sweet scents waft through open windows whenever our bus stops to drop folk off on the open roadside. Tracks will lead them through the stony fields to their pueblo. A vulture wheels above very slowly. A vulture spreading its pinfeathers like fine fans. No fan made by human hands, though, has ever held anyone so high above the world, so free, so finely.

Also published by Piwaiwaka Press:

Into the Woods: The healing power of birds
Helen Mae Innes

A funny, painful, powerful story about the strange ways grief moves through us. Helen's path of recovery, from a bed she doesn't want to leave towards a natural world she doesn't know, is full of recognisable difficulties and unlikely connections. This frank and bracing little book has a bass note of personal tragedy but a top note of surprising joy.

Damien Wilkins

It happened during the spring when the kākā had first appeared in the valley. I noticed a grey warbler fledgling outside my window who couldn't get the tune quite right. He'd start singing, get a note wrong and falter, then try tentatively again. Like a child learning the recorder, I thought to myself … like a child ...

Oracles & Miracles & Zombies
Stevan Eldred-Grigg & Helen Mae Innes

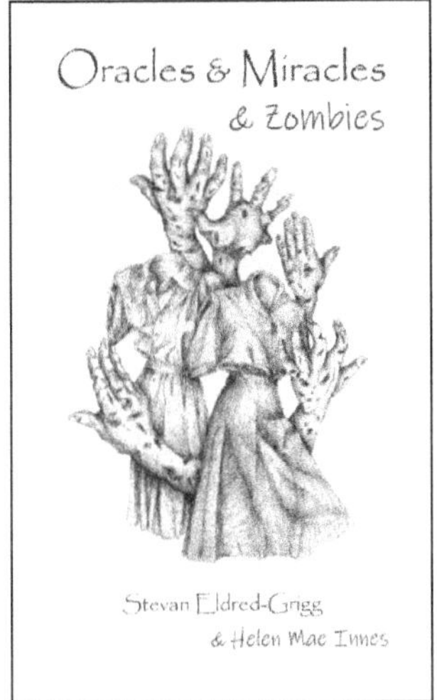

Stevan Eldred-Grigg's best selling, award-winning novel is back – with zombies!

Little has been written about how the biters created by the 1918 virus affected the lives of women, especially working-class women. This black comedy shows us how twin sisters, their sharp and shrewd mother, and many other women struggled to avoid being bitten by biters, cared gingerly for hunches who didn't want to eat their brains (just yet), and watched as the 'cured' lurkers started to take their jobs. Even during pandemics girls grow up, worry about boys, go out to work, get married, and have babies, all while trying to keep their brains safe inside their skulls. At the beginning the twins are small, fearful and helpless. By the end of the story they're armed and ready to go after the enemy ... but who's the real enemy?

Green Grey Rain
Stevan Eldred-Grigg

Rain on iron rooftops. A radio streaming the latest hit songs. It's the early 1950s. Valerie is a singing, slanging, pregnant daughter of the slums. Gilbert is the well-spoken son of a landed family. They already have three kids. Gilbert has just taken a job as paymaster at a coal mine. The family is about to start life in a green and black and red township on the West Coast. A little boy is born and named Stevan.

Green Grey Rain tells the story of the first years of that little boy. A story told by Stevan. A story told too by the hit songs he hears on the radio. And a story told by Valerie – who, with her sister, has already spoken to us in the pages of Oracles and Miracles. A story of working and playing, dreaming and singing, crying and laughing, hoping and wishing, bush, rain, rust, and the sooty streets of Blackball.

And the Birds Fled to the Bush
Helen Mae Innes

The valley is calm, quiet, waiting. Mrs Henderson thinks it's earthquake weather but doesn't say anything, doesn't want to make a fuss. It's probably nothing. No one else notices it's quiet, too quiet, until everyone does at the same moment, like at a party when everything goes silent and no one wants to be the first to speak. Suddenly, all the birds are airborne, and the whole valley … holds … its … breath.

Those living in post-earthquake suburbia are trying to survive everyday life, eviction by authorities, and infighting between different factions. Meanwhile a geeky student specialising in birdsong arrives hoping to conduct research. Anton's project is regarded with ire or indifference by many, except for Timothy, a weird loner whose speech is odd and behaviour odder.

My Dad
Anneke Gerbrands

My Dad is a beautifully illustrated simple story about a kid and their dad. Its short, simple sentences and use of dyslexia friendly font make it suitable for young readers and full-page colour illustrations make it attractive to toddlers. A great little book for dads and kids to bond by reading together, to give as a gift, or to help children learning to read.

Written by children's author Anneke Gerbrands and illustrated with delightful, quirky watercolour illustrations by Ingrid Kamp.

Pru Goes Troppo
Stevan Eldred-Grigg

Pru has been married to Guy for a quarter of a century. She hasn't had sex for ten years. 'Why the hell do I live my life this way?' she says to herself. 'I mean – really!' Change comes from out of the blue when odd old Uncle Bertie dies in Samoa and leaves his property to Guy. On a whim, the couple decide to go and take a look at what they know must be a tropical paradise. Not their usual stamping ground, you understand. Daringly, they fly to Apia. Pru soon finds herself thinking things, feeling things, doing things she's never till now come close to thinking, feeling, doing.

Pru Goes Troppo is a comic novel about the ups and downs of two people who are privileged parasites, yet curiously innocent.

Tatami Burns
Madden Hay

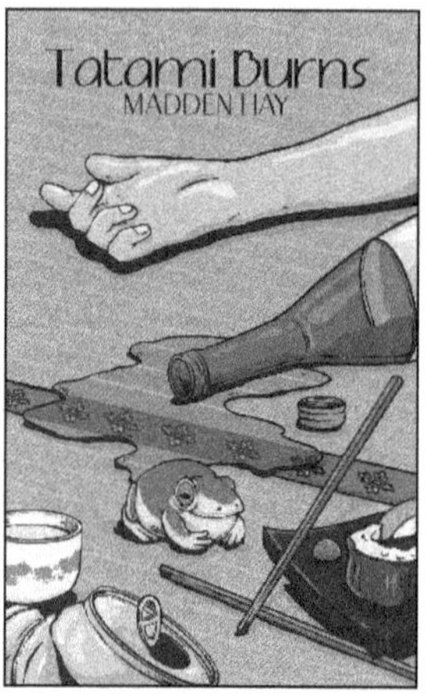

Lynley suddenly finds herself unexpectedly alone in Japan after her girlfriend cancels her teaching contract at the last minute. They'll have a long-distance relationship and meet up again in a year to travel together, she thinks. Or will they? Loneliness and anxiety threaten to overwhelm Lynley. Luckily another expat's living nearby, a flamboyant, fun-loving, sometimes obnoxious fag who she can hang out with.

A story about young expats discovering and questioning themselves, each other, and the world. A touching, funny story about understanding and challenging the rules of groups, both large and small, of relationships — and of boundaries.

Making Maths Add Up
Maggie Tu

This colourful, fun, clear, and sound approach to teaching mathematics takes a new approach to teaching maths by starting from scratch and breaking complex maths concepts down into their core parts, then building upon each foundation skill clearly and intuitively.

Children can jump in at the point they feel comfortable for each topic, allowing them to focus on the maths skills themselves and not arbitrary 'levels' and leaving room for revision, learning, and extension.

It starts at the level of 2 + 2 and teaches skills that quickly make equations like 680 + 70 easy to solve. It seamlessly incorporates algebra, word problems, and mnemonic storytelling. The relaxed, chatty style with cheerful, colourful images puts kids at ease.